As soon as the two missiles were launched, Lieutenant Felconi increased the shuttle's speed and climbed out of harm's way, accelerating rapidly enough that Lon thought he was near to graying out as the g-forces pressed him back against his seat. There was a roaring in his ears, the feel of blood pressing against his skin.

"Right on target, Colonel," Felconi announced. The view on one of Lon's monitors changed, showing smoke coming up from under the trees in the valley below Xavier's Beak.

"Good shooting, Lieutenant," Lon said. "Get ready to go in close to provide covering fire when Delta's shuttles arrive."

"Yes, sir," Felconi said. "I show them about forty seconds from touchdown, coming fast from the southwest."

"Let's get the bad guys, Lieutenant," Lon said.

Ace Books by Rick Shelley

UNTIL RELIEVED
SIDE SHOW
JUMP PAY
THE BUCHANAN CAMPAIGN
THE FIRES OF COVENTRY
RETURN TO CAMEREIN
OFFICER-CADET
LIEUTENANT
MAJOR
CAPTAIN
LIEUTENANT COLONEL

LIEUTENANT COLONEL

RICK SHELLEY

ACE BOOKS, NEW YORK

LIEUTENANT COLONEL

An Ace Book / published by arrangement with
the author

PRINTING HISTORY
Ace edition / May 2000

The Penguin Putnam Inc. World Wide Web site address is
http://www.penguinputnam.com

Check out the ACE Science Fiction & Fantasy newsletter
and much more on the Internet at Club PPI!

ISBN: 0-441-00722-8

ACE®
Ace Books are published
by The Berkley Publishing Group,
a division of Penguin Putnam Inc.,
375 Hudson Street, New York, New York 10014.
ACE and the ''A'' design are trademarks
belonging to Penguin Putnam Inc.

PRINTED IN THE UNITED STATES OF AMERICA

10 9 8 7 6 5 4 3

The year is A.D. 2823. The interstellar diaspora from Earth has been in progress for seven centuries. The numbers are uncertain, but at least five hundred worlds have been settled, and perhaps well over a thousand. The total human population of the galaxy could be in excess of a trillion. On Earth, the Confederation of Human Worlds still theoretically controls all of those colonies, but the reality is that it can count on its orders being obeyed only as far as the most distant permanent outpost within Earth's system, on Titan. Beyond Saturn, there are two primary interstellar political groupings, the Confederation of Human Worlds (broken away from the organization on Earth with the same name, with its capital on the world known as Union) and the Second Commonwealth, centered on Buckingham. Neither of those political unions is as large or as powerful as they will be in another eighteen decades, when their diametrically opposed interests finally bring them to the point of war. In the meantime, humans who need military assistance, and do not want the domination of either Confederation or Commonwealth, have only a handful of options. Those who can afford it turn to mercenaries. And the largest source of those is on the world of Dirigent. . . .

1

Major Lon Nolan allowed himself to accept the deception that he was standing in front of a ten-foot-square window looking out at the one world he had spent nearly twenty years telling himself he would never see again. But he *had* seen that world, spent nearly five months *on* it. Now he was leaving again, and this time there was absolutely no doubt in his mind. He would never return to Earth. He could not imagine ever *wanting* to return again. *I finally broke the strings,* he told himself.

From Over-Galapagos, the space city in geosynchronous orbit roughly over the islands that gave it its name, the world looked as Lon recalled it. Two decades could not bring changes large enough to alter the view. But the months he had spent on the surface had convinced him that Earth had changed—far more than he would have deemed possible in the years since he had left to go to the mercenary world of Dirigent to fulfill his childhood ambition of a career as a soldier.

Now, Lon's principal thoughts were of home—and Dirigent was home now, not Earth. He had spent a month traveling to Earth, five months there, and it would be another month before he could get home. He had traveled in civilian clothes, under an assumed name. Prior to his departure from Dirigent, he had undergone genetic-level nanosurgery to make absolutely certain that his true identity

3

could not be discovered from fingerprints, retinal pattern, or DNA testing of his blood or skin.

There won't be anything to tie me to Earth in a few months, he thought. He had hesitated to accept the mission to Earth, but once he had, Lon had decided to make the best use of the unexpected opportunity. After finishing his work for the Corps—and *only* after finishing that work—he had contacted his parents, then gone home to visit them at his childhood home on the eastern side of the Great Smoky Mountains, near the city of Asheville. Even then, Lon had been forced to stay incognito. Had his true identity been discovered by the authorities, it was a virtual certainty that he would have been arrested, that he never would have seen his wife and two children again.

The purpose of Lon's trip to Earth had been espionage.

He had needed nearly the entire month he had with his parents to convince them to emigrate. Although both his mother and father wanted to see their grandchildren, the ties to Earth were strong. They needed time to convince themselves.

"I've got my work at the university," his father had said when Lon first proposed the move. "And your mother has her garden, her friends."

"Dirigent has a university, and students who are there, are there because they want to learn, because they hope to make a difference to mankind. What have you got? You've told me yourself that most of your students are just hoping for a miracle that will help them climb out of the circuses into something—anything—better. You don't even go to the university but—what?—once each term? And then you need an armed guard. You can't go into town safely. This pleasant little country compound you both treasure, even it's an illusion, with electric fences, guard dogs, and armed patrols to keep the real world out. Once you get beyond the fences, casual violence is almost impossible to escape for long." Casual violence, happenstance, had worried Lon more during his months on Earth than the possibility that his mission might be discovered by the authorities.

"This is where our life has always been," his mother had added, in a voice that sounded more fearful than nostalgic. "Except for you and your family, everyone we know is here."

"All locked away safely in guarded compounds like this one," Lon replied.

It still took a lot of talk to get his parents to change their minds. When the decision was finally reached, they couldn't all travel together. Lon had a schedule to keep. He had to get off-planet and out of the reach of Earth's police and what remained of Earth's Confederation of Human Worlds, the old Colonial Office whose authority no longer ran beyond the solar system. His parents would wait a few weeks, sell what they could, then book passage by a circuitous route to Dirigent. By the time they arrived, Lon would have a cottage lined up for them.

Night was beginning to move across eastern North America. Lon stared until he saw the terminator line move across the mountains, past his parents' home, out of what had once been North Carolina into what had once been Tennessee. He saw lights in the cities and along the major connector routes. The cities were urban jungles, with the majority of people crowded into areas known as circuses, slums where the common denominators were poverty and lack of hope.

Lon turned away from the videoscreen that masqueraded as a window and left the observation compartment to return to his transient quarters two decks below. He would not be able to board the ship that would take him on the first interstellar leg of his trip back to Dirigent until the next afternoon. Twenty hours from now, he would be on his way out of Earth's solar system.

If his false identity remained safe another day.

· · ·

Seven months earlier, Lon might have thought that the DMC had no surprises left to spring on him, that he had seen the full repertory. He had been an officer in the Corps for nineteen years, gone out on more contracts than he could easily recall, seen every variety of life in garrison, including the political byplay that suffused the higher officer ranks. He had not even considered that anything out of the ordinary might be in the offing when Major Cavanaugh Zim, number two man in the DMC's Office of Strategic Intelligence (OSI), had asked him to stop by his office at Lon's "earliest convenience." The two men had known each other for some years, and occasionally paired up in bridge tournaments in Dirigent City.

"I remember when you used to work for me in the audit department, back when you were a lieutenant still learning the ropes," Zim had said after the usual opening pleasantries.

"Seems ages ago, Cav," Lon had said, nodding. Lieutenants in the Corps spent one day a week, while they were in garrison, away from their troops, helping out, learning a little bit about other parts of the Corps than their own assignments.

"And then some," Zim had agreed, returning Lon's nods. "When I filed my performance report on you, at the end of your tour here, I added an observation that you might, in time, be uniquely qualified for a special mission."

That had been enough to make Lon sit up straight—the first indication that the invitation had not just been for a stroll down nostalgia drive. Lon had cleared his throat. "A special mission?"

"You know our mandate in OSI—to obtain, catalog, and analyze information about as many of the settled worlds as possible. We're always years behind. New worlds are settled, and it might be decades before we even hear about them. Conditions change, often dramatically, on worlds we do know about. The Corps would like to have up-to-date intelligence on every settled world, at least every world we might possibly be called upon to serve, or oppose." Zim had shrugged. "Not that that rules out any world. And we can never count on being anywhere near up-to-date on any world but Dirigent."

"I don't need the lecture, Cav. Just what are you working up to?"

"We want you to do a job of work for us, Lon."

"Tell me something a cadet couldn't have figured out by now."

"Think about it, Lon. What sort of intelligence mission would *you* be uniquely qualified for?"

Lon had blinked twice, slowly, as it hit him. "You want me to go to *Earth*?"

"The boss and I talked about it at length. Then I chatted with Matt." Matt Orlis, now a lieutenant colonel, commanded 2nd Battalion, 7th Regiment. Lon was his second-in-command. "Matt agreed that you would be perfect for the job, so we put the proposal before the Council of Regiments. The General remembers your work here. He mentioned your analysis of the Aldrin contract." There was only one *General* at any given time in the Dirigent Mercenary Corps, head of government for Dirigent as well as commander-in-chief of the Corps, elected each year by the colonels who made up the Council of Regiments. The current incumbent was Jorge Ruiz, who had commanded the Contracts Section at Corps headquarters—which included OSI—when Lon was a lieutenant doing one day a week in Contracts. "The General okayed the mission, providing you were willing to volunteer. It will mean being gone for six months, more or less, but you've been away nearly that long on contract before."

"My son is fifteen. My daughter is nine," Lon had said. "I've missed a third of their lives already, being away from Dirigent. I know—it goes with the territory. I need time to think about this, Cav. And I need to talk it over with my wife."

"Of course. I didn't expect an answer right now. This isn't like a contract where you take the luck of the draw and go out when it's your turn. The General was adamant. Accepting this mission has to be voluntary. Entirely."

"The first rule any recruit learns is 'Never volunteer for anything,' " Lon mumbled as he settled himself for sleep that night in Over-Galapagos. He had not agreed to the mission lightly, or quickly. Just thinking about the possibility of returning to Earth had brought him new nightmares. Part of him wanted to go back, almost desperately, but another part of him was frightened by the prospect. It had been two days before he even mentioned it to his wife, Sara.

"Of course you'll go," she had said at once, and she proceeded on the assumption that he would.

Lon had needed a lot longer to convince himself. The chance to see his parents for the first time in twenty years was what settled the question. "Maybe I can get them to move here," Lon had told his wife. "I've been suggesting it for years. Maybe, face-to-face, I can convince them."

Sara had giggled. "Or just kidnap them and sneak them off-planet."

He had spent two weeks learning his cover identity and undergoing the genetic manipulation that would ensure that he could not be identified as Lon Nolan when he reached Earth and Earth-controlled space. He went as a trade representative from Calypso, a world he had some personal knowledge of. If necessary, the government there would vouch for his identity . . . but if that became necessary, it would mean that something had gone wrong, that he had made some mistake along the way.

Real-life espionage had nothing in common with the vid-adventure variety. Lon had carried neither weapons nor ultra-high-tech snooping devices. He had done no furtive sneaking about, no suborning of government officials. His information was collected through far more prosaic methods. He had talked to people. He had kept his eyes open, looking around, questioning what he saw, what he heard. He had copied libraries of data—books, newspapers, and magazines—transferring everything to scores of high-density data chips. Fourteen ounces of chips had been enough to record everything published on Earth in the past quarter century. It would give the analysts and auditors in OSI plenty to do for the next couple of years.

There hadn't even been much real danger when he had contacted Dirigent's resident agents and factors on Earth. Their covers were also impeccable. As long as his cover story and identity passed casual scrutiny, no one in authority would give him a second thought. It wasn't until he returned to areas where he had been known as Lon Nolan that there was any serious reason for nervousness, for insecurity. Someone might recognize him, even after twenty years, and wonder.

But nothing untoward had happened. His few encounters with authorities had been the result of what had appeared— to them—to be the casual violence they saw every day, and there had been no reason to look too deeply into Lon's cover. Lon had his reunion, spent time with his parents, even spent time hiking around in the mountains, just as he had done when he was young. Those few weeks had made the entire mission worthwhile.

Waiting to board the ship that would carry him from Over-Galapagos to Calypso was, in some ways, the most difficult part of the entire mission for Lon. His mind kept conjuring up ironic climaxes—the sudden appearance of uniformed police officers, weapons raised, shouting for him to raise his hands and surrender; being carted back to

Earth and a lifetime lease on a six-by-eight-foot prison cell. Or worse.

His baggage, including the data chips, was loaded aboard ship two hours before the four passengers were allowed to board. Lon spent most of those two hours in the observation deck, watching Earth below, saying a private, final farewell to the planet of his birth . . . for the second time in his life. *This breaks the strings,* he told himself—several times. The image remained strong: *Earth strings*—they reached out to every world humans had settled.

Once the ship started accelerating outbound, Lon started to relax a little. He would not feel *really* safe until the ship made its first jump through quantum space, five days out from Over-Galapagos—the first of three jumps it would make to reach Calypso. By the time of the first jump, it would be too late for the authorities from Earth to recall the ship or to intercept it. He would be out of their reach. Forever.

Five days, five nights. Lon slept lightly, when he slept at all. Dreams came, the same fanciful worries he had felt in Over-Galapagos, failing to get away, being intercepted at the last possible minute and carried back to Earth to stand trial . . . or simply being "made" to disappear without trial.

Five days of constant acceleration, farther and farther from Earth and its dependent colonies within the Solar System. When the first warning came over the ship's communication system—"Q-space insertion in thirty minutes"—Lon had bit his lip. *So close. Could escape possibly be snatched from me now?*

On a civilian ship, there were frequent warnings leading up to the Q-space transit. While the ship was in the void of quantum space, all the power of its three Nilssen generators—which provided artificial gravity aboard ship as well as propelling the vessel through Q-space—would be diverted to force the transit. Passengers were required to be in their bunks, strapped in, during the period of zero gravity—for their own safety . . . and to keep them from being a distraction to the crew, or worse, without weight to hold them in place. A crewman went to each passenger's cabin to make sure everyone was strapped in, then hurried to his own duty station to strap himself in for the duration.

"Thirty seconds until Q-space insertion."

The final ten seconds were marked by a countdown. Lon held his breath until he felt the slight shudder of the ship as its Nilssens ratcheted to full power and drew a bubble of Q-space—in effect, a pocket universe just slightly greater in diameter than the longest dimension of the ship and theoretically tangent to every point in the "real" universe—around it.

"Safe." Lon was not concerned that he had spoken the word aloud. He was in Q-space, outbound from Earth. *Safe*. It was not important, at the moment, that he was still more than three weeks from home, from Dirigent. Every interstellar passage took fourteen days, or slightly more: five days out before the first jump, three days before the second and third jumps, and from three to five days from the final jump into the destination. And Lon had to go to Calypso before he could transfer to another ship, *a DMC ship*, to get to Dirigent. And his family.

2

Lon was surprised to learn that there were *two* staff floaters waiting for him at the civilian spaceport in Dirigent City. The explanation came quickly, though. Cavanaugh Zim had come in one from Corps headquarters to take the case of data chips off Lon's hands.

"We'll do a full debriefing next Monday morning," Major Zim told Lon. "And I have a message for you from Matt Orlis. He doesn't want to see hide nor hair of you until after that."

"A full week off?" Lon asked. "Somebody gone soft?"

"We'll talk about it a week from today. Now, I've got to get back to work, and you've got better things to do."

It was at that moment that one door of the other floater—ground effect vehicle—flew open and Angie Nolan jumped out and ran toward her father. Three weeks from her tenth birthday, Angie was still happy being "Daddy's little girl." She squealed with delight as she jumped up to let him catch her and whirl her through a full circle. Angie was tall for her age but slightly below average in weight, blue-eyed and blond—her hair was nearly as light yet as it had been when she was a baby. She threw her arms around his neck and kissed his cheek, then pressed her cheek against his.

"How's my favorite girl?" Lon asked, easing her to the ground and prying her grip loose—with difficulty.

"I'm first in my class again," she announced.

By that time, Major Zim's car had pulled away and the other two passengers from the second vehicle were close—Sara and Lon, Junior. Junior was sixteen now; his birthday had come not long after his father had left for Earth. He hung back just a little. He did not want to seem too . . . effusive. Lon tousled Junior's hair, then took Sara in his arms for a serious hug and a couple of long kisses. Junior looked away.

"How was Earth?" Sara asked when the first rush of greetings was over.

Lon shrugged, turning her toward the car. Angie took her father's free hand. Junior trailed along behind.

"Dirtier than I remembered, and more crowded," Lon said. "Half a dozen small wars going on. Some people think the planetary government is losing all control. Maybe they're right. My parents will be coming here to live. They're probably already on the way."

"Gramma and Grampa?" Angie asked, excitement boiling out of her words. "Coming to *stay*?"

"Coming to stay," Lon agreed. Nothing had been said to the children before about Lon trying to get them to move, because he had been far from confident that he would succeed.

"I was afraid you wouldn't be able to convince them," Sara said. "The letters we've had from them over the years. Your father always seemed so dead set against leaving Earth."

"It wasn't easy talking him into moving," Lon said. A porter had already transferred Lon's bags to the rear compartment of the floater. The driver, a sergeant from the regimental motor pool, got out to hold the rear right door open for Lon and Sara. She got in first. "I think it was news about the battle in Panama City that turned the trick."

"Where?" Sara asked.

"Panama City," Junior said from the front seat. Angie had gotten in back on the left, next to her mother. "On the isthmus between North and South America, where the canal between the two oceans used to be."

"He's right," Lon said. "Militia forces of the Colombian district of South America and the Mexican department of the North American Union fought a major battle, more than ten thousand killed in four days of fighting. Both sides were hurt so badly that neither could honestly claim a victory, though both tried."

"Ten *thousand*?" Sara said.

"The death toll was little more than a footnote in the news stories," Lon said. "Earth's population has gone back above six billion. If a hundred thousand had died, it might have rated a few cheers at least, but ten? That's neither here nor there, as far as most people are concerned."

"That's awful," Sara said.

"You won't get an argument from me," Lon replied. "Or from Dad. 'Ten thousand killed and they don't mention it until the last line of the story?' he said—shouted—when the news came in. I couldn't recall ever seeing him that angry."

The driver had not waited for instructions. As soon as all his passengers were in the floater, he had started driving, exiting the spaceport and taking Freedom Boulevard, the direct route from the spaceport across town to the main camp of the Dirigent Mercenary Corps. It was a ride Lon had made many times in his career. He felt no need to look out the windows. It was much more pleasant to sit with his arm around his wife, holding her close, reassuring himself that they were really back together again.

"How long do we have to get things ready for your parents?" Sara asked, her mind going to practical matters.

"Probably at least a couple of weeks. They were going to need a bit of time to wrap up things before they left. They might have left in the last day or two, or maybe not. But they'll have to make two trips, just like I did. There aren't any direct flights between Earth and Dirigent."

"Find them a small house here in the city? Or an apartment?"

"A house. Mom wants to garden. She's always grown flowers and a few vegetables. She was quite definite about that."

"A good neighborhood, fairly close," Sara said. "And, as soon as we can after they get here, we'll have to take them to Bascombe East to meet my folks."

Lon started chuckling. "We don't have to start making plans this very minute. Give me at least a few hours to relax. What's been happening here?" Not only had Lon been away for six months, he also had been completely out of touch for that time. There had been no chance to exchange message chips while he was undercover on Earth. It would have been far too deep a breach of security practices.

Sara hesitated, trying to think back over what might interest Lon the most. Then she knew what she had to tell him. Bad news. "Matt Orlis's older boy was killed on contract, not a month after you left. It was his first time out."

Lon closed his eyes for an instant. "Mark was just—what—nineteen?"

"Nineteen," Sara confirmed. "Matt and Linda still aren't over it. I've done what I could, but . . ." She shrugged to show how helpless she had felt.

"There's not much anybody can do," Lon said. Glancing at his son was an involuntary reflex, and so was the almost invisible shudder. Junior was doing everything but counting the days until he would be old enough to join the Corps. "I'll go over to his place this evening."

"No, you won't," Sara said firmly. "Didn't Cav tell you that Matt doesn't want to see you until you report back for duty next week?"

"Sure, but that was business. This is . . . different."

"No. It's this, too," Sara insisted. "Matt didn't even want me to tell you about Mark until then."

Lon declined to continue that conversation just then. He couldn't speak freely with the children close enough to hear. This was not the first time Lon had felt haunted by his own past. As a child on Earth, all Lon had ever wanted to be was a soldier. It had taken him to The Springs, the military academy of the North American Union. Then, when the government decided to draft the top students from Lon's graduating class into the federal police—duty that would have centered on preventing and putting down riots in the urban circuses, slums too densely populated by people who had lived on government largess for generations—Lon had conspired with the commandant of the military academy to escape that duty and go off-world, eventually to Dirigent, where he could fulfill his dream of being a soldier. *All I ever wanted to be was a soldier:* Lon couldn't begin to estimate how many times he had uttered that sentence, or thought it. Now Junior kept saying virtually the same thing. All *he* wanted to be when he grew up was a soldier.

It was the *last* thing his father wanted for him. *I've seen too many friends die,* Lon thought. *I'd do anything I could to protect Junior.*

Short of shipping the boy off-world, to some colony where there were no soldiers, there was little Lon *could* do, except try to persuade his son to look elsewhere for a career, but as long as the father remained in the Corps, his arguments all fell short. And Lon knew it. Junior was sixteen now, and on his eighteenth birthday, he would be eligible to enlist in the Corps, whether or not his parents approved . . . and he had often announced his intention to do so, on that very day.

"Why is it that whenever I get a few days off, I always seem to be busier than when I'm supposed to be working?" Lon asked Sara halfway through the week of furlough. They were waiting for the call to board the shuttle to Bascombe East with Junior and Angie. Right now, the children were busy. Angie was in the arcade, playing video games. Junior was sitting off by himself, reading on his portable complink, intent on whatever had caught his interest.

Lon felt as if this were the first chance he'd had to sit and do nothing since getting home. The past three days had been busy, spent catching up on gossip and making arrangements for the arrival of his parents. Taking a couple of days to visit Sara's parents was a natural part of the furlough. Lon enjoyed being around his in-laws, and the children always liked to visit the only grandparents they had ever known—except through recordings that came in letter chips a couple of times a year.

Sara tried hard to suppress a laugh but failed. "Just balance, I suppose," she said. "So you don't forget what real work is like."

"Very funny." Lon let out a long breath, noisily. "At least it looks as if it might be quite a while before the battalion goes out on contract. We're not too near the top of the battalion or regimental rotas for assignment. Could have several months to help Mom and Dad get settled in and learn their way around Dirigent."

"You know, I was thinking last night, after you went to sleep," Sara said, turning on the bench to look directly at her husband. "If you decided it was time to retire from the Corps and take over the pub, we could get your folks a place in Bascombe East, too, and we'd all be together." Geoff and Mildred Pine, Sara's parents, ran the village's only pub, the Winking Eye. And Geoff had been making noises about retiring and turning the pub over to Lon and Sara since their marriage seventeen years before.

Lon did not reply immediately. First he looked around to see where the children were. Then, almost in a whisper, he said, "If I thought that would be enough to get Junior's mind away from joining the Corps, I'd do it in a second, but I don't think it would work."

"No, probably not," Sara said. Unlike Lon, Sara had long since accepted that there was little chance of diverting their son from the Corps. "Every boy wants to be like his father, and you've set high standards. Besides, this *is* Dirigent. The Corps is what we are, in a lot of ways. Without it, we wouldn't have much of anything." The Corps, and a thriving munitions industry that exported as much as it sold domestically, generated virtually all of the world's income. The importance of the Corps found reflection in the fact that the head of the DMC was also the head of state for the planet.

"With his intelligence, he could work in R&D, probably do more good for the Corps than he could do slogging through mud and getting shot at," Lon said.

"He figures he'll have time to do both," Sara replied. "Spend enough time in the Corps to learn just what ideas might be useful, then go off to a lab and turn ideas into practical gear."

That conversation lapsed because their flight was called. Sara gathered the children while Lon checked with the porter to make certain their baggage got aboard the shuttle.

Lon polished pint beer glasses with a bar rag. He enjoyed giving his father-in-law a hand around the pub on visits. It helped Lon relax. In any case, the Winking Eye could not close just because family came to visit. The Nolans had been in Bascombe East a little over six hours. The pub was closed for the night. Junior was sweeping the floor. He wasn't happy with the chore, but he had limited his complaints to a single groan of protest. Lon helped Geoff clean up behind the bar. Sara and Angie were in the pub's kitchen helping Mildred clean up and get ready for the next day. The food served in the Winking Eye was all prepared fresh, not assembled from raw molecules in a food replicator. That was part of the allure of the Winking Eye.

"Enough," Geoff Pine said. He filled two glasses with

his best beer and slid one of them in front of his son-in-law. "Take a swig of that, then we'll go over and take a load off while the women finish in the kitchen."

Lon didn't protest, and neither did Junior when his grandfather told him he could quit rearranging the dust.

"I'm going outside for a few minutes," Junior announced. Lon just nodded. There was little danger or trouble the boy could get into in Bascombe East.

"So you've been on Earth all these months," Geoff said when the two men were seated at a table near the front door. "Sara wouldn't tell us where you'd gone, said it was all hush-hush."

"Officially, even she wasn't supposed to know where I was," Lon said. "Undercover stuff. But, yes, I was on Earth most of the time, except for the transit time, of course, a month each way."

Geoff shook his head, then took a long drink. "Earth belongs to the past. It's not the future, hardly even the present. They don't give a damn about us, and there's nothing we need from them."

"Earth could give us a lot of trouble," Lon said. "Maybe it's just that I was looking at things with older eyes this time, or had a different perspective after twenty years away, but there's a feeling of desperation to just about everything and everyone on Earth these days. Too many people, too little hope. A constant race against disaster."

"The final collapse they've been talking about for centuries?" Geoff asked, arching a skeptical eyebrow.

Lon shrugged. "Let's just say it wouldn't shock me if civilization on Earth melted down."

"If it wasn't for all the suffering people would do, I'd say good riddance," Geoff said. "Find some way to lock Earth up in a Q-space bubble and let the rest of the galaxy get on with its business."

"I see your point, but it's awfully hard for me to feel that way, even as an intellectual exercise."

"No, of course you couldn't see it the way I do, lad. I'd be shocked if you did, coming from there and all. But the only thing Earth really has to offer the rest of us is trouble. They could start shipping off thousands of people to colony worlds, try to shovel their troubles off any way they could."

Lon managed a smile. "Part of the trouble is that they can't possibly ship people out fast enough to make up for the population increase. If they had a thousand ships, each carrying a thousand people out-system every month, they could hardly make a dent in the situation, and there's no way they can find the money or materials to do that."

"Used to be, Mother Nature took care of overpopulation," Geoff said, leaning back. "War, pestilence, and famine. And science has pretty much taken care of two of those."

"Not entirely. There are people starving to death on Earth, even with food replicator technology being hundreds of years old. You still need the raw materials to feed into the system."

"And people still know how to kill each other off," Geoff said. He drained the last of his beer and stood. "That's the shame of it, but if they didn't, the problem would be even worse. I'm just glad it's Earth and not Dirigent."

3

Lon slept well Sunday night, after getting back to the family's home on base in Dirigent City. Bascombe East and the Winking Eye always brought welcome relief to Lon. *Someday* he would take Geoff at his word and retire from the Corps to take over the pub. But not soon—at the moment, the pub was a good change of pace, an escape from the usual. That would change if it occupied his every day.

Monday morning, Lon woke before his alarm could sound at six o'clock. He shaved, showered, and dressed while Sara fixed breakfast—first for him and then for herself and the children.

"I'll try to get home early this afternoon," Lon told Sara. "The realtor has three places for me to look at for Mom and Dad. Maybe we can get to all of them today."

"If we don't, we can take the rest of the week," Sara said. She understood Lon's excitement, and their children's. To a certain extent she shared it.

"The sooner we pick a place and finalize the contract, the sooner we can start getting it ready," Lon said. "I want to have everything finished before they get here, and we don't know when that will be." A message from the ship when it came out of its final Q-space transit would give them just three days' warning.

"Yes, dear," Sara said with mock resignation.

• • •

Lon took the shuttle bus that served the married officers' section of the base to Corps headquarters instead of getting off at the stop it made near the edge of 7th Regiment's area. He would have preferred to visit his office in 2nd Battalion first, talk to others on the staff, but his instructions were clear: Get the debriefing out of the way first.

Cavanaugh Zim was waiting for him.

"We've started the preliminary assessment of your recorded reports, Lon," Zim said as they got settled in his office. "And the cataloging has started on the publications you picked up. I imagine we'll be picking your brain pretty regularly for years to come, trying to get every detail we can out of you. This morning I just want to get some sense of your impressions. I've got a few questions here."

A few *dozen* questions. Zim asked his questions, then sat back and let Lon talk, sometimes asking follow-ups, or prompting Lon for greater detail. The session was being recorded, sound and video. That did not bother Lon. Often he closed his eyes while he talked, using that to help him focus his thoughts, his words. At intervals Zim called for a break. They would take five or ten minutes, have coffee brought in, or leave the office to stretch their legs and breathe different air.

It was very close to noon when Zim said, "I think we'd better call it a day, Lon. Let's go over to the officers' club and I'll buy lunch."

Lon got to his feet and stretched. "Thanks for the offer, Cav, but I think I'll pass. I want to get over to battalion and find out how badly they've screwed everything up the seven months I've been gone. Probably take me a month or more to get things back the way I like them."

"*After* lunch will do just fine for that, Lon. I really have to insist."

"Why is everyone going to so much trouble to keep me away from 2nd Battalion? I heard about Matt's boy getting killed, but that can't explain all this. Something must be up."

"Keep your shirt on, Lon. Indulge us, please." Zim guided Lon through the door. "It'll only be another hour. Then Matt can explain everything. Trust me."

Lunch did not go down easily for Lon. He felt annoyed and concerned. He could not imagine what all the secrecy was about, why his return to his unit was being stalled so thoroughly. Zim had to do most of the talking. Lon's replies were generally monosyllabic. It was a reversal of how the conversation had been in Zim's office through the morning.

"Come on, Lon, don't go working yourself into a lather," Zim urged. "It's just that Matt wants this to go just right."

"Wants *what* to go just right?" Lon shot back.

Zim shook his head slowly. "There's a time and a place for everything. Just let it drift. One more drink and it'll be about time."

Lon rushed through his final drink. Zim dallied, stalling as long as he thought he could without getting Lon too upset to think straight. Then Zim got up. "I guess it'll be time by the time we walk over to your battalion headquarters," he said.

The central area of the DMC's main base had been laid out in a regular and orderly way. The largest building on base was Corps Headquarters, which also served as Government House for the world. A broad parade field extended from the west facade of Corps Headquarters all the way to the main gates. The fourteen line regiments were arranged along the long sides of the parade ground, 1st through 7th on the north, 8th through 15th (there no longer was a 9th Regiment; it had been virtually destroyed on a contract that—in retrospect—should never have been accepted, and the 9th had never been reconstituted) on the south. Each regiment had its headquarters at the far end of its section, marking the "bottom" of a long, narrow horseshoe, battalions on the flanks, with battalion headquarters in the center of the company barracks. Ancillary units—armor, artillery, and support services, for example—were quartered farther from the central parade ground.

Since the main officers' club, where Lon and Zim had eaten, was south of Corp headquarters, they had only a moderate walk to the offices of 2nd Battalion, 7th Regiment, across the parade ground and down Seventh Street, which ran between the battalion areas. Only a few soldiers were visible in 2nd Battalion's area, policing the ground—a regular fatigue detail.

"You could at least give me a hint what to expect," Lon said as they neared the entrance to 2nd Battalion's headquarters.

"No way," Zim said. "This is Matt's show. I'm not going to give you a peek at the script."

Zim stayed at Lon's elbow, herding him directly toward Matt Orlis's office on the ground floor. Zim knocked, but scarcely waited for the muted "Come in" from the other side of the door. Zim pushed Lon in first, then closed the door behind the two of them.

"Glad to see you back, Lon," Matt Orlis said as he got up from the chair behind his desk. There was no gladness in the voice, though, and Lon was immediately struck by the drawn—almost haggard—look on Matt's face.

Lon met Matt halfway across the office and they shook hands. "I was sorry to hear about Mark," Lon said. "Nobody would let me come see you until today."

Matt Orlis's shrug was minuscule, as if any more effusive gesture was beyond his physical capacity. "It's a risk we all take," he said. "As for the delay . . ." He did not complete that sentence. "Have a seat. You, too, Cav. You might as well stick around for the rest of this."

Lon hesitated. Matt had simply turned his back and retreated to his position in the rear corner of the office, behind his desk. Cavanaugh Zim went to a chair at the side of the room, out of the way. Finally, Lon took the seat near the corner of Matt's desk.

"What the hell is going on, Matt?" Lon asked.

Orlis leaned back in his chair but met Lon's stare. "This time tomorrow, I'll be a civilian. I'm retiring. You take over 2nd Battalion. Your promotion to lieutenant colonel is effective at midnight tonight. Vel Osterman from Delta Company will be your executive officer. His promotion to major will be on the same general order as your promotion."

"Matt . . ." Lon started, but Orlis cut him off before he could get more than the name out.

"Save it, Lon. It's a done deal. I made my decision ten weeks ago and there hasn't been a single second thought. I've put more than thirty years into the Corps. It's time to get out. Linda and I need to spend more time with each other, and with our children, our remaining children." Lon could almost feel the pain in Matt's voice. "I would have left sooner, but I wanted to wait until you got back."

"You could have been the next regimental commander, Matt," Lon said. He leaned forward. "A seat on the Council of Regiments. Maybe a term as General before long."

Matt shook his head. "No. I don't want it. I don't want any of it."

Once more, Lon hesitated before he spoke. "I'm sure you know your mind, Matt, but I still think it's a shame. You're a damned good officer, and you've always been a terrific friend."

"You'll be needing a new battalion lead sergeant, too," Matt said. "I talked Weil into sticking around through the end of the week to help you get settled in, but he's also retiring. Hell, he's got more time in the Corps than I do." Weil Jorgen had been a platoon sergeant in the battalion's

A Company when Lon first arrived as an officer-cadet, and had moved up the line through the years.

Is anyone staying? Lon wondered. "I'll want Phip Steesen as my lead sergeant," he said. "If he's not retiring, too."

Matt ignored the sarcasm in Lon's voice. "I told Colonel Black it would be Steesen. Regiment will cut the order promoting him effective Friday, when he takes over from Weil officially. I'll tell Weil to have Alpha send him over so you can tell him yourself."

"I've got to get back to the shop," Zim announced, getting up from his chair. He went to Lon and offered his hand. "Congratulations on the promotion, Lon." They shook hands, then Zim turned to Matt. "I'm sorry to see you go myself, Colonel, but I do understand why."

As they shook hands, Matt shook his head and said, "Not entirely, Cav, not entirely," very softly.

After Zim had left, Orlis used the intercom to tell Weil Jorgen to get Phip Steesen in as quickly as he could be located. Then he turned to Lon again.

"It hasn't been easy, these last months," Matt said. "You'd think that after thirty years of losing friends and comrades, seeing some of them die, a man would get used to death. Especially in the Corps." He shook his head. "It ain't so, Lon. It just ain't so. There are still nights when I wake up crying, feeling a knot in my stomach the size of a soccer ball."

"Some things you can't get used to, Matt. There are nights I lie awake worrying about Junior. He wants to be a soldier as much as I did when I was a kid. And I can't think of any way to keep him from joining the Corps, as soon as he's old enough."

"My father was in the Corps, and both his brothers. Both my grandfathers. It goes back nearly two hundred years in the Orlis family," Matt said. "Soldiering is what we do on Dirigent. It makes the world turn. But, *dear God*, this hurts." Matt's voice broke. He seemed to be near breaking into tears. It took him more than a minute to get his emotions under control. Lon sat quietly, not moving at all, trying to keep his own worries about Junior from getting to him in response.

"Sorry, Lon," Matt said when he could speak without showing anguish in his voice. "I shouldn't have laid that on you."

"Don't worry about it, Matt."

Orlis took a deep breath, held it a moment, then let it out. "Weil can give you a better briefing on what's going on in the battalion than I can. Delta and Bravo have new officer-cadets since you left. Wallis Ames moved to regimental staff six weeks ago. He's handling communications and transportation." Matt shrugged. "After twenty-three years as a captain commanding Bravo Company, something finally turned up that let him become a major." Ames had been a competent but unimaginative line officer; never any strong black marks against his record but also without any special flair for the business of combat.

"Charlie Company is number two on the rota for company-sized contracts," Matt said. "The rest are farther down, and we've got a way to go to get to the top for battalion- or regimental-sized contracts."

"I know. I checked the rotas last week, just after I got in," Lon said. Contracts came in all sizes, depending on the needs and resources of the client. The Corps maintained separate listings to make sure that every unit got its fair share of contracts. Contract pay was higher than garrison pay, and—especially on a combat contract—there was always the chance of a completion bonus.

"If we had been closer to the top, I think I would have retired sooner, Lon. The way I've been, it wouldn't have been fair to the men for me to command the battalion in combat."

"You'd have done it up right, Matt, the way you always

have. That would have been better than sending the battalion off without either of us."

"I'm just relieved the situation didn't come up."

Lon's office, across the hall from Matt's, was much as Lon had left it before leaving for Earth. There were a few recent papers on the desk, and the complink screen showed a list of files that he needed to check out. No sooner had Lon sat at his desk when there was a knock at the door.

"Come in."

Lon looked up to see Lead Sergeant Weil Jorgen enter. "Good to see you back, sir," Weil said.

"It's good to be back, sort of," Lon said. "Sit down, Weil. I hear you're running out on me, too."

Before he sat, Weil glanced at the door, almost as if he could see through two doors, to where Matt Orlis was. "It's time for me to hang it up, sir," Weil said. "Getting awful hard to stay in good enough shape. I'd rather choose when I go out than just turn up deficient on a physical training test. Last one was awful close. Too close."

"What about the colonel?" Lon asked, very softly.

Weil shook his head. "It's been rough for him, losing his oldest boy that way. Like the life just drained out of him. At first, we all thought it'd pass, that he'd get back to something like normal. Maybe not all the way, but . . . well, you know, sir. But, if anything, it's just dragged on him harder. Sometimes I could see him cringe at the sight of battledress uniforms. Like to broke my heart, seeing him like that. We've been on a lot of contracts together, all the way back to when he was a raw lieutenant and I was a squad leader. Ages and then some."

Lon nodded. "He's changed, that's for sure. I'm bringing in Phip Steesen to hold down your desk when you go. I'm glad you're sticking around a few days to help us all get up to speed. Phip, me, and the new exec."

"Well, sir, Major Osterman's been hanging around several weeks now, acting as executive officer, so he pretty well knows what's going on already. Steesen, now . . ." Weil grinned. "Well, I'll lay you ten to one he spends thirty minutes bitching about you ruinin' his life again."

Lon matched the sergeant's grin. "No bet, Weil. Phip's bitched every time we put another stripe on his sleeve. Keeps saying he wishes he was still a private taking orders, not stuck in the middle taking and giving."

"He can carry on, but he'll do the job right as anyone. You get under the crab hide, he's a damn fine soldier— but don't you dare tell him I said that, sir."

"Your secret's safe with me, Weil. Any idea how long it'll be before he gets here?"

"Shouldn't be long."

"Send him straight back as soon as he comes in."

Lon recognized the pattern of the knock on his office door. "Come on in, Phip," he said. He leaned back and grinned as Phip opened the door and seemed to peek around it before coming all of the way into the office. "Have a seat. Relax."

Phip Steesen had been one of the first friends Lon had made when he came to Dirigent and joined the Corps as an officer-cadet. Phip, Janno Belzer, and Dean Ericks had been in the fire team Lon had been assigned to. The three of them had taken him under their collective wing, as it were, and the four of them had quickly become close friends, spending much of their off-duty time together as well. Janno had gotten married and left the Corps little more than a year later. Dean Ericks had been killed on contract, nine years back, on Bancroft.

"I see you made it back in one piece," Phip said as he sat in the chair at the side of Lon's desk. "Get all the cobwebs swept out?" The relationship the two men maintained was delicate. They were close friends, but on duty, Lon was an officer and Phip a noncom, and Lon had been above Phip in the line of command from the day he received his lieutenant's pips.

"I think I finally cut the strings," Lon said. "Earth could hardly be more alien. My folks are moving here. Should arrive some time in the next few weeks."

"Hey, that's good news!"

Lon smiled. "It is. Now, I've got more news for you, and I'm not sure you'll think it's quite as good."

"Oh-oh. When you start out like that, it's odds on that I'm not going to like the finish."

"You've got until ten o'clock tomorrow morning to turn Alpha Company over to your successor as company lead sergeant. Matt Orlis is retiring tomorrow, and Weil checks out Friday. You're Weil's replacement. He's finishing out the week to help us both get settled in."

"Oh, Lon. Why'd you have to go and do that to me?" Phip said, and Lon wasn't certain if the remark was serious or in jest. Or somewhere in between.

"You know the reasons as well as I do," Lon said, struggling to keep from laughing. "If nothing else, you know how I like things better than anyone else I might pick, and—most of the time—I know what to expect from you."

"Don't polish my brass. We've known each other too long."

This time Lon couldn't hold back the laugh. "Exactly. That's why I need you in the front office when I move across the hall. Besides, I'm sure Jenny will find use for the extra money you'll draw as battalion lead sergeant."

Phip groaned. "Jenny could find use for the extra money if I was General." When Phip had finally "broken down" and married, four years before, it had been news almost of the magnitude of "Man Bites Dog."

"Does Captain Girana know you're shanghaiing me?"

Lon shook his head as he reached for a key on his desk complink. "Weil, get Captain Girana on the line," Lon said when Jorgen answered the intercom call. It took no more than thirty seconds before Tebba Girana appeared on the screen.

"Tebba, you need a new lead sergeant," Lon told him. "I'm taking Steesen."

"You mean it's official now?" Tebba asked.

"What's that supposed to mean?"

"Well, I've been figuring you'd steal Phip since I heard you were getting the battalion. Wil Nace will be the replacement."

"Good choice," Lon said. "I'll have the order published. The effective date will be Friday, but I'm pulling Phip over here tomorrow, as of the change-of-command ceremony."

"You can have him now, if you can find him," Tebba said, chuckling. "Just send him back to clean out his desk."

"No respect. I don't get no respect at all," Phip said, loud enough for Tebba to hear.

"He's here with me now," Lon said.

"I know, Lon," Tebba said. "At least, I knew he had been called over to see you. I'll tell Nace he's finally moving up. He's been due the promotion for years. Thought I'd end up losing him to another company so he could get it."

"He coulda had my job any time he wanted it," Phip said.

Once Phip left, Lon called Sara to tell her the news about his promotion. "This is one you didn't pick up on the back-yard net," he said then. "The grapevine must have broken." Over the years, there had been times when the officers' wives appeared to know when everything happened before their husbands did.

"I thought Matt would change his mind," Sara said. "I just couldn't believe he'd go through with retiring."

"You and the kids coming to watch the ceremony tomorrow?"

"Of course," Sara said quickly. "I was just trying to decide just what-all I've got to get done."

"I'll probably be home late this evening, tomorrow evening, too," Lon said. "All the time I've been gone, I'm going to have a lot of work slipping into the new job."

"You don't have to do everything the first twenty-four hours," Sara said. "You'll have months to get it all to your satisfaction. I know how far down on the rotas you are."

"New CO, new exec, new lead sergeant—Weil is retiring Friday, and I'm bringing Phip over to take the job. Bravo has a new company commander. Several new platoon sergeants and a new company lead sergeant. Two officer-cadets in the battalion. This and that. We've got to get in a lot of training before we're back at the level where we need to be."

There *was* plenty of work that needed doing, but after Lon closed the link to Sara, he just sat and stared at the blank complink monitor, not even blinking for more than a minute. In that time, Lon's mind was nearly as empty as the screen. Finally he shook his head, as if that might help clear away the sudden cobwebs. The day was far from over, and there had already been so much in it.

Everything at once, he thought. All of the day's events were fighting for his attention again. There was the agony he had seen in Matt Orlis, but that touched a raw nerve; Lon fought against thinking about that. *Lieutenant colonel.* Lon shook his head again. *I thought it would be years before I made it.*

That put him back in command of troops, not merely a staff officer. *Puts the load back on my shoulders,* he thought, *for a lot more men than ever before.* Being second-in-command behind Matt Orlis had been soft duty most of the time. Now the decisions would be Lon's, as well as the responsibility. *More than eight hundred men.*

If I screw up on a contract, a lot of good people could pay the price. There was always that burden.

"At least I've got the best batch of officers and sergeants anyone could hope for," he said softly. He got up and walked over to the window. He opened the blinds and looked out. Barracks and sky. "And I had a good teacher."

That brought his thoughts back to Matt Orlis, but not the years that Lon had served under him as both climbed the ladder in the Corps. All he could see was the anguish on Matt's face, thinking about the death of his son.

That could be me someday, he thought, and he felt suddenly cold all over. *Would I react any differently if Junior were killed on contract?* It was a question he couldn't—didn't want to—answer.

A change-of-command ceremony, in garrison, was a spectacle—with the scale increasing almost exponentially the higher the level of the change. The annual ceremony during which the newly elected General replaced his predecessor was as elaborate and ornate as any coronation of a hereditary monarch had ever been on Earth.

The uniform of the day for the ceremony transferring command of 2nd Battalion, 7th Regiment was full-dress. Since it was autumn, that meant iridescent blue-green tunics over dark green trousers with ceremonial swords for the officers, solid dark green tunics and trousers for enlisted men.

Colonel Hiram Black, commanding officer of 7th Regiment, was present to formally hand 2nd Battalion over to the Corps' newest lieutenant colonel, Lon Nolan. The DMC band was present, brilliant in scarlet and black uniforms, to play properly martial music for the ceremony. The men of 2nd Battalion stood at attention, ordered by platoons and companies, in ranks and files so straight they could have been used to lay out the foundation of a building. Families of married officers and sergeants had seats in temporary bleachers set up for the occasion. The families of the few married privates, lance corporals, and corporals had folding chairs, just a little farther than the other families from the platform where the handover would take place.

To the strains of a stirring march, an honor guard arrived carrying the flags of Dirigent, the Corps, 7th Regiment, and that regiment's 2nd Battalion. The flags were placed in stands at the rear of the platform. The officers of the honor guard—from other battalions in 7th Regiment—took up places at either side of the platform. The regimental chaplain offered an opening prayer, then introduced Colonel Black.

Colonel Black spent ten minutes extolling the martial virtues of the retiring battalion commander, noting Matt Orlis's length of service and the most notable of the combat contracts he had been part of. He mentioned the death of Matt's son, the "great personal sacrifice" that all members of the Corps had to be prepared for. Then Colonel Black spent an equal time touting the new battalion commander, mentioning—almost with his first words—that Lon had come from Earth to join the Corps, going on to talk about his achievements, rapid promotion, and so forth, right to veiled comments about his most recent mission, though Earth was never actually mentioned.

Next, Colonel Black read the text of the general order transferring command of 2nd Battalion from Orlis to Nolan. The captain who had carried the battalion's flag reclaimed it from its stand as the band went into another snappy tune, and marched crisply up to Matt Orlis, who touched the standard briefly with both hands. The captain then carried the flag three steps, to Lon Nolan, who touched the standard the same way. Then the flag was returned to its place at the rear of the platform.

Both lieutenant colonels saluted the colonel, who returned the salutes. The band segued into a different march while the three men exchanged handshakes and private words. The honor guard picked up the flags and started carrying them away, off to the left, to turn a corner—out of sight of the men of the battalion and their families— before dispersing.

Lieutenant Colonel Lon Nolan was now commander of the battalion he had served in since joining the Dirigent Mercenary Corps—responsible for the lives, well-being, and *performance* of more than eight hundred men.

4

By Friday afternoon, three days after he had taken command of 2nd Battalion, Lon was telling himself that it had been the most difficult week of his life—worse than recruit training on Dirigent or Hell Week at The Springs on Earth. From six every morning until as late as eight or nine in the evening, it seemed to be hurry, hurry, hurry, one thing right after the other, never enough time, always a half dozen more items on the schedule.

On Tuesday afternoon he had held an officers' call for all of the officers under his command. There had been several meetings with staff officers and company commanders, meetings with the officers and noncoms of each company. He attended briefings at regiment. He read incoming reports, read and signed outgoing reports, dealt with planning the battalion's training schedule for the next three months . . . and on and on.

Each morning he had taken calisthenics with the battalion, including the two-mile run that always concluded the exercise session. When he could, he squeezed in an hour's workout in the regimental gymnasium late in the afternoon. An officer in the Corps, no matter how high his rank, had to meet the same physical conditioning standards that a private—perhaps twenty years younger—had to. Lon worried that he had let himself get too far out of shape in the months he had been gone. On the ships he had traveled aboard and on Earth it had rarely been possible to get as

36

extensive a workout as he would have liked. Now that he was back, he was anxious to correct the situation as quickly as possible. He had started his program the morning after returning, and kept it up even during the two and a half days in Bascombe East. Back on duty, he increased his demands on himself.

As if he didn't already have more than enough to do, twice during the week he took time away from base to look at cottages his parents might be interested in, properties Sara had already inspected and decided were good enough for him to consider.

"I'm going to take off a couple of hours early today, Vel," Lon told his executive officer shortly after lunch Friday. "We're closing the deal on a place for my parents."

"Why not take off now?" Osterman suggested. They were sitting in Lon's office, drinking coffee. "No use burning yourself out at the start. You've been driving hard all week. I can handle things until quitting time." The major was three years older than Lon and had been in the Corps since the week of his eighteenth birthday. He had made captain shortly after Lon was commissioned as a lieutenant, and had only one promotion since, against the three Lon had won. Osterman's progress in the Corps was far more nearly typical.

Lon glanced at the timeline on his complink screen. "I told Sara I'd meet her at the realtor's office at three. It's not one-thirty yet."

"So stop at the officers' club for a kiss-the-week-goodbye drink first," Vel suggested. "Get out of here, away from the office. I'm serious. It'll do you a world of good."

"We're having company for dinner this evening, so I can't start drinking now," Lon said with a smile. He stretched, then stood. "But I guess I can get in fifty minutes at the gym."

• • •

Lon did not try to deceive himself. Although he was still in excellent physical condition, he was not the athlete he had been as a teenager. No matter how conscientious he was about his training, every year saw an erosion in his numbers—as much as a half second off his best times for the mile, for example. It had been three years since he had broken the four-minute mile. At The Springs, when he was nineteen, he had come within three-tenths of a second of the world record for the distance. He had accepted that all he could hope to do was minimize the inescapable erosion that age brought to performance.

He pushed himself hard for forty-five minutes, using several exercise machines, then running laps, attempting to match his last time for the mile. While he walked a final lap of the indoor track, cooling down, he thought about that. *I'm not trying to beat my best, just trying to meet what I've done lately.* He shook his head. *Age. It catches up with all of us.*

"Comes a time to face it and move on," he muttered. The average life span on Dirigent—ignoring the downward bias caused by military casualties—was 115 years, near life expectancy on most developed colony worlds. Most people remained healthy, active, even vigorous until very nearly the end. There simply came a time when nanomedical implants could not repair and regenerate tissue and organs as fast as they wore out, and the nanosystems started generating their own errors.

Exercise, a shower, and vigorous toweling always served to help Lon relax and put aside his current worries. Even his preoccupation with the effects of aging on his physical capabilities did not survive the routine. By the time he was dressed, ready to leave, he had almost fully put aside his workday thoughts and was looking forward to meeting Sara and concluding the deal for a home for his parents.

One of the perks of being battalion commander was that

Lon was authorized a staff car and driver from the regimental motor pool. Both were waiting when he emerged from the gymnasium attached to regimental headquarters. I ~~laxed in the backseat. The driver knew where to The realtor's office was in the city, along Free-ulevard—the route mercenary units took to the /ort when they were going out on contract.

ra was just getting out of a taxi when Lon's driver .ed up to the curb behind it. "Good timing, Corporal," ɔn said before his driver got out to open the rear door.

"Yes, sir," the corporal said as he held open Lon's door. "Just takes the right knack and a lot of luck."

"We shouldn't be too long. This is all supposed to be ready for signatures."

"I've got nowhere else to go, Colonel," the driver said.

When Lon got home shortly after four o'clock, he changed into civilian clothes—loose shirt and trousers, and soft moccasins he had purchased on Earth. The tag had said "genuine Cherokee handcrafted," but Lon was not convinced of the truth of that claim. It didn't matter. They were comfortable, and as far from boots or dress shoes as he could get without going barefoot.

Sara went into her busy mode, making final preparations for the evening's dinner, drafting both Junior and Angie to help. That the guests would not arrive for two hours didn't slow Sara at all, though there was little enough she needed to do. Lon made a perfunctory offer of help, which, predictably, was refused.

Lon allowed himself a single mixed drink and nursed it while he watched the news feed on the entertainment console in the living room. After his long absence, he still needed to click over to background material to make sense of some of the ongoing stories. Almost a third of the DMC was off-world fulfilling contracts, most of which were training missions. Only one contract was for a full regiment, the 8th. They were en route to a world Lon had never heard of before . . . not an unusual occurrence.

There was a paucity of other off-world news, and much of that was labeled as unconfirmed rumor. News traveled slowly through interstellar space, leaping from world to world with whatever ships happened to be leaving port, each transit aging the story by two weeks. One report that did have official confirmation, three months old, said that a son had been born to the Windsor king of the Second Commonwealth and his wife, on Buckingham. That carried the usual links to the history of the Second Commonwealth and the royal genealogy.

"I'm going to get changed," Sara announced a half hour before their guests were supposed to arrive. "Is that what you're going to wear?"

Lon glanced down at his clothing. "I planned to," he said. "What's wrong with it?"

Sara hesitated before she said, "Oh, I guess it'll do. It's just not very appropriate for a battalion commander."

The laugh jumped out before Lon could stop it. "We're not hosting the spring ball, dear," he said. "Just an informal evening with friends."

Sara opened her mouth, then closed it—trying not to smile. She shook her head, then left.

"What's wrong with the way I'm dressed?" Lon asked softly, with no one to answer.

Twenty minutes later, Sara was back, looking as fresh as if she had spent the entire day primping for the evening. She was not wearing anything fancy, but still managed to look elegant—more so by comparison with the way Lon was dressed.

"*That's* why you thought I should be more formal," Lon said as she pirouetted to give him the full effect.

"You've got time to change, if you hurry."

"I don't think so. My neck still chafes from wearing that

high-necked dress uniform the other day. Look at it like this: The seedier I look, the better you look by comparison."

When the entertainment console beeped to signal someone at the door, Lon went to answer. Phip and his wife, Jenny, were there with their year-old daughter and Jenny's brother, Kalko Green.

"You'd better water Phip's drinks tonight," Jenny said as soon as the greetings were out of the way. "He's already had to stick on one killjoy patch to sober up after the retirement party for Weil Jorgen."

"That's sacrilege, love," Phip said. "We never water our liquor. Goes against everything the Corps stands for. Besides, you've probably got enough killjoy patches in your purse to sober up the entire battalion."

They moved into the living room. Junior took the sleeping baby from Jenny Steesen and set her in the crib Sara had borrowed from a neighbor for the evening. Junior and Angie had volunteered—after only minimal coaxing—to tend little Mary Steesen while the adults had dinner; they had eaten earlier.

Sara came out of the kitchen, and the greetings started over. Phip had known Lon years longer than he had known Sara, but Sara claimed credit for introducing Phip to his wife.

It all went back to the court-martial. Nine years before, Kalko Green, then a private in the DMC, had been convicted of manslaughter for killing a sergeant who had been abusing him and threatening his young sister, Jenny. Lon had been one of the members of the court-martial. Afterward, Kalko had become something of a *cause célèbre* because of the court-martial testimony of his sister. Many people saw Kalko as more of a victim than the dead man— as a hero, even. Sara and a number of other officers' wives (calling themselves the Committee for True Justice) had petitioned the General for clemency for Kalko, taking the case public and enlisting growing support—including four of the five members of the court-martial. It had taken nearly three years, but the case finally found a sympathetic ear, and the current General had commuted Kalko's fourteen-year sentence to time served. The committee was still working, attempting to obtain a full pardon for Kalko, to restore the civil rights his conviction had cost him. He could not vote or hold any government position. It was during that continuing effort that Sara had introduced Phip and Jenny. Two years later, they had married.

Kalko was now a factory shift supervisor. The title sounded more impressive than it was. Each shift consisted of six workers to tend the machinery and the computers that ran them.

"I heard a rumor this afternoon you might be interested in, Lon," Phip said near the end of dinner. "At the party for Weil I got to talking with the lead sergeant from Contracts at Corps HQ. There's a ship inbound, just came out of Q-space this afternoon. One of the passengers is the governor of Bancroft."

"Bancroft?" Lon's eyebrows raised. Phip nodded and repeated the name of the world.

"Something special about that place?" Kalko asked.

"We were there some years back," Lon said.

"Nine years," Sara said. "Right after the court-martial."

"A good friend died there," Lon said very softly. The memory of Dean's death brought a quick pang. Lon shook his head and looked toward Phip again. "Was there anything more to the rumor you heard?"

"Just the name. Sosa is still running Bancroft. The ship won't reach parking orbit until Monday. They must be looking for help again, and it must be really serious if the governor came himself."

"Somebody trying to raid them for their mineral wealth

again, no doubt," Lon said. "Probably the same cartel as before. Oh, well, Bancroft will be somebody else's problem this time. We're too far down the rota unless they ask for a couple of full regiments."

"Not likely," Phip said. "They pinched pennies to hire one company to train their militia last time." He turned toward Jenny and Kalko. "Lon's the guy who actually talked them into offering a piece of the action when we amended the contract to go out and actually have a shot at the bad guys, a percentage of the gold, and other stuff we recovered."

Lon lowered his head, looking at his plate, remembering Dean Ericks. "We know a little more about the Colonial Mining Cartel now," Lon said, almost talking to himself. "I looked up everything I could find about them while I was on Earth. They've pretty well strip-mined everything in Earth's Solar System that didn't have people sitting right on top, and they've been working their way out through extrasolar colony systems as quickly as they could, local residents be damned."

"Earth's *that* desperate for those things?" Jenny asked.

"That desperate and more," Lon said, looking at her. She was scarcely half Phip's age, but that didn't seem to detract from the quality of their relationship. "They have to bring in gold, platinum, and even more common metals like nickel and copper as fast as they can just to keep Earth functioning."

The evening had progressed to dessert and wine before the complink signaled an incoming message. Lon excused himself and went to the living room to answer the call there. When he pressed the accept key and the call was connected, Lon's jaw dropped. He was looking at his mother.

"I've been trying to call for six hours," she said. "We

couldn't get an open channel until now. All tied up with official business, they told us. We're going to arrive Monday afternoon, they tell us, about two o'clock your time. Your father and I."

5

It was a hectic weekend for Lon and Sara. They had assumed that they would have at least another week to prepare for the arrival of Lon's parents. The house had been bought, but it had no furniture—or anything. Saturday started with a frantic furniture shopping tour, and a certain amount of pleading to get the basic necessities delivered before noon Monday. Some things they took with them, to drop off at the house that day.

On Sunday they hung curtains, bought towels and washcloths, sheets, silverware, and everything else they had been able to think of. By that evening, both were tired.

"I wish I could take off tomorrow morning to help get the furniture set up," Lon told his wife while they were getting ready for bed Sunday night—an hour earlier than normal. "But we've got the colonel's weekly meeting at eight, and I can't miss my first one as battalion commander." The Monday conference was a tradition—the regimental commander and his staff heads met with the battalion commanders to rehash the previous week's events and plan for the new week and beyond.

"Don't worry about it," Sara said. "I'll be there, and the delivery men will put everything where I want it and carry off the containers. As long as they show up when Mr. Hastings said they would, everything will be set before your folks get on the shuttle to land."

"Still, I *should* be there."

"Go to sleep."

The commander's conference Monday morning was uncomfortable for Lon. It wasn't simply because he was distracted by the impending arrival of his parents or the work that Sara had to do without him to make sure the cottage was ready. The meeting started with Colonel Black formally introducing Lon to the other battalion commanders and his staff—although Lon had known all of them for years. Lon was younger than the other battalion commanders—in one case, half the age—and the others all had at least ten years more service than Lon. He felt embarrassed, as if the others were staring at him throughout the meeting.

There was little substance in the conference—routine reports, measuring last week's activities against the program set out at the previous meeting, establishing criteria for the current week, discussion about the current state of affairs for the Corps—specifically, how long it might be before contracts came up for 7th Regiment or its constituent units.

The conference dragged on for two hours, and by the time Colonel Black finally dismissed the meeting, Lon was about ready to run for the door and keep going. He realized that it was irrational. He had attended a few of these meetings in the past, standing in for Matt Orlis or because he had something specific to contribute, but this was definite. Now, he *was*—in the jargon of the Corps—2nd Battalion, not a temporary substitute.

"Lon, stick around for a minute, if you would," Colonel Black said when the meeting was over.

Lon sat back down and waited for the rest of the officers to file out of the conference room.

"How are things going for you in 2nd?" Hiram Black

asked when the two were alone. "You getting settled in right?"

"No complaints," Lon said. "Being away from the battalion for seven months complicates things a little, but I've got good people. They're getting me up to speed in a hurry."

"Good, good. I know you'll do your usual bang-up job. Ah, by the way, I had a call from the General this morning."

"About me?"

"In part. The governor of Bancroft is arriving today, and the General suggested that you should be part of the official reception committee." Lon started to interrupt, but Black waved him quiet. "I know. I told the General that your parents are arriving on the same ship, that you need to meet them and get them settled. The General agreed, rather reluctantly, but said that since you'll be at the spaceport anyway, you ought to be able to take a few minutes to greet Governor Sosa."

"Yes, sir. Of course," Lon said. "I'd have tried to do that even without the General's . . . invitation."

Black smiled. "I was sure you would. I told the General you'd be eager to renew your acquaintance with the governor."

The way it worked out, Lon's floater was nearly part of the official procession from the base to the spaceport. That was accidental. Sara was at the cottage they had purchased for Lon's parents, and after picking her up, the driver had turned onto the boulevard a couple of cars behind the convoy that included the General and two regimental commanders as well as a number of other functionaries and aides. The band was already at the spaceport, warming up—or getting in a last rehearsal.

There was a certain amount of confusion when the official welcoming party piled out of the staff cars and limousines. Lon's driver managed to get into the reserved area where the other vehicles were parking, closer to the place where the shuttle would discharge its passengers than the public lot was.

The General, Jorge Ruiz, spotted Lon and had one of his aides bring Lon and his wife over.

"Good to see you again, Nolan," Ruiz said. "I hate to impose on you when you've got family coming in, but Governor Sosa asked after you by name."

"I look forward to meeting him again, General," Lon said.

"A few words now, a promise you'll be available to talk with him later on his visit, and we'll let you get on with your reunion," Ruiz said. "Seems the people of Bancroft are having the same sort of trouble you helped them with some years back."

"I guessed that, General, when I heard that the governor was aboard the incoming ship. Seems it might be worse this time if the governor himself came."

"We'll find out soon enough. The thing is, they were impressed enough with the Corps to come to us again, perhaps with a larger contract in the offing. That says a lot for the job you and your lads did for them before."

"Yes, sir. Thank you. How long will it be before the shuttle lands?"

The General glanced at his watch before he answered. "Twelve minutes, if the information I was given is correct."

If it isn't, somebody's butt will be hot, Lon thought. *You don't give the General bad data.*

The General turned his attention to someone else, and Lon and Sara moved a few steps away. Unlike the official welcoming party—all decked out in full-dress uniforms—Lon was wearing off-dress blues, the standard uniform in the offices. He stuck out like a banana in a bowl of grapes.

Off to the side, the band had gone quiet. They were done

rehearsing, or warming up, and the director was dressing the lines, making certain the military formation was perfect.

A red carpet was rolled out from the stand where the General and his entourage would wait. They were just starting to move up onto the platform.

"You think the pilot will be able to stop with the door right over that rug?" Sara whispered to her husband.

"Not one of our shuttle pilots, so who can tell?" he replied out of the side of his mouth. "Any of ours could, and would do it without being told. With an outsider . . . I wonder if the General's staff has made bets on how far off it'll be."

Sara giggled. Lon glanced at her and almost missed the gesture by the General's aide, calling for Lon to join the rest on the platform. The aide had to make the gesture a second time before Lon saw it and nodded.

"Come along, dear," he said, taking Sara's elbow. "Give you a chance to feel what it's like."

"They don't want me," she protested.

"Maybe not, but *I* do."

The shuttle arrived precisely on schedule, as Lon had assumed it would. Lon, along with most of the people who had come to greet the visiting dignitary, watched the shuttle come in from the west, gliding in for an easy landing— not at all like the combat landings a military shuttle practiced to get troops down and out of "the box" as quickly as possible when hostile forces might be in the area. A small dot in the sky, ten degrees above the horizon, was the first indication of the incoming craft. It "grew larger" and came gently lower.

From where Lon stood, the landing appeared to be as near perfect as possible. A hundred yards from the welcoming stand, the shuttle lowered flaps and reversed thrust on its engines, braking noisily as it went on past the waiting officers. The delay was short, though. As soon as the shuttle came to a stop, the pilot got it turned around and taxied back to where it was supposed to land.

Lon was almost disappointed that the passenger compartment's hatch only missed aligning perfectly with the red carpet by inches. A ramp was rolled into place, and the door was opened. The question in Lon's mind was whether Governor Sosa would come out before any other passengers or wait until the rest were off.

He came off first, accompanied only by two aides. Lon thought that one of them looked familiar, but after nine years and a lot of intervening faces, he was far from certain.

The band had started playing again while the shuttle taxied toward the stand, getting through one song and launching into the next as the door opened. The General and part of his entourage came down off of the platform to greet the governor at the bottom of the ramp. Lon was moved forward to accompany the General. He brought Sara with him, holding her arm so she couldn't slip away.

It was obvious the moment that Governor Sosa spotted Lon. The governor's face broke into something approaching a smile. He lifted a hand and waved, and his pace picked up a little.

"Welcome to Dirigent, Governor Sosa," the General said as soon as the visitor stepped off the ramp. They shook hands, and the General started introducing the functionaries with him. Then, "You might remember Lieutenant Colonel Nolan, Excellency."

"Of course I do," Sosa said, his tone not as completely diplomatic as it should have been.

"Lieutenant Colonel," Sosa said, turning his attention completely to Lon. "Another promotion, I see."

"Just recently, Governor," Lon said. "This is my wife, Sara. Sara, Governor Roger Sosa of Bancroft."

"Pleased to meet you," Sosa said, bowing to her before

he spoke to Lon again. "I understand there are a couple of other people aboard the shuttle you're waiting for, Colonel. I shared several delightful meals with your parents during the journey."

"Yes, sir," Lon said. "I'm sure we'll have other occasions to talk during your visit, but . . . with your permission?"

"Of course, Colonel. I'm counting on having a long talk with you later."

Lon glanced at the General for permission to leave the group, and Ruiz nodded, just enough for Lon to be certain.

Lon and Sara went on up the ramp into the shuttle.

Maddie Nolan embraced her son as enthusiastically as she had on Earth after not seeing him for two decades. His father, Lawrence, hung back a step, giving his son a wan smile—as if to apologize for Maddie's exuberance. Father and son shook hands, both looking almost embarrassed at that show of affection.

Lon introduced Sara to his parents then, and his mother went through the same sort of emotional embrace. "The children are in school," Lon said. "They should be home in an hour or so. I hear you've been hobnobbing with the big shots."

"Governor Sosa?" Lawrence said. "A remarkable man, I think. You worked for him?"

Lon nodded. "A contract, nine years back. Bancroft had trouble with the Colonial Mining Cartel raiding for precious metals and rare minerals."

"Yes. The governor pumped me for anything I could tell him about CMC. I hope I wasn't wrong—helping the little I could. He said they're back, worse than before."

"You couldn't be violating any security regulations, Dad," Lon said. "And, well, I rather guessed they might be having the same trouble when I learned the governor was coming."

"The governor had a lot of nice things to say about you," Maddie said. "Like you were the hero of some adventure vid."

They all laughed at that.

One of the shuttle pilots came back from the cockpit. "Okay, folks, you can disembark now. The bigwigs are leaving. Sorry for the inconvenience, but we weren't given much choice."

There wasn't much baggage. Maddie and Lawrence had each left Earth with only two suitcases—clothes, data chips with family holographs and home videos, and a few small mementos. The cost of transporting more would have been prohibitive. Lon had his driver take them first to the house he had picked out for his parents. A quick tour, words of satisfaction from both parents, and a ritual handing over of the keycodes for the doors and communications system.

"It's a shame we can't be closer to you all," Maddie said, "but I understand that we can't get a place on base. I'm certainly not about to let your father enlist in your Corps just for that." It was good for a polite laugh. At eighty-five, Lawrence Nolan was fifty years past the maximum age for new recruits, even though he was in good physical condition.

"You know, Dad," Lon said as they headed toward base and his quarters, "the Corps does use civilian intelligence analysts. If you get bored with retirement or teaching part-time, you might think about it. With your background in education and the fact that you come from Earth, you'd be a cinch."

"I don't bore easily," Lawrence said with a chuckle, "but I'll keep it in mind." The question of whether he would continue to work or simply retire had been left unsettled when Lon left them on Earth.

Junior and Angie had arrived home from school just minutes before their parents and grandparents got out of the staff car. Thanks primarily to Angie's exuberance, the meeting quickly became chaotic.

6

The reunion continued well past midnight. Once Junior and Angie had been seen off to bed, Lon and Sara accompanied Lon's parents back to their new home and spent time helping them settle in. The elder Nolans kept saying that they weren't tired, that they hadn't adjusted to the new time zone yet. By the time that Lon and Sara got home and into bed, it was nearly two o'clock.

Lon got up at his usual time Tuesday morning, but chose to forego calisthenics with his troops. He did not get to his office until just before work formation at eight o'clock.

"You're wanted at Corps Headquarters at oh-eight-thirty," Phip informed him. "Office of the General."

Lon blinked. "Must be to talk with Governor Sosa," he said after drawing a blank for a couple of seconds.

"Maybe they want you to negotiate the contract," Phip suggested. "After all, you got Sosa to agree to a percentage when we were there."

"Probably just want to pick my brain. We've been there, know the terrain, and might know what the traffic can bear. I'd be surprised if they didn't want my input. Contracts would want that on any repeat business. Besides, Sosa was clear about wanting to talk with me when I saw him at the port yesterday."

"If they'd waited a few months, they could have had us again," Phip said. "Now somebody else will have the pleasure of spanking their bandits."

"We've got our hands full here," Lon said. "We need those months to make sure the battalion is up to snuff with all the changes—new command structure here and in Bravo and Delta Companies, two officer-cadets, one raw lieutenant who hasn't seen combat since he earned his pips. We've got a lot of work." That was something Lon had trouble putting out of mind for more than a few seconds at a time. Responsibility. It came with the job, and there were no good excuses for less than excellent results.

"Yes, sir, and the work starts now. Time for morning formation," Phip said, gesturing at the clock.

Major Cavanaugh Zim was waiting for Lon on the broad stairs along the front of Corps headquarters—pacing.

"I was worried you wouldn't get the message in time," Zim said as Lon got out of his car. "They're waiting upstairs."

"What's so urgent?" Lon asked. Zim was already guiding him up the steps.

"The governor of Bancroft wants you to be part of the contract discussions from the outset," Zim said. "Says you know what he's up against, what he has to work with. I guess you really impressed him when you were there."

"I'm nine years out of date on Bancroft, Cav. I figured Contracts would want to pick my brain, but Sosa?"

"I'm just the messenger, Lon. The General said to get you over on the double. This could be a big contract."

They took a lift tube to the third floor and a room known as the informal lounge—forty feet square. The General, Governor Sosa, and three other men were sitting around a low octagonal table near the French doors on the east side of the room. All of them stood when Lon and Zim entered. The other three men were all colonels, regimental commanders—Nicholas Demetrios of 4th, Hiram Black of 7th, and Johan Ellis of 12th.

"Gentlemen," the General said after the formal introductions and greetings were completed and everyone, including Major Zim, was seated, "Colonel Nolan is here at the request of both Governor Sosa and myself. It was Nolan's company that helped the Bancrofters nine years ago, set up a training program for their constabulary militia, and took part in a successful action against raiders from off-world. In addition, Colonel Nolan has recently returned from an extended visit to Earth, which may offer additional insights into the problem Governor Sosa has come to us with. Governor, I'll let you take over from there."

Sosa nodded, then cleared his throat. "Nine years ago, we were faced with raiders striking our mining camps and communities, stealing refined metals and minerals, and killing many of our citizens. The problem was too large for us to handle without help at the time. We came to Dirigent to hire a company to train our fledgling constabulary militia and to set up a continuing training program we could maintain. During the course of that contract, the raids increased and we negotiated an amended contract to have the company of Dirigenters assist us in a punitive mission against the raiders. That was successful, if more costly in casualties than we all would have hoped.

"After your people left, our militia had to do some minor tidying up, taking care of a couple of dozen raiders who had not been accounted for earlier. To give us some additional hope for the future, we continued our constabulary militia, raising it in time to two thousand men and instituting a broader scheme to put all young men through basic training to constitute a reserve that could be called on if needed. We also took what diplomatic actions we could, protesting officially to the government of Earth, since the Colonial Mining Cartel, which had financed and supported the raiders, operates under the direct auspices of Earth's Confederation of Human Worlds. We also made certain that other worlds knew what had happened to us, including the government of the Second Commonwealth on Buckingham and the other Confederation of Human Worlds, on Union. Those alliances each wield considerably more power than any other grouping of worlds, and are in position to perhaps cause some restraint on Earth." Sosa shrugged. "That was our reasoning at the time.

"It seemed to work," he added after a pause. "The Colonial Mining Cartel left us alone, and we received no reports of similar attacks on other worlds. That changed about eight months ago." Sosa took a couple of sips of coffee, then set his cup back on the table before he resumed his narrative.

"We still do not have an adequate warning system, not enough satellites in orbit to give us continuous coverage of our near space, and we don't have the weapons or delivery systems to prevent unauthorized landings. I believe we were lucky to spot one ship that came and shuttled people in. We have reason to believe that there were at least two other ships that we did not spot. The raiding started again within days. Although we had militia garrisons in place at all major targets, it wasn't enough. Over the past nine years we have managed to expand our mining operations, nearly doubling the number of active sites. We have managed to inflict casualties on the raiders, but they have hurt us worse. We need help, which is why I came here."

"How many of these raiders do you estimate there are on your world?" Colonel Demetrios asked.

"At least four hundred," Sosa said without hesitation, "though it is possible that there are twice that number, or even more. And they have at least five armed shuttles, of the variety that Colonel Nolan's people encountered before."

"Against your two thousand militiamen?" Demetrios said.

"When I left, we had twenty-three hundred men in uniform—seven hundred of those, reservists called back to active duty. They are undergoing refresher training now, and should be ready to go into action before I return. After eight years without trouble, the number of active militia had fallen, and there have been casualties, keeping us from reaching the numbers we hoped to achieve."

"Colonel Nolan," the General said, "I had OSI extract everything in the data you collected on Earth concerning this Colonial Mining Cartel and do several analyses of the material. According to the summary they gave me, there is no mention of the CMC maintaining any military or paramilitary force, or doing raiding of the sort that Bancroft has experienced."

"No, sir, I'm sure there wasn't. That sort of material could not be published or archived anywhere I had access to. Reports of government activities are very tightly controlled on Earth. I heard rumors, clearly labeled as such in my reports. Among other things, several dozen army officers have apparently retired to work for CMC. That, in itself, proves nothing. CMC has always been on the lookout for military types to run off-world operations, as have dozens of other companies. There's nothing implicitly sinister about that. Retired military officers make good management material, or so I've been told."

That garnered a few chuckles around the table.

"On the other hand," Lon continued, "we know CMC was behind the raids against Bancroft nine years ago, and I have no reason to doubt that CMC is likely behind these new incursions. It also stands to reason that they would commit more assets this time than they did before, to try to avoid the same result."

"Colonel Nolan, can you estimate the capabilities of CMC?" Colonel Ellis asked. "How large a force could they sustain in operations against Bancroft?"

Lon hesitated. "In theory they could sustain a force large enough to conquer Bancroft—or just about any other colony world they decided to. CMC is, officially, a private concern, three corporations functioning together under government charter. The corporations have long since lost their individual identities, and much of their initial zones of operation, since most of the Solar System was stripped bare of useful materials long ago. Recycling has never been one hundred percent, so they have to keep looking for new sources. The CMC has become wholly dominated by the old Confederation of Human Worlds based on Earth, so it has—in theory—all the resources of the government to draw on."

"You keep saying 'in theory,' " Ellis pointed out.

"Yes, sir. Theory and practice. With six billion people on Earth, and another half billion on Earth's moon, Mars, and around the Solar System, Earth doesn't have anything approaching unlimited resources. In practice any extrasolar . . . adventure has to pay for itself in fairly short order, and Earth has to avoid anything so—I guess the word I want is 'brazen'—that it would cut off the commercial sources of raw materials they can still tap. Those are drying up quickly enough as it is, since Earth can't afford to pay the prices that, for example, Buckingham or Union can. So the question of how large a force they can sustain on Bancroft, and for how long, depends on how much they believe they can extract from the world. That's a calculation I can't make. Perhaps OSI can provide a reasonable estimate."

"A rough guess, Colonel?" the General prompted.

"Unless Earth is prepared to conquer Bancroft completely and bring in additional labor resources, I would guess that they wouldn't hazard more than the equivalent of a couple of battalions, but please remember, General, that is just the wildest guess, without any hard data to back it up."

"General?" Major Zim waited for a nod before he continued. "OSI's initial appraisal is that Earth would not dare an open invasion. It would totally alienate those colonial governments that still trade with Earth, either freely or under moderate intimidation. This might simply be another raiding mission, on a somewhat larger scale, or it may be leading up to something more. If Earth could put in enough troops to unseat the current government of Bancroft through extended guerrilla operations, they might be able to portray it as a popular coup carried out by dissatisfied citizens of the world, then bring in whatever additional manpower they might need."

"Governor, have any of the attacks so far seemed directed more at your forces than at raiding?" General Ruiz asked.

"Not clearly," Sosa said. "The raids have always been against mining targets, and where the raiders have carried the day, they have looted. Of course, if they continue to be successful at raiding, it would eventually have the effect of destabilizing the government. If we cannot protect our people, we aren't doing our job."

The General nodded. "Governor, before we end this session, just what sort of help are you looking for from us?"

"Our resources are not unlimited, unfortunately," Sosa said. "We hope to hire at least one battalion of troops, and preferably two, for long enough to help us eliminate the current threat from these raiders. In addition, we would like to hire a squadron of aerospace fighters and their carrier, to prevent reinforcements or resupply from reaching the raiders and to prevent them from getting the metals and minerals they have looted off Bancroft."

"Thank you, Governor. That gives us a good starting point. We'll start the feasibility studies immediately. Our people in OSI would appreciate a few hours of your time, Governor, to help us get all the details we can about the situation. We can resume our talks tomorrow morning, if that meets your approval?"

Within minutes after the meeting broke up, Lon was called to the General's private office.

"I have two questions for you, Colonel," Ruiz said. "I'm going to impose on you for quick answers, but I'll want you to consider the matter over the next few days and give me whatever else you can then."

"Yes, sir," Lon said.

"I've only had time to go through the summary of the initial analysis of the material you brought back from Earth. We're going to be looking at that for months. I have some concerns about this whole matter of Bancroft. We stymied Earth there once. Now, if a contract can be reached, we'll be going back to attempt it again. The Council of Regiments has to consider the possibility that Earth might turn its attention directly to us if we oppose them in force. My questions are these: How much chance do you think there is of Earth deciding to attack Dirigent? And can they mount an attack in enough force to succeed?"

"The answer to the second question is easy enough, General. Do they have the ability to attack Dirigent in enough force to succeed? Yes. For every soldier we have, they have hundreds. For every ship we could hold in orbit to defend us, they could attack with twenty. The various military academies on Earth commission twelve hundred new officers every year compared to the two or three dozen new lieutenants we commission."

"You don't sound very encouraging," the General said.

"No, sir. One of the first lessons I learned was that a commander has to be prepared for what a potential enemy is capable of doing, not what one believes the enemy might care to do. But there are reasons to think that the practical situation is not quite that dire. There are enough jealousies among the various political divisions on Earth that getting agreement to conduct any major offensive push at a distance would be difficult. And, just as in the case of Bancroft, Earth can hardly afford to mount an operation when they can't expect to pay for its own costs in fairly short order. They can't go too far without totally alienating those extrasolar worlds that still trade with them or offer at least lip service to the remaining part of Earth's Confederation of Human Worlds."

"But, short of all-out invasion, they might launch some sort of punitive strike?"

"That is possible, General. They might hope to scare us off with a show of force, but I'm not certain they would dare to take the risk that we might retaliate in kind. Any attack on Earth might destabilize conditions so much that the planetary government would fall apart and the regional federations and unions go to fighting each other. Again. The political situation back there seems to be quite . . . delicate."

The General leaned back, steepled his fingers together, and stared at them.

"Off the top of my head, General," Lon reminded him.

Ruiz nodded absently. "It's something the Council of Regiments will have to take into consideration before we decide whether to accept a contract with Bancroft."

"It's worlds like Bancroft that provide us with our livelihood, General," Lon said. "If we start turning our back on customers, how long will it be before we don't have enough customers to stay in business? And if that happens, what happens to Dirigent?"

7

The Office of Strategic Intelligence provided estimates and analyses of manpower and support requirements, tactical and strategic possibilities, casualty potentials. The accountants provided costing and overhead for various contract scenarios. The primary negotiating sessions took place each morning and lasted up to two hours; Lon was present at each of those. It wasn't until the fourth meeting, on Friday morning, that Governor Sosa delivered the bomb Lon had feared.

"We would, of course, want Colonel Nolan to command the force we hire, with as many of the people who helped us before as possible. We know they are familiar with our circumstances, and we have confidence in them."

The General explained that units of the DMC were chosen to give everyone equal opportunity for combat contracts and that Lon's battalion was not due for such an assignment.

"Nevertheless, I must insist," Sosa said. "We would waste time learning to trust a new commander, and we can't help but believe that it would lessen the effectiveness of the partnership between our militia and your people. Since we will be paying for the arrangement, it seems there should be no question."

"I'll have to refer this to the whole Council of Regiments," the General said, but Lon was under no illusions. If the customer wanted a specific battalion, it would get it.

Later, in private, Lon would raise the question of 2nd Battalion's readiness for a combat contract, the need for another month or two of training, but he knew it would not be enough.

Lon wasted no time once he got back to his office. He called a meeting of his company commanders and staff officers, and included Phip Steesen.

"This isn't final, so I don't want any word to leak out of this room," Lon started once everyone was seated in the conference room. "No one in the battalion is going to be drawing fatigue details near term, and we won't have junior officers tripping off one day a week for whatever secondary assignments they've been doing. We redouble our training, and that includes working evenings. There is a chance—unfortunately, a very good chance—that we'll be going out on contract soon, out of turn. Bancroft wants us, specifically, and even though the contract committee may drag its feet, in the end they'll almost certainly give in."

Lon paused, waiting for objections, but there were none, not immediately. Vel Osterman, the executive officer, stared straight ahead, no emotion on his face; Lon had briefed him before the meeting. Captain Torry Berger, the adjutant, closed his eyes, as if starting to make plans. The company commanders—Tebba Girana of Alpha, Brock Carlin of Bravo, Sefer Kai of Charlie, and Ron Magnusson of Delta—looked around among themselves. Even Phip Steesen kept his mouth shut, though Lon noted that his lead sergeant had his lips pressed tightly together, forcing himself to remain silent.

"I don't know what time frame we're talking about," Lon continued, "how long it will take to finalize the contract, and how long after that it will be before we ship out, but I want us working every possible minute, and that includes putting in a half day tomorrow—and yes, I know tomorrow is Saturday. Small-unit tactics, Alpha versus

Charlie and Bravo versus Delta. Monday we practice combat landings. The intent is to get in three before the day's out. If we're here next week, we'll work half of Saturday again, unless we're on notice to ship out.

"Concentrate on your officer-cadets, new lieutenants, new noncoms, new men in the ranks. People who aren't used to working together. That includes us here in battalion. We'll be in this as much as possible as well. Brock, Ron, I know this puts an extra burden on the two of you, since you're both new to your commands. And I'm new in my job, and so is Major Osterman. Ditto for Lead Sergeant Steesen. It's going to be a bitch for all of us, but better to oil the wheels here than on contract, when we might have bad guys shooting at us."

"You're going to have one hell of a lot of angry men when they hear they're gonna be working Saturdays," Phip told Lon after the meeting. "You'd better carry a fire extinguisher, 'cause your ears are gonna be burning."

"I know, Phip, but we can't say anything about why we're doing it until there's something signed and sealed."

"Even if people start bitchin' about what a hard-assed new CO we've got?"

"Even then, Phip. I'm not happy with the situation either, not with my folks just getting here. I figured to have several months helping them get settled and meet people before I'd have to think about a contract." *And make up for a lot of years we've been apart,* he thought.

Phip turned and started to leave the office. He stopped with his hand on the doorknob, then turned his head back toward Lon. "Bancroft. That's where we lost Dean. Dean Ericks."

Lon nodded. "I haven't stopped thinking about that since Governor Sosa landed."

• • •

"What about the units ahead of yours in the rota?" Sara asked that evening. "Won't they raise a fit?"

"There's an old saying, 'The customer is always right, even when he isn't,'" Lon said. "Sure, some of the battalions ahead of us might protest, but it won't wash. We'll take this one, and be pushed that much farther down the list for the next one. We lose out on time at home now and make up for it later. Besides, this might turn out to be a fairly short contract. We're talking about a three-month engagement, and it could be shorter than that if we can close it out faster."

"But you just got home after being away more than six months," Sara protested.

"That was something entirely different, not part of the routine," Lon said. "We knew that before I left."

"But . . ." Sara gave up. She knew she could not change the answer.

Lon had no difficulty arranging access to training areas for Saturday morning. In general, Saturday training was remedial, for individuals or units that failed to meet the standards of the Corps during the normal work week.

Trucks carried the battalion's companies to prearranged points in the forested training area east of the main base. The men had been briefed in the scenario they would act out. Observers drawn from other units would travel with each company, to referee the small-unit encounters and to report on unit effectiveness afterward. Lon split the headquarters detachment. He would take half to monitor the bout between Bravo and Delta Companies. Vel Osterman would take the rest to monitor Alpha and Charlie.

The DMC went to great lengths to make training as realistic as possible. Slug-throwing rifles and pistols were loaded with soft chalk bullets propelled by minimal powder charges—enough to be felt, not enough to cause serious injury. Beamers, coherent energy weapons, were restricted in power—a hit by one of those would leave the equivalent of a minor sunburn on skin.

"Working on Saturday's gonna make for some mean fighting," Phip told Lon as they drove toward the center of the area that Bravo and Delta would be contesting. "You tellin' 'em they'd do it again this afternoon if they screwed up didn't help."

"We'll work it out of them here," Lon said. "If we're going out in a week or two, we can't baby anyone. I want to see all the weak spots now."

The two men were in full combat gear, except for weapons. They spoke over a private radio channel. DMC battle helmets offered a variety of communications channels—more for command personnel, officers, and noncoms. Lon planned to scan channels to eavesdrop on operations. At every level.

"Bravo and Delta both have new COs," Phip said, as if the boss might possibly have forgotten such a basic fact. "I expect they'll do most of the screwing up."

"We'll know where to put the effort then, won't we," Lon said. "I'm trying to set up a full battalion exercise against another unit for Thursday or Friday. It means juggling some schedules, but the General okayed it. Just need to pull the wrinkles out of the rope."

"By the time we get through that, some of the men will be wishing they were still pulling fatigue detail, even whitewashing the rocks in front of headquarters."

It was three in the afternoon before Lon released the men, after relaying the deficiencies the referees had noted. When Lon got home, he found that Sara and the children had gone to visit with Lon's parents. Lon called, talked to his mother for a few minutes, but decided against driving over. "I'm too beat to walk out to the curb," he said. "We've got tomorrow free. We'll all do something together then."

When Sara and the children got home two hours later,

Lon was asleep in the living room, sprawled out on the sofa. Sara left him there until supper was ready.

"Your mother and I have it all worked out," Sara said while they were eating. "If you're on contract, we'll go to Bascombe East over the Christmas break. The five of us. I've already introduced your parents to mine over the net. We spent thirty minutes chatting, letting them get to know each other."

"That's good," Lon said. "If this contract works out the way I expect, we might not be back till the end of February."

"Are you going to miss my birthday again, Daddy?" Angie asked.

"I'm not sure, princess," Lon said. "It's going to be close, I'm afraid. If it looks like I will, we'll move your birthday up a few days, okay?"

"The whole time I was on Earth, and especially on the way back, I thought a lot about what we could do when I got home. I figured I could take a month's furlough after my parents arrived so we could do some sight-seeing, spend a lot of time together. Maybe travel to Deradine Falls," Lon said after he and Sara went to bed. Deradine Falls, named after the pilot who first saw it, was *the* natural wonder of Dirigent—as broad as Niagara Falls on Earth, but dropping half a mile in one clear fall down the escarpment of a rift valley two thousand miles from Dirigent City.

"Hasn't any of it worked out," Lon said. "The new command, then this Bancroft thing. I can't even be sure that when we get back from Bancroft I'll be able to take that much time, not right away. It depends on how the contract goes." There was no need to define that qualification—how many casualties the battalion took, how much rebuilding was necessary when it got home.

"So we'll work it in when we can," Sara said. "We're getting to be good at that."

"I know, but—"

"Just go to sleep."

Sleep. Although he was tired, Lon had difficulty finding the void. At first, it was thoughts of what he needed to do, what the battalion needed to do, to get ready for Bancroft: training, drills, lectures, planning. He recalled the rough terrain on Bancroft, the forested valleys and hills where most of the mining settlements and camps were, the difficulty of moving men on the ground. That led to memories of Dean Ericks, the friend who had died there. In his mind, Lon saw Dean lying on the ground dying; dead. He could almost hear Dean's voice. He remembered happier times, pub crawls in Camo Town, the area of Dirigent City that existed to serve off-duty soldiers . . . at almost anything they might want. The Three Musketeers and D'Artagnan they had been at the beginning. Phip, Janno, and Dean had been the musketeers. Lon had been the new man, D'Artagnan. Janno got married and left the Corps. Dean got killed . . .

Sleep, when it came, did not end the memories. They continued in Lon's dreams. So many friends and comrades had died over the years, or left the Corps—for one reason or another. It was not a restful night.

A day of rest that was not restful, away from the Corps in body but not in thought. Then, Monday, Lon was back to the grind, along with every man in the battalion. Vel Osterman substituted for Lon at Colonel Black's regular Monday conference. Lon was at Corps headquarters, sitting in on yet another session in the negotiations with Governor Sosa. Those had reached the technical stage, money and assets, details. By the time the meeting recessed, Lon was convinced that agreement could not be far away, perhaps no more than a day or two. After that, departure would likely come quickly—within seventy-two hours. It was traditional, when possible, to give men going out on contract two days off before departure, time for a last fling in Camo Town or a last visit with relatives.

"I don't think we'll have to worry about working the men this Saturday," Lon told his executive officer as they ate lunch together in the officers' club on Monday. "I suspect we'll either already be aboard ship or on notice to leave."

"That close?" Vel asked softly.

Lon nodded. "It wouldn't surprise me if the final draft of the contract is drawn up tomorrow, signed tomorrow afternoon or Wednesday morning. After that, I'm sure Governor Sosa is going to be in a hurry to get us moving toward Bancroft."

"We *are* in pretty good shape, Lon," Vel said. "A little rough around the edges, but it's not as if we had twenty percent new people. We've had a long time to get most of the rookies integrated into the companies."

"I know, but I hate going in not being confident that we're one hundred percent. Basically, this will be counterguerilla warfare, and that can be more difficult than squaring off against another army in an open fight."

"It's what we do, like beer and chips," Vel said. He shrugged. "I understand how you feel. We wouldn't be worth much as leaders if we didn't want our people at their best. It gives everyone a better chance to get home safe."

Lon nodded, then finished his drink and signaled for another scotch and water. The waiter had just arrived with the new drink when Lon had a call from Colonel Black.

"Governor Sosa just okayed the deal, Lon. They sign the contract this afternoon. You leave Friday morning."

8

There was the usual caravan of buses, led by two limousines and several staff cars, across Dirigent City from the DMC base to the spaceport—the usual parade leading up to the departure of soldiers on contract. Governor Sosa, his aides, and the General were the reasons for the limousines. The Bancrofters would be going home aboard the Dirigenter ship.

Second Battalion formed up next to the runway at the spaceport, dressed the formation, and stood at attention in their battledress uniforms with the faceplates up on their helmets and their rifles on their shoulders. There was a short ceremony, with the governor of Bancroft and the General each saying a few polite words. The band played. Nine shuttles stood waiting to carry the battalion and the Bancrofters up to *Long Snake,* the transport that would carry them to Bancroft. Baggage and supplies had been carried up to *Long Snake* earlier.

After the ceremony ended, the order was given to board shuttles—a maneuver carried out with well-practiced precision by the mercenaries. Lon's shuttle, which carried his staff, headquarters detachment, and the Bancrofters, was the first off the field. With outsiders aboard, the pilot made a more decorous takeoff than he might have otherwise. Forty-five seconds later, the other shuttles started taking off, two at a time, thirty seconds between pairs.

Here we go again, Lon thought as his shuttle quit accelerating to coast toward its rendezvous with *Long Snake*. He no longer kept track of the numbers, how many combat contracts, how many training contracts, the interstellar passages, the jumps through Q-space. He no longer *wanted* to remember.

There were formalities when the shuttle docked and was brought into one of *Long Snake*'s hangars. The ship's captain, Eldon Roim, was on hand to welcome Governor Sosa and Lon. Lon went to the launch and recovery center, which protruded from the side of the ship, offering a view of the hangars. Captain Roim escorted the Bancrofters to their cabins forward, in the crew section of *Long Snake*.

The last pair of shuttles were just being hoisted inboard by the ship's grapples. The launchmaster, *Long Snake*'s number three officer, was in control of docking operations. Lon stood out of the way and waited until the last hatches had been closed and the hangars pressurized. The launchmaster turned to Lon then, saluted, and said, "All shuttles aboard, sir. No problems."

Lon returned the salute and thanked him. "How long before we head out-system?" Lon asked.

"We'll be under way within minutes, Colonel," the launchmaster said. "*Taranto* and *Tyre* will follow us out." *Taranto* was a fighting ship; it carried a squadron of sixteen Shrike fighters as well as beam and projectile weapons of its own. *Tyre* was a transport being used to carry additional munitions and supplies for the battalion. "Captain Roim is task force commander."

The command structure included a little fine balancing. The naval arm of the DMC was considered an auxiliary service. Once the task force reached a contract world, the senior *army* officer—in this case, Lon—was in command of the operation, even though one or more naval officers might theoretically outrank him. The skippers of both *Long Snake* and *Taranto* were captains, the naval equivalent of a full colonel in the Corps. *Tyre* was captained by a commander, theoretically equal in rank to Lon. Interactions between Lon and the ships' commanders would be conducted with extreme diplomacy, built up from protocols that were centuries old.

Once *Long Snake* secured from recovery stations, the launchmaster escorted Lon to his quarters near the front of the battalion's section of the ship. Vel Osterman and Phip Steesen were waiting.

"Everyone is aboard and accounted for," Major Osterman said. "The men are getting squared away in their quarters now."

Lon nodded. "We're under way, heading toward our first jump point." With *Long Snake*'s Nilssen generators providing artificial gravity inside the ship, there was no sensation of movement. "Phip, get the meal arrangements confirmed and start working on training schedules for the trip." Facilities aboard the ship were limited, even though *Long Snake* was five miles long. The soldiers would eat, exercise, and train in shifts. Dirigent's Dragon-class transports, such as *Long Snake,* were being phased out—one every four years. Their replacements, the Raptor-class transports, were 10 percent larger, more modern, and better armed. In five years, the last Dragon would be retired.

"I'll get right to it, Colonel," Phip said. There could be no informality between them on duty with anyone else present. The forms had to be observed.

"I'll speak with the men at lunch today," Lon said. The officers and noncoms had gone through an intensive mission briefing—and everyone knew the basics of the contract. Lon would give more than a pep talk to the lower ranks, though. It was Corps policy to keep everyone as fully informed as practical. *No matter how badly the command structure might be shattered on contract, the Corps will be prepared to continue at whatever level of command might remain, even if the senior soldier is a private,* was how it was phrased in the contract manual.

Lon's luggage had been delivered to his cabin. The duffel bag stood next to the bed; the suitcase lay on it. That was one of the perks of command, allowance for more than just one duffel bag. Another perk was that the cabin was slightly larger than those the battalion's other officers were assigned, and Lon had a small office attached to his cabin and a private bathroom—"head," in naval parlance.

A few minutes alone. Lon shoved the suitcase to the end of the bed and sat next to the suitcase. He leaned back until his head and shoulders rested against the metal bulkhead of the cabin. He closed his eyes and took a long, slow breath. Lon was not at all surprised to find that he had the beginning of a headache. He knew it was psychological. The nanosystems that kept him healthy would prevent a physical headache, or cure it almost before he could notice a pain, but this kind . . .

It was always the same, heading out on a contract with the lives of others depending on his decisions, his abilities—his mistakes. A prayer that he not fail his men, that no one die because he wasn't up to his job. Each time out, the prayer was more intense, more deeply felt.

Maybe it would have been better if I hadn't tried to be an officer, if I had stayed in the ranks, let others make the big decisions, he thought. *Maybe Phip has the right of it, bitching every time he gets promoted.* That brought the edge of a smile. *I wanted to be a soldier, just a soldier, and being an officer gets in the way, more with every promotion.*

Lon was surprised by a knock on his cabin door—surprised because he had actually dozed off. He hadn't slept well the last two nights at home. Each night he had lain awake, worrying, wishing that he didn't have to leave his family again so soon.

"Come in." Lon sat up straight as the door opened and Phip entered.

"I've got the eating arrangements set up with the mess

officer," Phip said. "The first shift eats in thirty minutes."

"I'll eat with Alpha, this meal," Lon said. He made no apology for the fact that he had a soft spot for A Company. He had spent most of his career in that company, until promotion to major had sent him to battalion. "Make my talk after I get some food down. I'll have to have supper with the ship's captain and Governor Sosa." The military commander eating that first supper with the ship's commander was hidebound tradition in the Corps.

"Alpha's the first shift for lunch today," Phip said. Phip had spent even more years in that company than Lon had. The order in which the companies ate would rotate each meal so the same men didn't get to eat first all the time.

"You ever ask yourself if it's all worth it, Phip?" Lon asked. He closed his eyes for an instant.

"All the time, Lon," Phip replied very softly. "What usually gets me out of it is thinking if it wasn't me doing the job, it'd probably be someone less qualified than I am. The same goes for you. You wouldn't have made it so far so fast if you weren't one of the best to come along in a lot of Q-space jumps."

There was no mirth in Lon's taut laugh.

"I mean it," Phip insisted. "I've got no reason to grease your boots. Another ten years and you'll be General."

Lon shook his head. "Don't put money on it, Phip. It'll never happen. I'm first-generation Corps, first-generation Dirigenter. Even if, by some wild chance, I do make it to the Council of Regiments someday, they'll never vote me in as General. I couldn't count on even one vote because I'm not sure I'd vote for myself. You've got a better shot at getting elected General than I do."

"They don't make sergeants General."

Lon got to his feet. "Nothing says you'll always be a sergeant, Phip." There was almost humor in his laugh this time. "You might wake up a lieutenant some morning. After that, it would just be a matter of time."

"That's a hell of a thing to say to a friend," Phip said, a look of something approaching terror on his face. "What'd I ever do to deserve a threat like that?"

He's right about one thing, Lon thought as they left the room. *We take the promotions because deep inside we figure we can do the job better than someone else might. It's the pat on the shoulder we always need.*

Nearly half the men in A Company were veterans of the previous contract on Bancroft. Most of the rest had heard stories about that contract—if only since the unit had been alerted for this job. That made the initial briefing easier for Lon. Most of his listeners had points of reference. It got a little more involved with the other companies.

"The people of Bancroft have good memories of the Corps," he told each group as he concluded his talk. "We did a job for them, and we behaved. I don't want anyone spoiling the image the Bancrofters have of us, either for the way we do our job or for the way we behave if—*if*—we get a chance to socialize off-duty. Best behavior. That means no 'drunk and disorderly,' no attempts to undermine the virtue of the local lasses. Anyone gets out of line, he'll think a shuttle landed on his head before I get through with him."

The pep talks did as much good for Lon as they did for his men; perhaps more. After repeating the same general spiel several times, he stopped thinking of his own doubts, started concentrating on what the battalion would need to do when it reached Bancroft.

This early, the talk could only be in general terms. Until *Long Snake* and the other ships reached Bancroft's Solar System after their final transit of Q-space, detailed planning would be impossible. By that time Governor Sosa would have been out of contact with his world for more than six weeks. The current tactical situation might have changed drastically. There would be updates once the Dirigenter ships emerged in normal space three or four days out from Bancroft, and then Lon, his staff, and the governor could begin to make firm plans for the battalion.

"Right now we can hardly rule anything in or out," Lon told his company commanders. "There is a slight chance that Bancroft's constabulary militia will have managed to get the upper hand on the raiders since Sosa left. There is also a chance that the raiders will have been so successful that the militia is more or less bottled up in Lincoln and the other towns, that they will have been forced to abandon the smaller mining camps and villages. Or the situation could be anywhere between those extremes."

"Can't go too far wrong assuming the situation will be closer to worst-case than best," Captain Kai of C Company said. "That way, any surprises are liable to be pleasant."

"If the miners all just pulled back to the cities and quit working, pretty soon the raiders wouldn't have any decent targets. They'd either have to do the hard work themselves or leave," Captain Carlin of Bravo said. "If what you said before about those raiding operations having to pay for themselves is right."

"Wouldn't make the government of Bancroft look very good to just pull back and hide," Lon said. "They'd probably be voted out of office as being unfit to govern if they couldn't do anything to protect the miners and keep production going. Not to mention how fast they might go broke."

"Same result if the miners go on strike on their own say," Tebba Girana of Alpha said. "It's the miners who are on the front line, in the line of fire when the raiders come around."

"The point is, make sure everyone knows why we don't have any initial plan of operations, and why we won't have one until we come out of our final Q-space jump and have time to get updated information from the ground," Lon said. "Work the men hard on the Bancroft database, especially physical conditions, flora, and fauna—the things that can't change all that much in a few years. The shuttles the raiders used last time—armed shuttles like ours, but smaller. The tactics the raiders used, on the ground and in the air. Those may have changed, but we need a starting point."

It was always a difficult job, finding practical use for the time in transit. Meals, sleep, and exercise could use only so many hours each day. There could be no field exercises in a troop transport. There were no furloughs, passes, booze, or women. Officers and noncoms tried to keep gambling to a minimum. But there were always empty hours, and giving men too many of them to lie in a bunk and think about what might be coming was no good either.

That included the commanding officer.

Lon tried not to be too intrusive, tried to be careful to avoid giving his men any reason to think that he might be nervous about the contract. *Put on an act if you have to,* his first commanding officer had advised. *You might try amateur theatricals if you need help.*

It was easier now. Lon had a lot of practice at projecting confidence. There were only a few men he allowed to see past the mask. Phip and Tebba were old friends as well as subordinates. Lon was learning to trust Vel Osterman enough to let him see behind the facade. In any case, if nerves did intrude, Lon could retreat to his office, the aloof commander pondering *Bigger Questions.* In private, he sometimes simply went through the personnel files on his complink, studying ID holographs as much as anything, wanting to be able to put a name with each face under his command, hoping to know a little about each of his men. He had been executive officer of 2nd Battalion long enough that it wasn't an overwhelming problem. He knew most of the men, at least enough to call them by name.

Five days out: one transit through Q-space, out from

Dirigent to one of the major navigational routes. Eight days out: the big jump along the well-charted travel lane. Eleven days out: the jump in toward Bancroft.

Immediately following the final jump through quantum space, Lon went to the main communications center just aft of *Long Snake*'s bridge to meet Governor Sosa and Captain Roim.

"We're waiting for my deputy governor to get to his office," Sosa said. "I'm sure you'll remember him, Dan Henks, former commander of our constabulary militia. Government House knows we're in-system. As soon as I give Dan the authorization code, they'll start transmitting everything they have for us on the current situation. Then we can make real plans for our landing and initial movements."

Lon nodded. "Captain Roim, are we picking up any sign of other traffic in-system?"

"Not yet, Colonel," Roim said. "All three ships are actively scanning, of course. We'll continue that as long as we're here. Ground as well as space, once we're close enough to do you any good with ground tactical."

"I always feel a lot better when I know we've got good eyes watching out for us, Captain."

That conversation was tabled when Deputy Governor Henks came on-line.

"Roger, am I glad to see you back!" Henks said, mopping sweat from his forehead. "We've had trouble. The raiders attacked Lincoln last night. It was just hit-and-run, not a lot of damage, but it's got people in a panic here."

9

Several small mining camps had been abandoned in the past weeks—sites where miners worked a month shift, than went home to families in towns or villages for a month. Militia garrisons had been strengthened in the permanent mining villages, but that drained manpower from Lincoln, the only real city on the planet. No mining was done in or right around the capital, but all of the refined precious metals, minerals, and rare elements passed through it before going off-world in Bancroft's normal trade.

As soon as Lon and the others had the initial data feed from Government House, they took time to study the material and confer. More updates came in. Dan Henks provided almost hourly reports on what was happening.

"It could have been worse," Roger Sosa confided to Lon and Captain Roim. "It's bad enough, the first strike against the capital, against *any* of our larger towns, but I've had nightmares about how bad it might have been."

Lon kept his face blank. He could understand what the governor was hinting at. "Fear was probably what the raiders were trying to sow, Governor. If a small raid against Lincoln forces you to hold forces back from protecting the mines, they've eased their primary job."

"It would have worked if we didn't have your people coming in," Sosa said. "We would have had no choice but to defend Lincoln and the other towns. We'll turn the entire militia camp over to your regiment, Colonel Nolan, the main camp, there at the edge of Lincoln, where your company stayed before. Unless there's a raid in progress when we get close enough to land, the best thing would be to put all your people down where folks in the capital can see just how much help we've got."

"I'll have A Company alerted for possible diversion in case there is a raid going on," Lon said. "That's where most of the men who were here before are. *Taranto* will have fighters ready to move in as well. Two or three Shrikes can put quite a hurt on ground forces that don't have any air cover, especially if the raiders aren't expecting attack from above. If there's no immediate action, they can do a flyover while the shuttles are landing, give you a little extra show."

"Is A Company the one trained with rocket packs?" Sosa asked.

Lon shook his head. "That's Charlie, and the packs are stowed on *Tyre*. We're not in position to use them going in, Governor. I don't want to risk one company when there's no chance to get reinforcements to them, not until we've had time to get a firsthand evaluation of the situation." Lon and his men had been surprised by raiders using rocket packs to land men in a heavily wooded area, where no shuttle could land, during their previous contract on Bancroft. "Besides, this is hypothetical, since we don't know that there *will* be a raid in progress when we're ready to land."

Governor Sosa was unable, or didn't try, to completely suppress a low sigh. "It would be nice to be able to hit them hard before they know that we've brought in outside help," he said.

"Nice, but not essential, Governor," Lon said, managing a smile. "I agree, it would be dramatic, but I don't think your problem is going to be solved that quickly."

"No, of course not, but still . . ."

• • •

OSI had done a remarkable job working with the material Alpha Company had brought back from Bancroft nine years earlier. They had edited tens of thousands of hours of video taken from ships in orbit, by shuttles during all of their operations, and through cameras mounted in the helmets of officers and noncoms. The resulting maps and overlays provided a high-resolution photographic atlas of a large section of Bancroft's primary continent, along with moderately detailed surveys of the rest of the planet's surface. The result was that 2nd Battalion was going in with far more precise knowledge of the physical conditions on the contract world than the Corps usually enjoyed ... "only" nine years out of date. For Lincoln, the three other main towns, and several of the largest villages, that meant that almost every building was pinpointed. All of the smaller villages and mining camps were located, though terrain or tree cover had prevented building-by-building charting.

Long Snake had the complete map database in its Combat Intelligence Center computers, which could feed information to the complinks and mapboards that officers and noncoms carried. The maps would be updated constantly once the Dirigenter flotilla was in position over the inhabited continent. New buildings, new villages, new mining camps would be added. Abandoned camps and villages could be annotated. There was a slow but constant shift to mining sites, apart from the movements dictated by the latest raids. Old lodes played out. New deposits were discovered.

Governor Sosa and his aides had pointed out where some of the new sites were. Those were indicated by a separate overlay on the map, to be replaced once direct video and topographical charting could be done.

"We've managed to increase our population substantially since you left here before," Sosa told Lon during one conference over the map. "We advertised for new settlers from some of the older colony worlds and brought in nearly twenty thousand people, and our people have also been doing their best to build up the population the old-fashioned way."

Nine years earlier, the DMC had estimated Bancroft's population at three hundred thousand. As a result of that first contract, the estimate had been increased by 20 percent. Now Lon suspected that the number was probably over half a million—still relatively small for a world that had been opened to colonization more than a century earlier.

"Remember, this is subject to last-minute change if there's anything going on when we get into the landers," Lon said as his staff and company commanders gathered twelve hours before the scheduled start of landing operations. "We hold Alpha back, in the shuttles but not launched, until the rest of the battalion is on the ground. Bravo will be first in, to establish contact with the constabulary militia and to provide a security perimeter around the militia base at the edge of Lincoln. My headquarters detachment will go in behind Bravo. Charlie and Delta will follow us. As soon as we're organized enough to be able to get Charlie and/or Delta dispatched to meet any raid, we bring Alpha in. We'll have Shrike coverage throughout the landing operation. *Taranto* will try to keep four Shrikes in position to provide immediate support during this phase. After that, I expect to keep the Shrikes on alert status, ready to lend ground support or to intercept any ships coming in-system."

"You going to keep some of the shuttles on the ground?" Tebba asked.

Lon nodded. "Probably half; rotate shuttles and crews between *Long Snake* and the ground. That gives us the means to move two full companies at a moment's notice, or to use shuttles for ground support." Dirigenter shuttles carried rockets and multibarreled, high-speed 20mm cannon pods. Though not as fast or as maneuverable as Shrike fighters, the assault shuttles were armed nearly as well.

"I expect we'll have at least one day, possibly more, before we begin mounting offensive action," Lon continued. "Subject, of course, to what the raiders do. I'd love to have two or three days to get us settled and making regular patrols before we have to react to enemy action, but that's beyond our control."

"If there's something going on when we get up in the morning, Alpha goes right in on top of it?" Tebba said. It wasn't really a question. He merely wanted to get the plan verified once more.

"That's the plan," Lon agreed, nodding. Lon had little doubt that Tebba Girana was his best company commander. Like nearly half of the officers in the Corps, Tebba had come up from the ranks. If he remained in the DMC long enough, Tebba would be a battalion commander someday. But that was a big *if*. Tebba already had thirty-seven years in uniform. He was also Lon's oldest company commander, by more than a decade.

"Make sure your men know the plan, and how it might change," Lon told his captains. *Don't let them think that the Old Man doesn't have a plan or can't make up his mind,* he thought. That would be bad for morale.

"At least we shouldn't have to fight our way ashore," Lon told Vel Osterman after the meeting broke up. The two were alone in Lon's office.

"Amen to that," Vel said. "No hot landings, no one targeting us before we can get out of the box."

The box: Infantrymen felt—and were—helpless in their landers, unable to defend themselves, subject to having their ride blown apart around them. Coming in on a hot landing—opposed by ground forces or enemy air cover—

could be the stuff of nightmares. Until a Dirigenter could get out of the box and in position to contribute to his own defense, he was as helpless as a chick still in the egg. And knew it.

"I know we didn't discuss this before, Vel, but I want you to ride in with Alpha. I'd rather go with them myself, but"—Lon spread his arms in a helpless gesture—"that would be setting a poor example. I need to ride with the bulk of the battalion, go in with the governor, and so forth."

Vel nodded, not mentioning the thought he had entertained, that Lon would choose to go in with his old company, especially if something was definitely happening on the surface when it was time to climb into the boxes. The executive officer had been prepared to argue the point with his boss. He was glad it would not come to that—not on their first contract together.

"Chances are we'll get in first," Vel said. "Be on the ground before the raiders hit anywhere. Sosa said the pattern has been several days between raids, sometimes a week."

"Not a firm pattern," Lon said. "They've been careful not to establish a hard pattern."

"It's what any professional would do," Vel said.

"And I expect we'll be facing professionals, Earth-trained officers who've had the time to train a cohesive fighting force." *Maybe some of them who trained at The Springs, took the same courses I did,* Lon thought. That could cut both ways, give him a slight edge on what the enemy might do . . . and give them some idea of what *he* might do. He got to his feet. "Let's get some supper, then try to get some sleep. Morning isn't going to wait for us."

Supper, a walk-through of the troops' bays, a few words here and there. By the time Lon got back to his cabin,

Drop Hour was less than nine and a half hours away. Reveille would be two hours before that.

This might be the last night of undisturbed sleep you get for three months, Lon told himself as he undressed. *You've got to take advantage of it.* He had a sleep patch laid out on the stand next to the bed; that would guarantee him a minimum of four hours' undisturbed sleep. In his younger days, he would have tried—and likely failed—to get by without the patch, tossing and turning while he fretted about everything that might conceivably go wrong, leaving himself in less than first-rate shape for the landing. With an entire battalion depending on him, he could no longer afford such a foolish indulgence.

"Don't let me fail my men," he whispered. He turned out the light, lay down, and put the sticky side of the patch against his neck. In five minutes he was asleep. There were no dreams to disturb his quiet . . . one more telling reason for him to resort to the help.

Morning. During the journey from Dirigent to Bancroft, the ships had gradually adjusted shipboard time so it would agree with local time in Bancroft's capital. On the day of the landing, sunrise was scheduled in Lincoln at 0627 hours, by the military clock. Reveille in the troop bays of *Long Snake* was at 0430 hours. The men would be ordered to their shuttles at 0615, and the landing craft would start the ride down to the surface at 0630. Clockwork. Schedules.

Corporal Jeremy Howell, Lon's clerk and aide, knocked on the bedroom door at 0415 hours—as instructed. He waited thirty seconds and, when he had heard no response from inside, opened the door and turned on the light.

"Colonel, time to get up," Howell said in a conversational tone as he closed the door behind him. "Coming up on reveille."

Lon opened his eyes a little, squinting against the glare

of the ceiling light. "I'm awake, Jerry," he said, though his voice was scarcely evidence of his words. "No problems?"

"I guess not, sir," Jeremy said. If there *had* been a problem in the night, the battalion commander would have been wakened and told long before his clerk learned of it.

"Okay." Lon sat up, still squinting. "I'll check with Captain Roim while I have breakfast. You check on the exec and Lead Sergeant Steesen. Ask them to eat with me. I'll need twenty minutes to shower and dress."

"Yes, sir. I'll see to it. The lead sergeant is already up. I saw him heading toward Alpha's quarters on my way here. He was already dressed for departure." Jeremy Howell had been four years old when Lon entered the DMC. Howell had earned his corporal's stripes on a combat contract a year ago, after less than six years in the Corps. And there was a good chance he would make sergeant following this contract. Lon had taken an almost parental interest in his aide, who had lost his own father, a platoon sergeant in Delta Company, when he was only three.

"Tell him about breakfast and see if Major Osterman is up, then get to your own feed."

"Yes, sir."

Lon waited until he was alone before he permitted himself a yawn that seemed to try to split his face wide open. He stretched, then put his feet on the floor and stood to stretch some more, twisting, trying to pump his mind the last distance up from sleep. He stripped off his underwear and headed into the attached bathroom. This morning, twenty minutes would be tight for getting ready.

At 0615 hours Alpha and Bravo Companies moved from the troop bays to their shuttles. Although there was no sign—yet—of any raider activity on the surface, the entire battalion would go in ready for combat, wearing camouflage battledress and battle helmets, magazines in weapons, but with safeties on and no rounds chambered. Lon moved into the command shuttle with his headquarters detachment just as the first two companies were being sealed into their landers. Charlie and Delta Companies started moving toward their craft five minutes later.

It was a busy time for Lon, so busy that he no longer had time to worry about anything but the essentials. He was in radio contact with the launchmaster, *Long Snake*'s bridge and CIC, his executive officer, and the company commanders, switching from channel to channel frequently. More rarely he spoke with Governor Sosa, who was seated next to him in the shuttle.

The command shuttle, a model only recently introduced, was smaller than those that carried the line companies. Instead of holding fifty people, it held—at most—thirty, with the same minimal standard of comfort. Slightly faster and more maneuverable, a command shuttle was armed and better equipped for surveillance and reconnaissance.

The hangar holding Bravo's shuttles was depressurized. The two landers were launched and started their descent, accompanied by the first Shrike fighters that had been launched a few minutes earlier from *Taranto*. Lon's shuttle was next out. There would be a delay before Charlie and Delta were launched, and the men of Alpha would remain sealed in their landing craft, in the hangars, until the rest of the battalion was on the ground. That wait would not make for happy soldiers.

Lon had three video monitors placed within comfortable viewing range. The shuttle's pilots had one showing *Long Snake;* the second the area approaching Lincoln, which was near the horizon, east of the ship's position; and the third tracking the two shuttles carrying Bravo Company.

Shuttles were not equipped with Nilssen generators to provide artificial gravity—an unnecessary "luxury," planners said. Passengers remained strapped in tightly, even during a "cool" landing, where gravity would reassert itself as much as fifteen minutes before the craft touched down.

Governor Sosa sat holding a portable complink, in contact with Government House in Lincoln. Without a Dirigenter battle helmet, he was effectively out of touch with everyone in the shuttle except for Lon. Even without any troubling news coming in, Sosa looked extremely worried. Part of that was just the fact of the shuttle ride. Like many people who rarely experienced zero gravity, Roger Sosa did not like the experience.

"We've all got a lot riding on this," Sosa said when Lon questioned him as the shuttle settled into its glide path for the landing at Lincoln. "I'm past worrying about the political ramifications of failure. If we fail to put an end to these raiders, Bancroft is going to suffer, worse than it already has."

Lon stared at the governor for a few seconds before replying. He *thought* Sosa was sincere, but he found it difficult to trust the words of any politician.

"We should have enough going for us, Governor," Lon said, lifting his faceplate to make it easier for Sosa to hear him.

Sosa did not hear much, though. The command shuttle banked hard to the right and started to accelerate. Lon received a quick alarm from the pilot at the same time.

"We're under fire from the ground, Colonel. Two missiles tracking us."

10

Thirty seconds before the attack, the views on the three monitors had all been focused on the ground—the militia base, Bravo's landers near it, and the closest portion of Lincoln. Once the shuttle pilot started violent evasive maneuvers and accelerated to get altitude, the views on the monitors flashed around so quickly that anyone watching them closely might have become dizzy. Lon gripped the armrests of his seat, fighting against the surge of blood away from his head as the shuttle climbed at more than an eighty-degree angle, trying to escape the two surface-to-air missiles that had been fired at it.

Seconds. The sound of the shuttle's straining rockets covered any other noise. Lon could not even hear his own heartbeat—which surprised him.

The shuttle flipped sideways, then dove, forcing blood toward Lon's head and threatening him with a revolt of his stomach. He swallowed hard to keep from vomiting. Governor Sosa did not manage to keep his breakfast down. It spurted. He dropped his complink. It flew away from him, a missile to ricochet around the passenger compartment.

One of the Shrikes dove in behind the shuttle, its multibarrel cannon firing at the two missiles. It detonated one of the small rockets. The other lost its fix on the shuttle and climbed until it ran out of fuel, giving another Shrike the chance to explode it before it could fall back to the ground.

The shuttle banked around again and the pilot cut the rockets, switched on the jets, and worked to slow the craft for a landing. This time the pilot did not concern himself with a gentle landing. He wanted to get his aircraft, and his passengers, on the ground as quickly as possible.

Lon heard the details, but late. As the shuttle braked to a stop near the southern wall of the militia base—scattering most of the welcoming committee—he was still receiving updates, piped straight through to him from the Shrike pilots, who had gone hunting the shooters on the ground. The two SAMs had been launched from within a mile of Lincoln.

The instant the shuttle stopped, Lon hit the release on his safety harness and staggered to his feet, still dizzy from the aerial gyrations. He spread his feet, slung his rifle over his shoulder, and then—carefully—leaned over to help Governor Sosa get out of his harness. Sosa appeared far more shaken. He still gripped his armrests as if he thought the shuttle were still in the air, maneuvering wildly.

"Come on, Governor. We need to get out of the box, in case there's more trouble," Lon said, half-lifting Sosa from his seat.

Sosa's eyes did not focus as their gaze crossed Lon's face. They started to rotate upward, and the governor started to black out. His knees buckled. Lon caught him and dragged him toward the hatch. Two men from the headquarters detachment came over and took charge of the governor, one on either side. The rest were already out of the shuttle, out of the box.

One platoon from Bravo Company had moved into position around the shuttle, covering three sides, weapons pointed outward. Another platoon was moving in the presumed direction of the SAM launches. Lon looked that way and saw a Shrike making a low pass, strafing the edge of a wooded area. The shuttles carrying the Charlie and Delta platoons had been launched from *Long Snake* but were being held in orbit. *Taranto* was launching an additional four Shrikes to cover the landings.

Slowly, Lon's attention caught up with the reports coming in, but he had to ask for repeats. The second Shrike pilot reported that they had seen a half dozen men running into the woods, and those were the targets they had gone after. "I think Zeke got a couple of them, Colonel," the pilot added. "Your boys are headed in the right direction—about six hundred yards."

A company of constabulary militia was also moving to intercept the raiders. Lon heard about their movements secondhand, from an officer in the Bancroft Constabulary Militia (BCM). At first Lon didn't recognize the man . . . he scarcely had a second to glance at him. Several minutes passed before Lon lifted his faceplate and really looked at the Bancrofter.

"Crampton, isn't it?" Lon asked.

"Wes Crampton," the local officer said, nodding. "Colonel now, commander of the BCM. Sorry about the reception. I thought we had sterilized the area around Lincoln."

"Your governor got more than he bargained for." Lon looked around and finally spotted Sosa, sitting on the ground with his back against the log palisade wall of the militia base, almost hidden by the people clustered around him. "Can't really blame him for the way he reacted. None of us did much better."

"Damned strange piece of luck," Crampton said. "Passing by the first two shuttles filled with troops and hitting the shuttle bringing you and the governor in. They must not have been able to get into position fast enough."

"If they didn't know we were coming, it isn't strange at all," Lon said. "They wouldn't have known anything was going on until the first shuttles came in. We just happened to be next."

"Maybe."

Lon stared. "You think there's something more?"

"Let's just say I can't rule it out," Crampton said. "It was no secret the governor went to Dirigent to get help. The debate over whether we should seek your services went on for weeks. If the raiders are tapped into our public comnet or have other sources of information, they might have been waiting."

"Other sources?"

"We've had a lot of new settlers since the last time you were here, Colonel. It's not impossible that some of them might have had, shall we say, suspect reasons for coming to Bancroft."

"Spies for the Colonial Mining Cartel?" Lon asked.

"I know that sounds melodramatic, but it is possible. Before, we had a tight social bond here. All our families had lived on Bancroft for generations. Now we have all these immigrants, different backgrounds, different customs."

"It's not something Governor Sosa mentioned," Lon said.

Crampton shrugged. "The governor has a more optimistic view of human nature than I do."

The discussion ended. Lon could hear gunfire off to the south—more clearly over his radio than directly. He was linked to the platoon sergeant chasing the raiders. The firefight lasted less than two minutes, ending before the BCM unit could reinforce the Dirigenters.

Lon turned back to Colonel Crampton. "Better have your men see if they can find the raiders hit by the Shrike, Colonel," Lon said. "Hope there's somebody still alive. The four men my people got . . . well, one of them is alive now, but probably won't survive to get to a trauma tube."

Crampton nodded and spoke over his own radio. The Bancrofters had battle helmets purchased from Dirigent now, one of the commercial contacts that had continued since the first time the DMC had helped against off-world raiders.

"We're closing in on them," Crampton reported. "Have to go in with a little care, in case there are any still capable of, ah, resisting."

"Of course. I've just spoken to CIC aboard *Long Snake,* ordered the next two companies in," Lon said. "They'll be on the ground in twenty minutes." Lon was ready to write off the possibility that any survivors would be taken in in good enough condition to question under truth drugs. "I just hope they don't have more SAM teams in position."

"We'll do what we can to make sure the route in is covered," Crampton promised. "I've got every available man moving."

"We'll be alert to the possibility as well, Colonel," Lon said. "If a tracking system locks on, we'll know." *Should have known before,* Lon thought. It was something to check on later, why his shuttle had not detected targeting radar locking on before those missiles were fired.

"I thought we had cleared the area after the raid the other day," Deputy Governor Henks said. It was past noon. The last Dirigenters were on the ground. Half of the shuttles had returned to *Long Snake.* The rest were parked on the new plascrete landing strip next to the militia base that had been turned over to the mercenaries. This meeting was being held in the commandant's conference room.

"It happens," Lon said. "We got lucky. I just wish we'd been able to take one of the raiders alive." The one wounded man had died, as expected, before medical orderlies could get to him with a trauma tube.

"I wish I could be as casual about it as you are, Colonel Nolan," Governor Sosa said. He had showered and changed clothes, but his face still seemed uncommonly pale, and his voice sounded weak. "That is something I don't ever want to go through again."

"No one likes to be exposed like that, Governor," Lon said. "It's something of an occupational hazard for us, but no training can truly prepare a man for it." One of the two pilots had reacted the same way Sosa had aboard the shuttle—vomited. "And it's something a civilian should never have to experience."

"It was my fault, Governor," Colonel Crampton said. "My responsibility."

Sosa made a dismissive gesture. "We're not looking for scapegoats, Colonel. Right now, the important thing is to get the situation on the ground in hand, rid our world of those bastards once and for all."

"There is one security measure I believe we need to take right away," Lon said. "Since the raiders might be able to receive any public comnet broadcasts, we have to make certain that they can't pick up anything that might give them any tactical advantage—anything about the positions and movements of DMC and BCM personnel and other assets; operations, plans, suppositions; casualty reports, intelligence of any sort."

"Censorship?" Henks asked.

"You don't tell the enemy where to point the gun, sir, or give him information on how well you think he's doing," Lon said. "You've been a military man."

"We have the authority under the emergency measures the council approved," Sosa said. "Do it, Dan."

"Yes, sir. I'll have my staff prepare plans this afternoon," Henks said.

Sosa shook his head. "We don't drag this out. Have an executive order ready for my signature in an hour and be ready to implement it immediately. I want you on top of this personally, Dan, and I want every possible leak plugged immediately."

"Of course, Governor," Henks said, a little stiffly. "If you'll excuse me, I'll get right to work." He pushed his chair back and stood, bowed abruptly, and left.

"It's something we've never had to worry about before," Sosa said after his deputy left. "We cherish our freedoms here, and censorship, even if it only means delaying the public release of information for a few hours or days, will not be easy medicine. I agree, though, Colonel Nolan. It is most certainly necessary that we not provide the raiders with any avoidable assistance."

"Yes, sir, I understand how you feel. But it is necessary. In some cases it might not be a matter of hours or days. Some information might have to be withheld until the raiders are eradicated, or until we are absolutely certain that they no longer have the capacity to use that information."

Sosa nodded. "Whatever the situation requires, Colonel."

"I'll have my executive officer coordinate with your people on this, Governor," Lon said. "We'll try to keep it from being too onerous."

The militia compound looked, on the outside, like something that would have been more at home in the Old West of North America a thousand years before. The walls of the compound were wood palisades, tree trunks planted next to each other with pointed tops. The headquarters building, barracks, and other buildings inside were also of log construction. The base would not stand up to attack with even small-caliber artillery or shoulder-launched rockets. To address that weakness, which Lon had pointed out nine years earlier, the Bancrofters had added additional cleared ground on three sides—all but the side that abutted the built-up sections of Lincoln, the planetary capital—and had set up defensive measures farther out, razor wire, pits, and electronic snoops that would warn if any enemy force came within striking range. Armed patrols were also routed around the base now . . . since the return of off-world raiders.

Inside, the buildings were thoroughly modern, with no

trace of the frontier design visible. Lon's office in the headquarters building was larger than his office on Dirigent, and the living quarters above the office were very nearly luxurious. By suppertime of his first day on Bancroft, Lon was confident that his men were ready to move to offensive operations. Liaison with the local government and the BCM were in place. His officers had direct radio links with their counterparts in the militia. Shuttles and Shrikes were flying reconnaissance missions to look for any concentration of raider forces. The computer map had already been fully updated.

"I think we're ready to roll, Phip," Lon said. The two men were alone in Lon's office.

"There's one good thing about being on a contract like this," Phip said. "We can stuff most of the red tape in a boot box and leave it until we're shipboard headed for home. Oh, by the way, they got your shuttle cleaned up. Sosa wasn't the only one who puked. And we've returned his complink—what's left of it. It got banged around pretty good this morning."

"That was too close, Phip," Lon said, very quietly.

"Don't look for an argument from me. All the years I've been in the Corps, that's the closest I ever came to a dirt pension. It'd really have been hell if three of the four of us went out on the same world. Maybe Janno was the smart one, getting out when he did."

Lon squeezed his eyes shut, briefly. The same thought had occurred to him earlier. Dean had died on Bancroft. Lon and Phip had almost followed, nine years later.

"I've got a mean itch up my back, Lon," Phip said after letting a silence grow for a minute or more. "Something tells me the trouble might be worse than these raiders just listening to the local compnet. That they might have had more direct news of us, like when we were coming in, maybe even the landing order."

"A spy in Government House or the BCM?" Lon tried

to make it sound light, skeptical, but did not completely succeed.

"They've had a lot of new people come in. Why couldn't Earth have planted a few ringers?"

"No reason, except maybe practicality." Lon never talked about the details of his own mission to Earth, the fact that Dirigent had resident agents working there.

"What practicality?" Phip asked. "Putting a couple of people out, every world they could, that might be the most practical idea they could have. Tell them where they might find easy pickings, what the target was worth, and have a helping hand available if they decided to come in. Like here."

"Okay, it's possible, and I'm sure the Bancrofters know that as well as you do. They still can't put everyone who's come here in the last nine years under truth drugs to ask. And we can't treat every member of the militia as a potential enemy. We've got to work with them or this contract is impossible."

"Maybe, but we should make sure our people know to keep their eyes open, even with 'friends' covering their backs."

"Go easy, Phip. Vigilance is one thing. I don't want to turn everyone paranoid."

"Sentry lists are posted," Phip said. "Besides regular posts, I've set it up so that one shuttle crew is on duty at all times, ready to use their weapons as well if the raiders try to have a go at us. I remember those little shuttles they used."

"*Long Snake* and the other ships are watching for surprises like that, Phip. We should have plenty of warning if any of them get in the air anywhere within a thousand miles."

"Yeah, right," Phip said. "Like when they hit us at that mining camp nine years ago."

"We didn't know the raiders had shuttles then, Phip. We know to look for them now."

"But we don't know how good their stealth technology is. They might be able to hide better than we can seek."

Originally, Governor Sosa had planned to host a formal dinner for Lon and his senior officers their first evening on Bancroft. After his close call, the governor decided to postpone that reception for twenty-four hours. Lon ate with his staff and company commanders instead, and it was a working meal, with discussions of each company's readiness and initial assignments.

One company would always be on alert, ready to board shuttles and head to any trouble spot within fifteen minutes. The other three companies would share responsibility for the security of the base—mounting guards and sending patrols out in the vicinity—until the Dirigenters had enough intelligence to go hunting the raiders. Already, CIC was putting together bits of information that might lead to action within a day or two. They were using new technology developed largely as a result of the previous Bancroft contract, techniques that might make it possible for the Dirigenters to find raiders without necessarily waiting for them to strike. *Might.*

"There's one thing that's been puzzling me," Captain Kai of Charlie Company said as the meal was winding to an end.

"What's that, Sefer?" Lon asked.

"That cave system where you had the raiders bottled up last time—did the Bancrofters ever open it back up to see if there were any other caches of stolen metals and minerals?"

"He wants to know if they still owe us any percentage," Tebba said, laughing.

"Deputy Governor Henks and I talked about that this afternoon," Lon said. "He was the one who brought it up.

They opened those caves thirty months after we left. They found only negligible amounts of stolen goods, supplies and munitions, and fourteen bodies—raiders who didn't make it out."

"Did they account for everyone who was here?" Kai asked.

"Henks thinks that maybe three or four weren't accounted for, that they must have died on their own, either prey to local predators or from starvation or whatever."

"Or maybe they survived until these new raiders landed," Captain Magnusson of Delta suggested.

"I don't think they'd be much use to the new lot if they'd been living in the wild for nine years," Captain Carlin of Bravo said. "More of a liability."

"In any case, not something we should have to worry about," Lon said. "Let's not borrow trouble. For now, we wait, ready to head out the minute we have a contact or a fix on raider positions from CIC. Nothing shows in the next couple of days, we start putting patrols out near the last few raids, see if there are trails to follow."

Lon's quarters on the third floor of the headquarters building were . . . considerable. The bedroom was twenty-eight feet square, with windows on three sides, high enough to look over the outer wall of the compound. He could stand on one side of his room and look out at the city of Lincoln, a growing, modern city. The tallest buildings were six stories high, and Government House was visible at the far end of a broad avenue. If Lon crossed the bedroom to look out the opposite windows, he could see across the cleared defensive zone into untouched old-growth forest—woodlands that stretched hundreds of miles with only minimal breaks. On the third wall, the view was mainly forest, but with the city beginning to intrude—new residential neighborhoods that had grown over the past nine years.

Sunset. Dusk. Night. The only light in the bedroom was

the dark blue glow of a blank complink screen on the table next to the full-sized bed—a bed larger than the one that Lon and Sara shared at home. Lon was in no hurry to try this bed, in no hurry to tempt sleep. He paced softly, slowly, then stood in front of one window or another to stare out, perhaps as long as ten minutes before moving to the next window.

Thoughts. Worries. Memories. Scenarios—growing wilder as the evening progressed.

What the hell am I doing here? he wondered more than once. This was the time for doubts he could not let his subordinates—even those who knew him best—see. Alone in the dark, he did not need to hold the mask to his face. The cracks in his public facade could widen. There would be time to repair them, time to sleep and let new mortar set.

Thoughts flickered through and vanished, often unconnected bits of trivia as the flip-flop blocks of random association struggled to fill the voids of consciousness. It was near midnight when a series of frames came together to pose Lon a question that jerked him clear of his reverie.

What happened to the second shuttle that attacked us the last time we were here? Two raider shuttles had come down that valley after dropping men on jet packs to hit the mercenaries with gunfire and rockets. One shuttle had been shot down, the wreckage available for inspection.

"We never found the second shuttle," Lon said. "It didn't show up while we were here. I wonder if the Bancrofters ever found it." He went to his complink and keyed in a note to himself, to ask the locals in the morning. Then he undressed for bed and put a sleep patch on his neck.

11

"**No, we never** found it," Daniel Henks said when Lon asked about the raider shuttle the next morning. They were speaking over a complink hookup. "I'd damn near forgotten about that, Colonel. We were so overjoyed at the way your lads and mine smashed the raiders in that last big fight it completely slipped my mind for the longest time. By the time I thought about it again, you had already made your first Q-space jump toward home."

"Did you look for it then?" Lon asked.

"I didn't have the facilities or equipment for an exhaustive search, but I did have our shuttle crews looking, off and on. We did spend time searching the area around those caves where we cornered the raiders, figuring it was most likely they'd have kept their transport close to base. From the air and on the ground. We found a clearing they had apparently used for shuttles, but no sign of anything other than the one your people shot down. Is it important?"

"I don't know yet. It could be. It's a loose end, something that popped into my head last night. If that shuttle got off-world, made rendezvous with a ship, it would explain where any stragglers got to, and it would mean that the CMC would know how we caught their people. Could mean they'll be ready for us if we use the same tactics we did last time."

"And if it didn't get off-world, that shuttle, or at least wreckage, should still be around, somewhere."

"Something like that," Lon said. "We'll look for it. Our close-in surveys ought to spot that much metal on the ground even if it's under trees or covered with camouflage netting. As long as we know what we're looking for."

"We know this new batch of raiders has similar shuttles," Henks reminded Lon. "We've never spotted more than two at a time, but that's no guarantee that's all they have."

"And we haven't spotted any of them yet," Lon said, as much to himself as to the deputy governor.

"This and that and three other things," Vel Osterman said when Lon mentioned the missing shuttle. "You'd think we'd be able to detect any craft on the ground. We're running electronic detectors, magnetic detectors, mapping scans on dozens of frequencies from ultraviolet through infrared, microwave, and I don't know what-all else in addition to visible-light video. And if any of them get airborne, we ought to know within seconds."

"That's the theory," Lon said. "The samples of the wrecked shuttle we had analyzed showed extensive passive stealth technology, but we should still be able to catch them."

"Active stealth?" Vel asked. "ECM?" *Electronic countermeasures.*

"If we're dealing with equipment from Earth, that's likely," Lon conceded. "Hard telling how advanced. That's not the kind of thing they let out." Lon wasn't certain if there was anything on that in the material he had brought back to Dirigent from Earth. There was so much material on the data chips that they had not been completely analyzed before the battalion left Dirigent and made its first transit of Q-space.

He leaned back and closed his eyes, letting out a soft sigh. "This is a little on the screwy side, Vel," he said. "Not a regular combat scenario at all, even though we're talking fairly substantial numbers. No fixed lines, areas of enemy control, or anything. We have to find the enemy before we can even begin to engage them."

"If they know we're here, and we have to assume they do, they might go to ground and just try to wait us out," Vel said. "Good chance we wouldn't find them."

"Wrong. We'd find them," Lon said. "We came prepared to look for caves this time. We can use echo ranging from the shuttles to find cave systems, if it comes to that, then send people in on the ground to do close-up slap-and-grab charting to see if the caves have anyone in them."

We'll find them. Lon kept telling himself that, but every hour that passed without any sighting, without anything that said *Here they are,* he felt his tension increase. It did not help much to remind himself that the battalion had been on the world little more than twenty-five hours.

CIC's computers had been running pattern recognition searches—location of raids, time between attacks, size of raiding party, even the specific metals and minerals stolen—looking for sequences that might help determine the location of the main base of the raiders . . . or the time and place of their next attack. So far the computers had not been able to find anything that could be definitely posited as more than random.

"There have never been two precisely simultaneous attacks. That's the only thing that's struck me so far," Lon told Phip when Steesen came in and found his boss staring at the complink screen, watching the computer sequence the location of attacks and the duration between them. Lon had been staring at various visual summaries for nearly an hour, often going for minutes without even blinking, nearly hypnotized by the program.

Lon turned away from the screen, swiveling his chair until he was directly facing his lead sergeant. "Two and a half hours apart is the closest two raids have come, and the targets were sixty-eight miles apart."

"In other words, it's just barely possible the same people hit both of them," Phip said.

"Can't rule it in or out," Lon said, nodding. "The lack of any recognizable patterns, either it's all blind luck or the opposition is being directed by a damned military genius."

"Or a good computer program," Phip suggested. "One that's able to outsmart our CIC brain boxes."

"Where's my shuttle?" Lon asked.

Phip glanced at his watch. "Should be leaving *Long Snake* right about now. It went up to refuel and load some of the extra scanning gear. Maybe to switch crews as well. I'm not sure about that."

"Pick out a good squad to go along. I want to get out and have a look around for myself," Lon said. "Maybe that will give me more ideas than staring at the complink."

"Can't hurt," Phip said. "You, me, Jerry, and a squad?"

Lon hesitated before he nodded. "Full battle kit, just in case. And make sure CIC knows what we're doing and has a Shrike or two ready if we turn up any worms."

The cockpits of the DMC's larger attack shuttles had three seats—pilot, copilot, and crew chief. A command shuttle, though it was smaller, added a fourth seat in the cockpit, above and behind the pilot—empty except when the infantry commander chose to occupy it. Lon strapped himself into the fourth seat, pulling his harness as tight as it would comfortably go.

"Just what do you have in mind, Colonel?" the command pilot, Lieutenant Art Felconi, asked.

"A little prowling, Art," Lon said. "I've got to see things for myself. Maybe we'll get lucky and stumble onto something."

"Like those rockets yesterday?" Felconi asked. "I'd

rather not go that route again just yet, thank you."

"That's not quite what I had in mind, but it *would* give us a location on some of the enemy. Let's start west. We'll make a tour over as many of the sites that have been raided as we can. Maybe follow a few valleys, see if we happen to turn anything."

"You're the boss," Felconi said.

Petty Officer Steve Tink, the crew chief, came into the cockpit and strapped himself in. "Everyone's aboard and the box is sealed tight, skipper," he reported.

"Colonel?" Felconi asked.

"Whenever you're ready," Lon replied.

Lon had ridden in the cockpit of a shuttle only four times before, in all his years in the Corps. The first time hadn't even been in a Dirigenter shuttle, but in one of the transports the Bancrofters used—*Taking off from this same place,* Lon thought as the pilot pushed the throttles forward and the aircraft started to tremble at power being held back by brakes.

When the shuttle lunged forward, quickly gaining speed, Lon forced himself to keep his eyes open, though his instinct was to close them. Seventy yards from standstill to airborne. The pilot pulled the nose of the shuttle up while the copilot opened the throttles farther. They climbed at a seventy-five-degree angle. Lon concentrated on his breathing as acceleration pushed him into his seat, telling himself that this would only last a few seconds. When the pressure eased and the shuttle nosed forward into level flight, Lon could feel blood moving forward in his head again. For an instant he felt almost dizzy, but a couple of deep breaths—covering an involuntary sigh of relief—brought him back to something approaching normal.

"Where do we start, Colonel?" Felconi asked.

"Head for the southwest limit of the primary sites," Lon said. "The valleys and ridges are all pretty much southwest to northeast, so we can go up and down for a while. I'm going to want to get low enough to have a look at the villages and larger camps." The weather was perfect. There were only a few wispy clouds, high, nothing that would obscure the view.

"The garrisons know we're coming? I'd hate to have even a friendly missile chasing my butt around."

"They're supposed to know, but I'll call Colonel Crampton's headquarters and make sure," Lon offered.

Hills and valleys, creeks and rivers, almost endless trees. Most of Bancroft, even in the area that had been settled, remained mostly as it had been before the first humans landed. There still weren't the numbers to do great damage to the environment, even though Bancrofters preferred to grow most of their food rather than use nanotech assemblers to construct it from patterns out of whatever organic materials came to hand. A hundred people here, a thousand there, only a handful of population centers were larger.

To Lon's right, the crew chief kept busy monitoring the scanning equipment, in case they got lucky and found human activity where it didn't belong. Lon watched out the front of the shuttle, mostly, supplementing that with glances at the two small monitors in the console in front of him.

The pilot kept the shuttle's airspeed low—slow enough that Lon could occasionally see more than just a blur of trees racing past. When they approached one of the mining villages or camps, the pilot made a series of S-curves, banking from side to side to give them more time overhead to look the terrain over.

I don't know what I hope to see, Lon thought after an hour of looking. *No one's going to stand in a clearing and give us the finger.* He didn't expect to spot raiders beginning an attack. That would be too much to ask for. *Maybe we'll turn up one of their shuttles.* That might happen, if luck was running with them. A magnetic or electronic signature that did not belong in unspoiled forest, a flash of matte black surface, the glint of light off a cockpit wind-shield. *Something*.

One of the monitors in front of Lon kept him posted on their position, indicating the names of villages and camps. The flight had been in progress just minutes short of two hours when they went over the cave system where Alpha Company had bottled up the raiders and then destroyed them nine years before.

"Let's take a closer look," Lon told the pilot. "We're just about out of valleys. Past the next ridge to the east, the ground starts to flatten out and slope toward the sea."

"You don't think they'd go back to the same place, do you, sir?" Lieutenant Felconi asked.

"Odds and evens," Lon said. "No, I don't expect that they'd go back to the same place. Even if there were no survivors to tell them what happened, they could see that the entrances had been destroyed by explosives and guess. But if they *thought* we'd think that, it might seem to be the safest place. With a few extra safeguards to try to avoid the same fate."

"You're making my head spin, Colonel. Here we go."

The shuttle made a gentle banking turn, losing five hundred feet of altitude. Lon had never seen the location from the air before. The perspectives were different. It was not until he spotted the narrow chimney along the northwest-ern end of the hill where he had first discovered traces of the enemy that he was able to orient himself. He had the pilot make several passes along the valley on the west side of the ridge, gradually picking out several of the other entrances to the cave system—mostly from rock that was colored differently, scars left by the explosions that sealed off the cave. The areas of heaviest fighting could be deduced from that, though there was no visible evidence of the battle after nine years.

"Okay, Lieutenant, I guess I've done enough sightseeing

for one day," Lon said finally. "Let's head back for Lincoln."

"On the way," Felconi said.

The shuttle was still climbing when Lon got the report. Raiders were hitting one of the newer mining camps, considerably to the northwest. Lon didn't hesitate. "Head for those coordinates, Lieutenant. This might be what we're looking for."

Felconi pushed the throttles all the way to the stops, and the shuttle went supersonic. The site of the attack was eight minutes away.

Lon was too busy to notice the ride. He linked to Vel Osterman to ensure that the alert company—Delta—was on its way. The men were already boarding their shuttles and were off the ground almost before Osterman could report it. Two companies of militiamen would be no more than five minutes behind the mercenaries; they were coming from two different locations.

"The mining camp is called Xavier's Beak, and don't ask me why," Osterman said. "There are about sixty civilians and forty militiamen stationed there. The mines produce copper ore and trace elements usually associated with copper deposits."

"Any sign of raider shuttles?" Lon asked.

"Negative, and we're doing a close scan of the area around Xavier's Beak. First reports from the camp say there are at least fifty raiders, but we don't have any way to confirm that yet. There is shooting going on now. The militia got three minutes' advance warning from snoops they had planted along the valley floor, so the raiders weren't able to just walk over."

Before Lon could say anything, Vel started talking again. "We've just lost radio contact with the camp. The uplink must have been blown." No more than fifteen seconds elapsed before he passed along confirmation of an explosion at the edge of the camp, spotted by *Long Snake* first, and then by several shuttle pilots almost simultaneously.

"Bravo has the base security detail?" Lon said, seeking confirmation. He didn't wait for Vel to agree. "Get Alpha and Charlie ready to move on ten minutes' notice. Get on to *Long Snake* to get shuttles down to carry them, ASAP. We hit them and hit them hard."

"CIC is monitoring our talk, Lon. There, I've got confirmation on another circuit. Two shuttles will launch in seven minutes. With what we've got on the ground, that will carry Alpha and Charlie."

"We should reach Xavier's Beak about ninety seconds before Delta. We'll stay overhead to provide close-in eyes, at least until they're on the ground and can engage," Lon said. "I'll decide what I'll do next when the time comes."

"Just stay high enough to keep out of trouble, Lon."

"We'll do our best."

The command shuttle deployed wing flaps to cut its airspeed once Xavier's Beak was in sight. The shuttle went subsonic and Lieutenant Felconi banked into a wide turn, orbiting the area at twelve thousand feet—high enough to ensure that they would be able to escape any surface-to-air missiles that might be fired at them.

"We've got a good fix on the raiders, Colonel," Felconi said before they had made one complete circuit. "I'm linked through to the militia commander and I've got the positions of his people and the enemy."

"Can we give them something to think about? A couple of rockets, maybe?"

"Coming up. We should get a little closer, though, to be sure we don't have a bird stray off in the wrong direction."

"Go for it, Lieutenant."

A transparent bubble came down over the crew chief's

head. Inside, he was in a virtual reality gunner's turret. The pilot controlled the missiles. The chief operated the two Gatling gun pods. Going in close, the cannon might be needed. With the assist of a targeting computer, the cannon might even be able to destroy a SAM coming at them.

Lon keyed the controls on one of his monitors to give him a constant readout of altitude and airspeed. They dropped below four thousand feet—inviting range for a shoulder-launched rocket. Their speed fell to 450 miles per hour—a crawl—as the pilot used air brakes and reverse thrust to slow the shuttle.

Not for long. As soon as the two missiles were launched, Lieutenant Felconi increased the shuttle's speed and climbed out of harm's way, accelerating rapidly enough that Lon thought he was near to graying out as the g-forces pressed him back against his seat. There was a roaring noise in his ears, the feel of blood pressing against skin, fleeing his face. It was difficult to draw a deep breath. Then it ended. Too much weight was replaced by a few seconds of virtual weightlessness as the shuttle nosed over.

"Right on target, Colonel," Felconi announced. The view on one of Lon's monitors changed, showing smoke coming up from under the trees in the valley below Xavier's Beak.

"Good shooting, Lieutenant," Lon said. "Get ready to go in close to provide covering fire when Delta's shuttles arrive. They're going to land right on the strip there at the edge of the camp. Let's give them a chance to get the men out of the box."

"Yes, sir," Felconi said. "I show them about forty seconds from touchdown, coming in fast from the southwest."

"Let's go get the bad guys, Lieutenant," Lon said.

Felconi nosed the shuttle over and started gliding toward the raiders, holding airspeed down to allow safe use of the Gatlings—if the shuttle were flying too fast it might overrun the bullets. Like the pilots, Lon watched for any indication of a shoulder-fired SAM coming toward them. Below five thousand feet, they were especially vulnerable.

The shuttle launched two more missiles. As soon as they were away, Chief Tink started strafing, using only the lower turret gun. The missiles exploded. More bits of the wooded hillside got thrown around. Tink's shells started chewing through leaves and branches. He kept firing even after the command shuttle had to bank away and start climbing again.

Two Shrike fighters made passes at the raider positions, one following the other, rockets and cannons chewing up more of the hillside. By that time, the attack shuttles carrying Delta Company had landed and the men were pouring out of the troop compartments and moving into their initial defensive perimeter. That drill took DMC soldiers less than thirty seconds.

"We'll hang around until the Bancrofter militia arrives," Lon said as his shuttle leveled off two miles above the mining camp. One camera had already picked up the local shuttles speeding in, though the aircraft were only dark points against the sky without magnification.

12

The two Dirigenter attack shuttles took off before the BCM arrived, and circled overhead—ready to contribute to the fight on the ground. As soon as the militiamen were out of their shuttles and moving to flank the raiders—while Lon's Delta Company kept them pinned down—Lon told Felconi to land.

"I want to see this from the ground," Lon said. He had been monitoring the radio traffic among Captain Magnusson and his platoon leaders and sergeants. The fighting was not heavy. Only scattered rifle fire was coming from the raider positions.

"Yes, sir," Felconi said, staring to nose the shuttle around to line it up with the landing strip. "The LZ should be secure."

"I should hope so," Lon said, more to himself than the pilot. Between Delta and the two BCM companies, the odds on the ground were about those of a battalion to a platoon—twelve to one—without considering casualties that Lon's shuttle and the Shrikes might have inflicted.

Still, as soon as the command shuttle came to a stop on the ground—along a ridge across the valley from the buildings of the mining camp—Lon was out of his safety harness and moving toward the exit as quickly as if he knew that hostile fire was coming. Phip Steesen, Jeremy Howell, and the squad Phip had assembled from the headquarters detachment moved out of "the box" with Lon and stayed around him . . . just in case. The firefight was continuing, but not with any great ferocity—scattered bursts of rifle fire, none of it near the landing strip.

"Just what did you have in mind, Colonel?" Phip asked. He and Corporal Howell were so close to Lon that they were physical shields—which annoyed Lon.

"I want to see what's going on, take a look at any raider casualties they leave behind," Lon said, moving away from his companions. They moved right with him, giving up only a few inches after a glare. The defensive squad gave them more room, arranged in a semicircular perimeter, facing out, rifles ready. "The sooner we get some kind of handle on the action, the sooner we can bring the contract to a successful conclusion. Let's move toward the camp, see what's going on with the miners."

The squad with Lon moved in a double column, keeping Lon, Phip, and Jeremy near the center. They detoured past the village on the opposite slope before descending and crossing the narrow valley, giving the firefight as much room as possible. That fight was beginning to move. The raiders were attempting to withdraw, but were being pressed too heavily by the DMC and BCM forces to have much chance.

Xavier's Beak mining camp consisted of a half dozen buildings—including the ore refinery—and five separate excavations. The latter included mine shafts and two deep bunkers for explosives. The buildings were hastily constructed in frontier style, using available wood—large log cabins for the miners and militia to use as barracks, a slightly larger building to serve most other functions—built along the slope above the eastern side of the valley, high enough to be safe from flooding if the narrow creek that marked the lowest contours ever flooded. Rough paths connected buildings and the excavations. A broader path led from the camp to the landing strip that was the only access between Xavier's Beak and the rest of Bancroft.

The largest building had been turned into a medical facility. The single trauma tube that the miners had was in use. The two tubes that Delta Company had carried were being set up as Lon arrived. One of Delta's medical technicians was directing several miners to help with the work and give first aid to a half dozen wounded men who had been brought in.

"We're doing pretty good, so far, Colonel," the medic said when Lon came up to him. "None of our people have been brought in yet. Several miners and local militia were wounded before we got here." He shrugged. "Don't know about the other side yet. Not much worried about *them*."

"If you need help, a couple of the men with me are trained as medics, and we've got another trauma tube in the shuttle," Lon said. The portable trauma tubes the DMC carried into the field were not quite as sophisticated as those that would be found in a permanent medical facility, but they did the job. If a wounded man survived long enough to get into a tube, he had better than a 98 percent chance of complete recovery. A tube provided life-support machinery plus hordes of medical-repair nanobots to repair damage done to the body. Only extensive damage to the nervous system or amputation were likely to require extensive periods for recovery and regeneration. Anything less and the wounded soldier would normally be ready to return to duty in four hours or less.

"Colonel, we can *always* use more trauma tubes," the orderly, Corporal Allison, said. "And I'll take any help I can get."

Fifteen minutes later, the fighting at Xavier's Beak was over. Three wounded prisoners were brought in for treatment. Captain Magnusson had two platoons, led by his senior lieutenant, pursuing the twenty or more raiders who had managed to withdraw. One militia company was also engaged in the pursuit.

"We've come off pretty good, so far," Magnusson said when he came to report to Lon in person. "I've got two men with minor wounds, no one killed. There are seventeen raider bodies out there." He gestured vaguely toward where the firefight had occurred. "I didn't want to risk men keeping any of the enemy from escaping, not at the start like this."

"You did right. I would have told you if I wanted more. I'd rather have them on the move, giving us some clue as to where their base might be. CIC has its eyes open, and the shuttles and Shrikes are doing what tracking they can. Were you able to get a good count on how many of them there were?"

Magnusson shook his head. "Three captured, seventeen bodies, at least twenty escaped. Might have been twice that number that got away, depending how they were originally deployed and whether any moved out before we got close. Doesn't look like they got close to any of the loot they were after. I've got men collecting weapons and equipment. And these." He pulled a small plastic tag, just over an inch in diameter, from a pocket and gave it to Lon.

"ID tag?" Lon asked, turning the disk over. There was no visible writing, just a sketchy logo that Lon did not recognize.

"That's my guess," Magnusson said. "All the bodies we've checked had them strung around their necks."

"The computers in CIC should be able to decipher anything on them," Lon said, giving the tag back to Magnusson. "We'll ship all of them up to *Long Snake,* along with samples of the weapons and equipment. They were using active electronics, shielded too well to let us get precise fixes on position."

Magnusson nodded. "Good battle helmets. Not exactly like any I've seen in my twenty-odd years with the Corps, but close enough. The rifles were the same ones shown in the database from the last time the Corps came here. Martian manufacture."

Lon looked around to make certain no Bancrofters were close. "How did the militia do?"

"No complaints. This wasn't really a good test, but I'd say they've kept their standards fairly high."

"I hope so," Lon said. "They had it quiet long enough that they might have relaxed."

"If these raids started a year ago, they'd have had time to whip their people back up," Magnusson said. "At least we don't have to train them from scratch."

Lon grunted. "Let's take a walk. I want to see what we've got left on the ground here."

Squads of Bancrofter militia were combing the area around the village, looking for bodies or wounded men. The dead were not being collected yet, but weapons, gear, and personal effects were—labeled as to which body, or fragment of a body, they came from. The smell of battle lingered on the hillside, a mixture of gunpowder, burned wood and flesh, and death. The cannon and rockets had done considerable damage to the trees. Outcroppings of rock were chipped and blackened.

The remaining militiamen, and the other two platoons of Delta Company, had established a wider perimeter around the mining camp, alert against the small chance that the surviving raiders might dare another assault against Xavier's Beak.

"Something bothers me about this attack," Magnusson said while he and Lon stood over the body of one of the dead raiders. Phip, Jeremy, and most of the squad that had come with them were close, still providing up-close security for their commander.

"Like what?" Lon asked.

"The timing, mostly," Magnusson said. "They came in the middle of the day, and managed to trip an electronic snoop before they were close enough to do any good. They should have been able to figure that we'd show up before they could neutralize the militia contingent here and make off with anything. I mean, we *do* assume that they know we arrived, don't we?"

"Almost a certainty, Ron. That might be the point of this raid, just to see how fast we can respond given the most favorable conditions for us."

"Waste that many men to feel us out?"

"We're not dealing with humanitarians," Lon said. "Earth has more people than it can deal with. They won't mind losses. We played hell capturing any raiders the last time here. It wasn't until the last battle that we bagged *any* live prisoners."

Magnusson turned until he was looking in the direction of the buildings. "We've got some now. Ought to be able to find out quite a bit about the opposition from them."

Lon nodded. "Whatever they know." *Maybe we'll be able to end this job in a hurry,* he thought. *Find out where the enemy base is and hit it hard.* Once the prisoners came out of the trauma tubes, they would be questioned under the influence of truth drugs that could not be resisted or fooled—at length, by men who knew how to get the most out of an interrogation.

"Colonel Nolan, we've got a big problem." The call came from Corporal Allison. Lon was still walking over the site of the firefight with Magnusson. "All three prisoners are dead."

"What?" The shout was unintentional. Lon grabbed Magnusson's arm, then gestured and they started back toward the buildings. Lon forced a brisk pace.

"Couldn't help it, Colonel. I infused them with stabilizers to keep them going until we could get them into trauma tubes. Less than five minutes later, they started going into convulsions. Before I could do anything, they were all dead. I've never seen anything like this before, Colonel. Never even *heard* of that kind of reaction."

"Any sign of any of the other wounded reacting?"

"No, sir, and I used the same batch of infuser on two Bancrofters."

The three prisoners who had died were lying on blankets, by themselves, along the east wall. Corporal Allison was standing over one of them when Lon and Magnusson entered.

"I just don't understand it, Colonel," Allison said. "This just shouldn't be possible. Look at them."

They were not pretty. The visible skin was livid, marked by blotches and lines of dark red going black. "It looks like massive hemorrhaging, as if all the blood vessels exploded," Allison said. "I don't know any way that *could* happen, not from what I gave them."

"It looks as if the enemy doesn't want us questioning their people," Magnusson said.

Lon glanced at him. "Some kind of booby trap in the blood?"

Magnusson shrugged. "Sounds like a good guess. Hit them with any nanobugs without neutralizing the defenses, and zap."

After a hesitation, Lon looked toward the ceiling and said, "Same thing might happen if we use truth drugs."

"Probably," Magnusson said. "Maybe we can get enough from a postmortem to find the triggering agent, and how to counter it."

"Colonel?" Allison waited until Lon looked at him. "You mean they rigged their men to die if they got captured?"

"That's what we're thinking. We need to get these three and some of the raiders who were killed outright to Lincoln for detailed examination. Ron, will you take care of that?"

"Yes, sir," Magnusson said. "I'll get my lead sergeant right on it. Send the bodies back on one of our shuttles."

"I'll have Major Osterman make the arrangements on the other end," Lon said. He turned and walked away, leaving the building.

Outside, he walked down to the bottom of the valley, near the thin stream, and looked up into the sky. After a moment he squeezed his eyes shut.

"No easy fix this time," he whispered. "Unless we find a way to counter whatever they've done, it's going to be just like before, hunt them out on the ground."

13

Lon could think of dozens of things he would rather do, or *should* do, that evening other than attend a formal dinner at Government House. But there was no avoiding Governor Sosa's invitation. The political aspect of leadership demanded Lon's *gracious* attendance, and that of his second-in-command.

"I really don't like for both of us to be away at once, Vel, but that's the way it goes," Lon said after they donned formal white uniforms. A car was coming to pick them up.

"A couple of hours, Lon, and it's not as if we had to jump to Q-space for it. We've got our radios and we can get back to base in, what, five minutes if we have to?"

"I know, it's just"—Lon hesitated for ten seconds or more—"I've never been comfortable with the highbrow stuff."

Vel laughed. "Seems that, once upon a time, I heard someone suggest that you got married just to escape going to all those junior officer functions, the grand balls and all that."

Lon couldn't help a smile. "No, that wasn't why I got married, but it sure as hell was a nice bonus. I couldn't get out of *all* the social nonsense, but once I had Sara along, it wasn't nearly as hard to bear. Three or four times a year, when we're in garrison, I can manage. Snag is, now that I've got the battalion, I'm going to have to go to more of those affairs, be on display, play the game." See and be seen. Talk with the right officers, smile at the right officers' wives. Play the game, the inevitable politics of command.

"How's the food at Government House?" Vel asked. The limousine was just pulling to a stop in front of the headquarters building in the militia compound.

"Okay, I guess, the two times I ate there. But that was a lot of years ago. They might have a different chef now."

Polite conversation. Soft music in the background. Introductions and meaningless smiles. Cocktails and hors d'oeuvres. Men in uniforms or dinner jackets. Women in fancy gowns, festooned with too much jewelry. Lon tried to give the evening all the attention he could, but it was difficult. He played the game, but absently, his mind wandering to the events of the day, the fight and the gruesome death of the injured prisoners. There were no final reports yet on the postmortem examinations. Tests were still being conducted and analyzed. *Maybe in the morning,* CIC had told Lon while he was dressing for the governor's affair. All the medical lab could confirm so far was that whatever had been added to the medical nanosystems of the dead raiders, it had self-destructed after death, making analysis difficult, perhaps impossible. They would try to reverse-engineer the nanotech agents. That seemed the necessary step if any antidote could be fashioned, but that might also prove impossible without too much time and better facilities than were available on Bancroft or aboard the Dirigenter ships.

The "dinner is served" announcement was a small relief to Lon. It meant that the end of the evening was a little closer. The preliminaries were over. An hour, maybe ninety minutes, would see the end of dinner, and it might be possible for Lon and Vel to excuse themselves not too long after the meal.

Most of the other guests seemed excited at the victory over the raiders, especially since it had been accomplished without any Bancrofter fatalities and without the loss of any of the metals and minerals that fueled the world's economy.

Lon scarcely noticed the quality of the food. He ate in mechanical fashion, keeping up a portion of his share of the table talk, trying to pay attention to what was going on around him. It wasn't easy, but he kept reminding himself that he had to play the game. Vel Osterman seemed to enjoy it. He kept the talk going, turning phrases that brought polite giggles from the women seated at either side of him and holding the attention of most of the people at the table.

Dessert. Brandy. Lon sampled both only sparingly. His primary interest in them was as indications that the dinner was nearing its conclusion. He watched. Either the governor or, more likely, his wife would stand and make some trifling comment. That would be the signal for everyone to rise. There would be a general migration toward the formal parlor and, after that, guests would be free to leave. He did not notice the servant who came up and leaned forward to whisper in his ear.

"Excuse me, sir," the liveried attendant said, "the governor requests you and Major Osterman to give him a few minutes after dinner. I will conduct you to the governor's office."

"Of course. Thank you," Lon said, thinking, *So much for a quick exit.*

The governor made excuses and promised his other guests that he would join them in the parlor as soon as possible. He moved toward a narrow door that was almost concealed by a tall cabinet at the side of the room. The servant conducted Lon and Vel through the same door, down a corridor to the governor's office.

"I'll only take a moment, gentlemen," Governor Sosa

said. He had remained standing. "I was most distressed to hear of the fate of the prisoners taken this morning at Xavier's Beak. I can't believe that Earth has become so barbaric."

"It was unexpected, Governor, but I can't say that I'm especially surprised at it," Lon said. "Shocked, yes, but not surprised. Human life doesn't carry the same value on Earth as it does on most worlds. It's obvious that Earth knows, or surmises, that prisoners were taken before and were questioned. They don't want to take the same risk again."

"Will you be able to find a way to neutralize whatever it is that causes such a ghastly death?"

Lon spread his hands. "I can't even make a decent guess. We're working on it, full blast, in the labs on *Long Snake* and *Taranto*, but it might be beyond the scope of what we can do here. A message rocket couldn't carry sufficient samples to Dirigent, and I don't want to detach one of my ships to make the trip."

Sosa started to speak, but stopped with his mouth open. Then he shut it and started over. "I see why," he said. "A month in transit for the round trip, and whatever time your ground labs might take to analyze the problem and come up with a solution . . . if there is one."

"I have a lot of faith in the research people back home," Lon said, "but this is something that might take years to puzzle out, if we can at all. Computer models can't take the last step, to verify anything they reverse-engineer, and this isn't the kind of thing we would ever consider doing live trials on."

"Of course not," Sosa said. "Nor would we." He paused, frowned. "This does complicate matters."

"Possibly. It certainly robs us of the easiest shortcut to solving your problem," Lon said. "But aside from the macabre fail-safe Earth seems to have infected its soldiers with, the encounter this morning was encouraging. Your garrison got word out of the attack fast, and both your people and mine were able to get to the scene fast enough to stop the raiders cold."

Sosa nodded absently. "They were not scoring every time they hit before, Colonel—not to belittle your contribution. But I wonder if part of our success this morning might have been due to the fact that you were in the air when the raid started and were able to get to Xavier's Beak even before your fighters."

"It's possible," Lon conceded. "There might be a lot of factors that went our way this morning. That particular raid might have been staged just to let the raiders gauge how we react to an attack, feeling us out, trying to figure out what changes they might need to make in their tactics."

Three in the morning. The dream was one that Lon welcomed being wakened from, even for bad news. The ghost of Dean Ericks, nearly transparent, defined more by dripping blood than form, had come to him. Though nothing had been said yet, the dream fit an all-too-familiar pattern. Lon was certain that Dean was coming to tell him that Lon, Junior, had been killed on contract.

"Colonel Nolan! Wake up, sir!" The voice was Jeremy Howell's.

Lon opened his eyes and blinked several times against the light in his room. He lifted his arm to shade his eyes. "What is it?" There was nothing sluggish about Lon's voice. He had wakened completely—the better to escape his nightmare.

"A raid. At least we *think* it's a raid," Howell said.

Lon swung his legs off the side of the bed and sat up. "Calm down, Jerry. Start at the beginning."

"Mining camp called Three Peaks didn't make a scheduled check-in at oh-two-hundred, then didn't answer when militia HQ called. There's no netlink with the camp. Then one of our Shrikes spotted smoke rising from the location."

Lon had gotten to his feet and stretched while Howell was talking. "Three Peaks—that's one of the places the raiders hit when we were here last time," he said.

"Yes, sir. I recognized the name."

"Are we responding?" Lon asked. His answer came from outside. He heard the engine sounds of two attack shuttles taking off just south of the militia base.

"That's Alpha Company, Colonel," Howell said as soon as the initial roar abated enough for easy talk. "And the militia OD said they'll have two companies on the way in five minutes."

Lon sat on the edge of his bed again. He glanced at the timeline on the complink on the nightstand. "You might as well get back to bed, Jerry. I'll stay up until we've got a report from Captain Girana."

"Would you like some coffee?" Howell asked.

"No. I want to be able to get back to sleep once I know what's going on."

Lon yawned as Jeremy left. His moment of peak alertness had passed. Then he moved a little, to get closer to his complink. He keyed in instructions and got a radio link to Girana aboard his shuttle.

"Tebba, I want a direct report as soon as you get on the ground and know what's going on at Three Peaks."

"We should be touching down in about twelve minutes," Girana said. "A few minutes to get into the camp, unless the landing is contested. I'll keep you posted."

Lon closed the link and yawned again, after noting the exact time. He was moderately surprised at the return of sleepiness. He felt no excitement, no nervousness. There was no urge to jump into battledress and take a shuttle to Three Peaks to see what was going on for himself.

Age, I guess, he thought. Trouble would come when it wanted to. He felt no call to go looking for it. *Twenty years of winning other people's wars with our blood.* He yawned. The thought was no longer novel, no longer revolutionary to his mind.

He sat slouched over, head occasionally nodding. There was a pleasant feeling of detachment as he hovered on the edge of the slide back into sleep, an anesthetizing warmth. Outside, there would be the chill of a spring night. It had been noticeably cool when he left Government House five hours earlier. Early spring. The nights could still get close to freezing in Lincoln.

When his complink buzzed to alert him to an incoming message, Lon was startled. Twenty minutes had passed since he had talked to Tebba. Lon had nearly been asleep. He reached quickly to accept the call.

"We're on the ground at Three Peaks, Colonel," Tebba Girana reported. "It's bad. Looks as if everyone here was killed, militiamen and miners. The raiders are gone, presumably with whatever was worth taking."

Sleep was banished. Lon could feel his heart start to beat more rapidly. He sat up straighter.

"First glance, it looks as if the raiders hit with grenades, got past whatever snoops the militia had planted, knocked out the netlinks before anyone could call for help," Tebba said. "The buildings were all torched—intentionally, I'd guess. It's been raining here, and one building didn't burn all the way to the ground."

"You send patrols to see which way they went?" Lon asked.

"Not yet. I thought I'd better check with you and give the Bancrofters time to get organized. They're still moving away from the landing strip."

"Right. You'll have to work with the senior officer. Get a perimeter set up, then put out patrols to look for the raiders' trail. Anything more might have to wait until daylight. Is it still raining there?"

"Yes, sir, and fairly heavy. Miserable. The pilot said the cloud deck extends all the way to the ocean and the ceiling is nine hundred feet—below some of the peaks in this area."

"Which limits what we can see from above," Lon said, more to himself than to Tebba.

"Limits what we can see on the ground, too," Tebba said. "The odd bolt of lightning hurts more than it helps, blurs the night-vision gear."

"Do what you can tonight, Tebba. I'm going to have to confer with Colonel Crampton before we fix anything past the immediately necessary. You know what to do."

The conference with the Bancrofter militia commander came sooner than Lon expected. Before he could call BCM headquarters, Colonel Crampton linked through to him.

"I heard," Lon said before Crampton could say why he had called. "I just got off the line with my senior man on the scene. Your people had just arrived."

"I told my company commanders to put themselves under your man," Crampton said. "I assume we go right after these raiders." There was no question in his voice.

"If possible," Lon said. "We're putting patrols out to try and pick up their trail. There's a lot of rain in that area now. That might make it impossible to find any trail we can follow."

"We can't let them get away scot-free!"

"If it's humanly possible to prevent that, we will, Colonel," Lon said. "Right now, we've got to give the men on the ground there a chance to do their jobs. Swimming blindly in the mud won't do us any good." *Neither will hysteria,* he thought.

"I'll be heading out there shortly," Crampton said. "Time it to reach Three Peaks at dawn. The forecast says the rain should let up by then. It's starting to rain here now, but Lincoln is right on the edge of the system."

"Tell you what, Colonel. Why don't you come over here

and we'll take my command shuttle. Takeoff in an hour, maybe an hour and a quarter."

Crampton scarcely hesitated. "I'll be there."

Coffee, a shower, more coffee. Lon gave orders to have his shuttle prepared, and had Phip wakened to gather a few men to ride with them. Shave, eat a quick breakfast, drink more coffee . . . go to the latrine. Lon plodded through the routine, as if this were just a normal morning. As far as he could, he put off thinking about Three Peaks. There would be time enough for that later. Once Colonel Crampton arrived, it might be impossible to escape discussing the raid.

Crampton arrived before Lon finished but did not intrude. Crampton went to the communications center and talked with his officers in Three Peaks—getting the latest tally on the disaster. The duty officer informed Lon that Crampton had arrived.

"I'll be down in a few minutes," Lon replied, and he made a point not to rush through the few remaining necessities. When he left his room, Lon was in full field kit, carrying his battle helmet under one arm and his rifle slung over the other.

"No warning this time?" Phip Steesen asked as Lon came out of the bedroom.

"Doesn't look like it," Lon said. "You ready to go?"

"We're ready. I've got a fire team in the shuttle, and the pilots should be through their checklist by now. Just waiting for you, me, and Colonel Crampton and his people."

"How many did he bring?" Lon asked.

"Just two. They'll fit."

"We can't let these raiders get away with an attack like this one," Crampton said while the men were walking across the compound toward the gate on the south side.

"We're talking about sixty people killed, most while they were sleeping."

"No one's letting anyone get away with anything," Lon said. He had his helmet on with the faceplate tilted up, away from his face. There was a steady rain coming down over Lincoln now, but without much wind to drive it. "That's why we're here, to stop these raiders. It just might take time."

"After this, we'll play hell keeping miners at any of the camps. We might even have to evacuate some of the villages, bring people into the towns. And *that* plays hell with the economy, on top of the way our citizens are going to feel about a massacre like Three Peaks."

Lon stopped walking and turned to face Crampton, almost colliding with him. "Look, Colonel, I know how you feel, but snapping your fingers and saying, 'We've got to do something this minute' won't accomplish one damned thing. We're here. We'll do what is possible, as fast as possible. You're a good officer, but you can't think straight getting emotional. Get a grip on yourself."

For a few seconds, Lon could see anger rising in the Bancrofter; his face started to get red; his jaw worked as he ground his teeth. Lon waited, ready for any kind of reaction, even violence. Finally, Crampton closed his eyes for a second, let out a long breath, and swallowed hard.

"You're right, Colonel," Crampton said, his voice sounding near strangulation. "I was letting myself get out of control. Please excuse me. But I am under pressure. I had a call from the governor. He wants action, and military facts of life mean less to him than they do to you or me."

"Our turn will come, Colonel," Lon said. "Come on. It'll be drier in the shuttle."

14

Three Peaks was no longer one of the most isolated mining camps on Bancroft, but it was still not in a well-populated area. There were several new camps, even smaller, within a radius of twenty miles, but all of them had been abandoned—temporarily, Colonel Crampton said, until the raiders were destroyed.

Only one shuttle was on the ground when Lon's craft made its approach. The landing strip, hacked out of rock, did not have facilities for multiple shuttles to sit around. There was barely enough room for aircraft to land. The mining camp and its landing strip were on a broad shelf on the flank of a moderately steep hill, some fourteen hundred feet above mean sea level. The camp got its name from three broken heights along the ridge on the southwest side of the ledge.

"Looks like some expansion since I was here last," Lon said to Crampton as the shuttle touched down.

"I think so, yes," Crampton said. "We opened two new shafts a couple of years ago, brought in more people to work them. And we had to build a barracks for the militia detachment."

Tebba Girana was waiting at the landing strip with a squad from his company's first platoon. One of the Bancrofter captains was also waiting to report to his commander.

"Doesn't look like the locals had any chance at all here,

Colonel," Girana told Lon as they walked away from the Bancrofters, toward the remains of the village. "They got hit hard and fast, without warning. The bodies I've looked at, most were killed by fire or shrapnel, most looked like they didn't even get out of bed before they died. I've only seen one body with bullet wounds, and the medic said those might have happened after the guy was already dead."

"You find any snoops planted around here?" Lon asked. "They should have had *some* warning."

"We've pulled three snoops, all nonfunctional," Tebba said. "I can't say if they were working when the raiders hit. Outside of that, it was raining and foggy. The clouds extended nearly five hundred feet down, more than halfway to the valley floor when we got here. Without night-vision gear, visibility would have been zero-minus. We haven't been able to determine which direction the raiders came from, or which way they went when they left. All the rain, we might never figure it out."

"We'll have to search, Tebba, at least until we *know* we're not going to find anything," Lon said. The rain had stopped, but there were still high clouds, thick enough to hide the sun.

"I've got three platoons out, and half the Bancrofters are out as well." Tebba glanced over his shoulder. "The other militiamen are taking care of the dead, getting them ready to take home."

"No survivors at all?"

"None that we've been able to find. I suppose there's a small chance one or two might have managed to slip away, to hide in the woods, but it's not likely. Odds are we'd have already come across them."

The walk had carried Lon and Tebba, followed by the squad that had been on the ground and the Dirigenters who had come with Lon, into the center of the burned ruins of Three Peaks. Even with the rain, the smells of fire and ashes—and burned flesh—were heavy, rank odors. Some of the remnants were still smoldering.

Three Peaks had been a narrow strip. A natural ledge along the hillside had been widened. Nowhere was the level cleared area more than a hundred feet wide, and the settlement, including the landing strip, was only six-tenths of a mile long. The buildings had been built against the back of the ledge.

I doubt anyone escaped, Lon thought. *They had only one way to go, and the raiders would have been waiting for them there.* He shook his head, a minimal gesture.

Bodies encased in plastic bags were being laid out on the wet rock. Two rows.

"Not much left to some of them," Tebba said when he saw Lon staring at the body bags. "Charred, some burned down to the bones. Hot fire." He paused, then added, "I wasn't the only one to puke. An' one of the Bancrofter militiamen went hysterical. They had to slap a sleep patch on him to quiet him down."

"I can imagine," Lon whispered.

"Weren't just wood burning, that's for sure," Tebba said. "We've taken scrapings of some of the charred wood. The raiders used something to make the fire burn hot and fast. Maybe just white phosphorus, maybe something more sophisticated."

"Won't make much difference to the people who died, but it might help us prove who's behind this," Lon said. "Not that it's ever going to get into a court of law."

"News gets out to enough worlds, it might make a difference," Tebba said. "Earth could pretty much cut itself off from the rest of the human worlds."

Despite the surroundings, Lon felt a smile cross his face. "Politics, Tebba? You?"

"A thing like this can do it to you," Tebba said, his tone completely serious. "News gets out we can prove Earth was behind this kind of raiding, it'll help Buckingham and

Union. And Dirigent. Folks'll maybe not hesitate so long to get professional help when things start happening on their worlds."

"If the Second Commonwealth and the new Confederation of Human Worlds get too big, it'll hurt business for us and the other mercenary worlds, Tebba. Time'll come when there won't be room for independent worlds like Dirigent."

"Not in my lifetime," Tebba said. "We're a long way from that."

Lon was not particularly surprised to learn that Governor Sosa was coming out to view the scene of the tragedy at Three Peaks. He did not look forward to hearing what the governor might have to say. Neither could be avoided, though; Lon also knew that. Because of the visit, the bodies were not removed. Sosa would take some of them back in his shuttle. The rest would follow in one of the militia shuttles . . . after Governor Sosa had been videoed walking down the line of the dead.

"We're going to close down more of the small camps, Colonel," Sosa said after he had performed the political rituals for the cameras. "We can't take the chance of having this happen again. Close the smaller camps, move the miners home, increase the garrisons at the mining villages and more important camps."

"That's probably wise, Governor," Lon said, relieved that there had been no irrational outbursts. Yet.

"They have escalated the conflict," Sosa said. "I suppose in retaliation for us bringing you in, and for their defeat at Xavier's Beak."

"None of the electronic snoops placed around Three Peaks were operational when we found them, Governor," Lon said. "Whether they were working earlier I can't say. Either the garrison had turned them off, or the raiders were somehow able to get around the security codes and shut them off themselves. Or the equipment was defective; that might be possible, though it seems extremely unlikely. The men in Three Peaks had no warning, no chance to call for help, no chance to defend themselves."

Sosa frowned at Lon. "I thought the encryption schemes used on the snoops were too secure for anyone to get around them. We bought them from Dirigent."

"I know. We pulled the snoops to check. And the security codes . . ." Lon shook his head. "The way it was explained to me is that it would take a dozen of the best computer nets a thousand years to hack through the protection. Hell, snoops that were around five centuries ago were too good for troops in the field to crack the security codes without setting off an alarm."

"If the codes can't be broken and it's so unlikely that all of the units would be defective, that would indicate that either the garrison had turned off the snoops for some reason or the raiders somehow managed to get their hands on the codes that would let them deactivate the devices?"

"Those are the only alternatives that I've been able to come up with," Lon said. "And neither seems all that likely."

"I can't imagine why the garrison would turn off the snoops," Sosa said. "That is too incredible. Their own lives were at stake and, especially right now, every garrison would know that it was snoops that saved Xavier's Beak. And only the garrison of the camp and perhaps two people at militia headquarters would have access to the specific codes that the individual snoops at this site used."

"Governor, I'd like to bring a couple of specialists down from *Long Snake*. We need to know for certain that we can account for every person who was in the camp, and that could mean sifting through a lot of ashes to make sure that none of the victims were burned too completely to leave visible remains."

"Are you suggesting what I think you are, that there might have been a traitor in the camp?"

"I'm suggesting that we need to be able to rule that in or out as a possibility."

Sosa nodded once, an abrupt gesture. "Do it." Then he walked away, waving for his aides to join him. He was ready to leave Three Peaks.

It was past noon before the sun came out over Three Peaks. The bodies had been removed. A preliminary count showed a discrepancy. One man—everyone at Three Peaks had been male—was unaccounted for.

"Can't be sure yet," Tebba reminded Lon. "Some of the bodies we did find, wasn't much left but a few bits of bone and more ash."

"I know," Lon said. "That's why we brought the lab people down to shift through the ashes and look for traces of human DNA or small bits of bone that might have survived incineration."

"You think there was a traitor in the camp," Tebba said. It was no question.

"I think that's the most likely explanation. Probably one of the men in the militia garrison. Turned off the snoops and got out of the way, left with the raiders. Maybe even set incendiary devices in the buildings where the rest of the miners and militiamen were sleeping. But we can't say anything until we know. Absolutely know." Lon shrugged. "The governor knows what I suspect. It was hard to miss the implications."

"The locals get to thinking they can't trust each other, that'd make the job a hell of a lot harder," Tebba said. "They'll be too busy looking over their shoulders, wondering which of their buddies might snuff 'em."

"And they've got ready-made targets, Tebba, all the new settlers who have come to Bancroft in the past nine years.

The militia has a bunch of newcomers. This could get really messy."

"There's something else," Tebba said, hesitating before he continued. "Even if there was a traitor here, nothing says the raiders had to take him away with them. They might have left his body just so we wouldn't figure it out."

Lon nodded. "Start pulling our people in. If we haven't found any trace of the raiders by now, we're not likely to. We go back to Lincoln and do some more waiting."

"We're not going to find anything. We've been out three miles in every direction, farther along the easy travel routes, and not a clue which way they went or came from. Hang on a second, Colonel, I've got Harley on the line now." Lieutenant Harley Stossberg was one of A Company's platoon leaders.

Lon waited, resisting the urge to switch channels on his helmet radio to eavesdrop on the conversation. It lasted less than a minute.

"Maybe we got something, Colonel, but not much," Tebba said when he had finished. "Four miles off, across the ridge to the southwest. First platoon found a clearing big enough for shuttles. They found scorch marks, coulda come from shuttle engines, and fresh tire tracks. Looks like the raiders came in and left by air."

"Harley get video?" Lon asked.

Tebba nodded. "And scrapings from the scorch marks."

Lon shook his head. "We didn't pick up anything in the air. That's not good, Tebba. Their stealth technology is beating us."

"They had good weather for hiding, Colonel. Don't forget that."

"Tell the militia commanders here what we found," Lon said. "I'm heading back to Lincoln now. That'll clear the landing strip so you can get your company out. I imagine the locals will be hanging around a while longer."

"That's the last word I had. I expect they'll want to look that clearing over for themselves."

Impatience did not help. Lon knew it would take time to get answers—both on the search for human remains and the investigation of the deactivated electronic snoops—but waiting was difficult. Back in the privacy of his office, Lon paced through much of the afternoon. He took reports—the return of A Company, the work of the lab technicians from *Long Snake*, the end of the collection process. He talked by complink with Colonel Crampton, then with Deputy Governor Henks.

The Bancrofters had begun the process of identifying the remains of the miners and militiamen. Before sunset, Henks was able to give Lon the name of the man who could not be accounted for, and had his DNA code transmitted to *Long Snake* so the lab could look for matches. "He had been in the militia more than three years," Henks said. "He came to Bancroft with his wife from Lorenzo seven years ago. We had thirty-odd families who came here after Lorenzo voted to join the Second Commonwealth."

Lon keyed a note to himself to check Lorenzo in CIC's database. "Dissidents?"

"I don't have details, Colonel," Henks said. "It's likely. And, to save you the trouble of asking, there are only two other Lorenzo immigrants in the BCM, and neither of those is posted to any of the mining garrisons."

"We don't know for certain that there's cause for worry there yet, sir," Lon said. "But since you brought it up, I assume you have also checked on the employment status of other members of that group?"

Henks hesitated before he said, "Yes, we have collected data on all of them. All in all, quite an accomplished group of people. Most live and work in Lincoln or the other towns. Two are lawyers. One of those works for the Min-

istry of Justice as a prosecutor. One is a chartered account-
ant who operates on contract from the government,
auditing mining and trade accounts."

Lon responded without taking time to consider his
words. "Someone who would know which targets might
be most valuable?"

Henks's hesitation was a *lot* longer this time. "That did
occur to us. Damn it, Colonel, I know we have to look
into these things, but this is all most distasteful."

"I understand, sir," Lon said. "I agree that it is most
distasteful, and the problems an investigation could raise
might be troubling long after the raiders are dispatched.
Especially since one cannot assume that *if* there are trai-
tors—still an unproven hypothesis—they must necessarily
all come from the same world, from the same batch of
immigrants."

"Colonel Crampton informed me that he has had the
security codes changed for all of the electronic monitoring
devices, and has restricted knowledge of those codes to the
officer in charge of each garrison. None of those officers
is a first-generation immigrant. Or second, as it happens.
If we can't trust people whose families have been here
three or more generations, we are in much deeper trouble
than we could possibly imagine."

You are indeed, Lon thought after the conversation
ended. *But it's unlikely.* That realization was little comfort.

"Gentlemen, we're at a standstill here." Lon was address-
ing his staff officers and company commanders in the conference room adjacent to his office in the headquarters
building of the militia base. Supper had ended fifteen
minutes earlier.

"Our surface scans have provided no clue to the
whereabouts of any raider bases or aircraft. We haven't
made any significant progress in determining what the enemy has done to their soldiers to cause death if they re-

ceive treatment from us, so we can't begin to search for an antidote that might keep a captured raider alive long enough to answer questions. We haven't established, for certain, that a Bancrofter traitor shut off the snoops around Three Peaks and left with the raiders after the massacre. We haven't been able to come up with a computer analysis of any pattern to the raider attacks that we could use to anticipate their next strike.

"What is infinitely worse, as far as I am concerned, is that there's damned little we can do immediately to improve our grasp of the situation. We have troops and equipment, but little useful way to employ them until we have more intelligence or catch a break. I dislike waiting for the enemy to make a mistake. Our contract is for three months, and every day that passes without making serious progress puts us that much closer to the possibility that we will fail to fulfill that contract on time." Lon paused and held up a hand to forestall interruption.

"I know. We can't make things happen simply by wishing for them, and I've seen several of the proposals that you and your lieutenants have come up with, war-gaming the situation." He smiled. "It's good to know that some things haven't changed. Encourage your platoon leaders to keep it up. There's a chance someone might actually come up with something useful."

Captain Kai raised his hand and waited for Lon to nod before he spoke. "Some of the men are getting a bit . . . restive, wondering when we're going to get off our butts and do something. Especially after we heard about what happened at Three Peaks."

"I know, Sefer," Lon said. "All we can do is what we always do. Be as open with the men as possible. Tell them why we're not doing much but chasing after raiders. Hell, we did get in a few licks at Xavier's Beak. Husbanding our strength until we have a reasonable chance of scoring against the raiders is infinitely preferable to putting two or three companies out in the woods to look around, just hoping to stumble on some sort of trail when we can't even guess where we should do our stumbling.

"We will respond to any alert, and keep our sentries and patrols working around this base. Apart from those duties, we keep the men eating and resting as much as possible, maintain the highest level of readiness. If the need arises, I want to be able to put the entire battalion in the field, anywhere on Bancroft, as quickly as transportation gets down here from *Long Snake*. Questions?"

"I've got one," Tebba Girana said. "We know the raiders are using active electronics this time out, helmets as sophisticated as ours. Did any of our ships or aerial patrols pick up anything last night, during the time when the attack on Three Peaks must have happened?"

"Almost," Lon said, and he paused for a beat before he explained. "Nothing identifiable was noticed at the time. Neither the computers nor the men monitoring the feed picked up anything more than a little static, not localized enough to be a helmet or portable complink, not strong enough to be a combination of emissions from a shuttle. After the fact, CIC put men going back over the recordings. The last word I had was that they're 'ninety percent certain' that there were signals, just too well protected for us to intercept. Their ability to mask emissions is better than our ability to detect."

"Ouch," Tebba whispered.

"CIC is trying to fine-tune our gear. We might be able to do a little better now that we know the problem, or at least once they figure out just what adjustments to make. That might take time . . . like everything else on this contract."

It had been a long day. Lon was exhausted by the end of the meeting. He went to his quarters and sat on the bed, his mind caught between the need for sleep and a sense of urgency—the need to find a key to allow him to move his men against the raiders as soon as possible. He had seen some of the newsnet coverage of the massacre at Three Peaks, sampled some of the responses posted on Bancroft's public nets. There was anger, and not all of it was directed at the raiders. Some was being vented against the government and the mercenaries brought in—"at tremendous cost," one respondent noted—to prevent such disasters from happening.

I can't do anything useful now, Lon thought, suppressing a yawn. *My mind has turned to mush. I need sleep. Hopefully, a full night's sleep. Maybe the answer will come to me in a dream. I'll wake up in the morning and know what we have to do.* He shook his head and nearly laughed at the absurdity of those thoughts—dream up an answer when his conscious mind could not provide one.

He glanced at the timeline across the top of his complink screen. It wasn't eight-thirty—2030 hours—yet. He shook his head slowly, then leaned over to open his boots and take them off. That was as far as he bothered to go with undressing. He turned off the room lights and flopped over on the bed, asleep almost before the bed's springs stopped vibrating. Deep sleep, void of troubling dreams—the sort of sleep only monumental exhaustion can bring.

It lasted less than four hours. His complink buzzed loudly, the volume increasing until he woke and hit the accept key.

Colonel Crampton was on the line. "More trouble, Colonel."

Lon came completely awake.

15

"A mining camp called Erskeine, almost three hundred miles due north," Crampton said. "One of our newer work sites. It's scheduled to be evacuated in the morning. Twenty minutes ago, the lieutenant commanding the militia detachment shot one of his own men who was attempting to deactivate the snoops. With the changed codes, he didn't have any luck. I notified your duty officer and alerted my own people. My aide has a line open to the commander in Erskeine. There's been no attack yet, but we expect it . . . soon. The men on the scene are as ready as they can be, militia and miners."

"My alert company will be in the air in ten minutes," Lon said. "I'll have a second company ready to go fifteen minutes after that. Maybe we can turn the tables tonight."

"I hope so," Crampton said, then cut the link.

Lon rang the officer of the day. "Who's alert company?"

"Charlie, Colonel. They're heading for the shuttles now." Harley Stossberg from Alpha had the duty.

"Turn them around quick. I want them carrying their rocket packs. We'll put them on the ground behind the raiders, have the shuttles circle overhead if they arrive before the enemy does." Rocket packs let soldiers jump in wherever they might be needed. If the shuttle didn't land, the troops weren't limited to setting down in the nearest clearing, which might be miles from where the men were needed. It was a tactic used sparingly in the DMC. Only

143

one company in each battalion trained routinely in the equipment and tactics. "Get the next company on the list moving. I want them out as fast as possible. They'll go in at the landing strip at this place—Erskeine. You have that located on your map?"

"On the complink and on my mapboard, Colonel. I phoned it in while Colonel Crampton was still telling me about it."

"Right. Wake Major Osterman and Captain Berger. Have them meet me in my office in ten minutes. Then get on to *Long Snake* and tell Captain Roim that I want the rest of our shuttles ready to head in on five minutes' notice. I'll contact *Taranto* myself to have them get Shrikes in for the attack."

"Yes, sir." Harley quickly repeated his instructions. "Anything else?"

"Not yet, Harley. I'll be down in ten minutes."

Lon made the call to *Taranto,* held that to thirty seconds, then pulled his boots on—grateful that he hadn't bothered to get completely undressed before going to bed. The uniform was battledress, so the lack of sharp creases was unimportant. He got up—hearing the roar of shuttle engines powering up for takeoff—and hurried down to his office. Lieutenant Stossberg was sitting at Lon's desk, but got up as soon as the door opened.

"What's the weather like at Erskeine?" Lon demanded as soon as he came through the doorway.

"Heavy cloud cover, snow flurries. Ceiling sixteen hundred feet, just above the hilltops. Temperature hovering right around freezing as of ten minutes ago," Harley said quickly. "The snow flurries should end within the next hour. No accumulation. Erskeine had less rain than Three Peaks. Ought to be ground soft but firm enough to hold prints if there's any dirt between the rocks. Of course, a couple of inches of snow would be better. We could damn sure track the raiders then."

Vel Osterman entered the office then, without knocking, and Torry Berger, the battalion's adjutant and third-in-command, was right behind him, with Phip Steesen right on *his* heels.

"You heard?" Lon asked, turning to face the new arrivals. All three men nodded.

"We put maximum effort into this. Charlie on the rocket packs. Delta going in at the camp's landing strip. I've got *Long Snake* on alert to send the rest of the shuttles down on short notice to move Alpha and Bravo if there's any need, but I hope we'll be able to hold at least one of them as a reserve—and a hedge in case the raiders stage a second strike while we're handling Erskeine. Maybe we caught the break we need. With a little luck we might nab a few prisoners who haven't been wounded. Maybe we can't use drugs on them, but there are other ways. Old ways."

"You going in right away?" Osterman asked.

Lon shook his head. "Not this time. I want to be here to coordinate everything. Once we get the first response out and know that the raiders actually are hitting the camp, you take off in the command shuttle. Take Phip with you. I'll keep Torrey here. I'll use you to handle things on the scene, our people and the Bancrofters. Crampton has two companies on the way, and I'll have him ready to reinforce them if necessary."

Only then did Lon bother to go around to sit behind his desk. He felt better than he had since hearing about Three Peaks. *Maybe this is the break we need,* he thought, leaning back in his chair. *I've got a feeling.*

Lon's anticipation grew quickly in the next few minutes. He had his mapboard open on the desk, the zone of coverage narrowed to an area with a two-mile radius around the mining camp at Erskeine. On the desk complink he had several communications channels open, to allow him to monitor anything that might be relevant . . . and to give commands when—if—necessary.

The first important message came from CIC aboard *Long Snake*. "Colonel Nolan, we're picking up the same kind of static we did during the attack on Three Peaks, about three thousand yards from Erskeine, northwest."

"How narrow can you focus on that static?" Lon asked.

"We're working on that now, Colonel. So far, we show static over an elliptical area a hundred yards long and sixty wide."

"Moving?"

"I'll be able to give you a better read on that in a few minutes, Colonel. We've just picked this up. If there is movement, it's slow."

"Can you highlight the area on the mapboard circuit for me?" Lon asked, pulling his mapboard closer.

A yellow oval appeared on the screen, drawn in roughly. "Right at the edge of a fairly large clearing, Colonel," the duty officer in CIC reported. "Easily large enough for a shuttle to land and take off from. It doesn't seem to be moving. Stationary. Hold on, Colonel, Captain Roim is here."

"Colonel Nolan, we've got as good a fix on this static as we're likely to get tonight. This is all on the edge of what we can get out of our instruments right now. We can't tell if this is men or maybe a shuttle. Should I vector Shrikes in to saturate the contact before they can get to the miners?"

Lon hesitated for nearly half a minute before he said, "Not yet, Captain, not without knowing what the target is. Have the Shrikes within range, high enough that they won't be heard, but hold off on any attack. I've got a company moving in with rocket packs. We'll jump them in behind the raiders. Have the Shrikes hit that clearing just before my boys jump. I'll have Captain Kai link directly to you to coordinate the strike. Okay?"

"We'll butter the bread, Colonel."

"We'll use the noise of your attack to put shuttles in at the landing strip in Erskeine as well," Lon said. "That'll give us a full company on either side of the raiders—whatever your Shrikes leave for us. Give me a minute, Captain, while I pass the orders on to my company commanders."

Lon linked through to Sefer Kai and Ron Magnusson together and gave them the orders for Charlie and Delta companies, and put them on an open link to CIC in *Long Snake*. After he switched back to Captain Roim and confirmed orders, it was time to sit back and wait. Again.

"I wouldn't count too much on getting prisoners out of this," Captain Berger said. He had remained with Lon after Vel Osterman left to get ready to take the command shuttle into the area. "Those Shrikes might not leave a hell of a lot."

"They'll leave enough, I think—if it's men on the ground *Long Snake* is picking up, and not a shuttle. No matter how heavy the attack, some men will survive. Big trees and rocks. We're not going to fry that entire valley. Remember, Torry, we don't even know how many raiders we're talking about."

"What if it is a shuttle?"

"The Shrike pilots know what to look for . . . and what to look out for. In a fight, our Shrikes have it all over the shuttles the raiders use."

"Those they used nine years ago," Berger said. "We haven't actually *seen* what they have this time, now have we?"

"Nope," Lon agreed.

"Can I make a suggestion?"

"Of course."

"As close a search as possible in the area behind the presumed raider party. If the contact *Long Snake* has isn't a shuttle, the raiders might still have one sitting on the ground somewhere in the vicinity, unless the men on the ground have been walking forever. Or a shuttle might be in the air, somewhere in or under the cloud cover, waiting for them to do the job so they can drop in and pick up the raiders and their loot."

Lon nodded. "Good point." He called *Long Snake* again and passed the suggestion on. Captain Roim was still in CIC.

"We're already working on that, Colonel," Roim said. "All three ships as well as the Shrikes and shuttles in the air. That offers the hope of triangulation and gives us the chance of putting together a full-dimensional picture of whatever is down there, if anything. We haven't turned up anything yet, but I'll keep you posted."

"I almost wish I'd kept Vel here and gone myself," Lon said after ending that conversation. "This all comes off smooth, it could be quite a show."

"Ought to ease the pressure the government is under," Berger said. "If we hit the raiders as hard as they hit Three Peaks."

"Better if we can pull a prisoner in one piece, but, yes, it will help," Lon said.

"If we hit the raiders before they reach the snoops—and learn they haven't been shut down—it should confuse the raiders. If nothing else." Berger shrugged. "Give them something to think about. If they get the word back to their headquarters on planet. Even more if these raiders simply disappear and they don't know what the hell happened to them."

"They'll find out something, eventually," Lon said. "We have to assume they have contacts among the immigrant population here, and almost certainly some way to get information quickly."

"And we can't keep it a secret that we hit them," Berger said.

"I don't think so," Lon confirmed. "The governor is going to want to show his people we're earning our pay."

Charlie and Delta Companies were in position. The area of static had faded so much that none of the Dirigenter gear could detect it. Four Shrikes were ready to swoop in to saturate the area between the clearing and the mining camp with rockets and cannon fire.

Lon remained a spectator. He had given the orders. Now he could only wait to see how the fight progressed. If there *was* a fight. "I've never been fond of waiting, Torry," he said softly, his attention on the complink and mapboard.

Torry Berger did not respond.

Four Shrikes began their attacks, going in one at a time, launching rockets first, then braking to give them more than a fraction of a second to use their rapid-fire cannons. Charlie Company started to jump, the men trusting their lives to metal and composite packs strapped to their backs, sixty-four seconds of rocket propulsion to get them safely to the ground. Delta Company's two shuttles started to make their hot landings seconds apart, leaving no room for error for either pilot. *Get down, get the men out of the boxes, get back off, out of the way as quickly as possible.*

"You ever jump in on fire cans?" Berger asked.

Lon shook his head. "Not on contract. Made the necessary practice jumps back home." He hesitated, then added, "And hated every single one. Worse than parachutes."

"I don't think I've ever come across anyone who likes the cans," Berger said. "It's a miracle we've still got them in inventory."

Video of the Shrike attacks started to come in over Lon's complink—infrared-enhanced to show as much detail as possible in the dark.

"There!" Lon jabbed a finger toward the complink

screen. "Men moving. They're in there, Torry. They're in there."

The scene on the screen changed abruptly. Lon saw a tail of fire coming up from the ground, and the Shrike's pilot started maneuvering violently to come out of his dive and climb away from the surface-to-air missile. The feed to Lon's screen changed, coming from one of the other Shrikes. The fighters were shooting at the SAM, then at three missiles as more were launched by the raiders on the ground.

One SAM exploded, low, before it came near any of the Shrikes. One missile suddenly veered sideways and ran into the hillside, destroying nothing but trees . . . and any wildlife unlucky enough to be in the kill zone. The third small missile kept coming. The pilot of the Shrike whose video Lon was watching pulled out of his dive and accelerated, at such speed that Lon suspected the pilot might have blacked out, at least momentarily. Lon was slightly dizzy just from staring intently at the changing view on his screen.

"Charlie Company's on the ground!"

Lon scarcely noticed that call, or the one ten seconds later that told him that Delta Company's shuttles were landing. The video he was watching shook violently. Light seemed to flash forward from behind the camera out into the field of vision.

"I've been hit!"

Lon did not recognize the voice of the pilot, but did not expect to. He knew few of the Shrike fliers well. The frame rotated through more than 360 degrees, then dipped. Lon found himself gripping the arms of his chair. He leaned forward, unaware of the way his body was moving in response to the view.

"I'm losing fuel. Can't tell how much damage to the bird yet," the pilot said, his voice sounding much calmer than Lon felt. "Vibrations, getting heavier. I'm going to have to look for a place to set down. Can't make it back to *Taranto*."

Get out while you can, Lon urged silently. *Get down in one piece. We'll pick you up.*

"Have *Taranto* send pickup, or do we do it?" Captain Berger asked—loudly, to make sure that Lon heard him.

Lon blinked and looked away from the screen. "See if Vel is close enough to track him in. If the command shuttle can't get to the site quickly enough . . . hell, that'll still be faster than waiting for *Taranto* or *Long Snake* to send a shuttle. Make the call."

Seconds. Minutes. Lon focused on the Shrike, listening to its pilot talking almost constantly—matter-of-factly—as the condition of his fighter deteriorated, seemingly by the second.

"Controls are getting flaky," the pilot said. "Can't be certain of landing safely. I'm going to have to eject."

"We've got pickup on the way," Lon said, hitting the transmit switch on his complink. "We're tracking you."

"Thanks, whoever you are. I see a clearing ahead, to my left. I'll come down as close to that as I can. Here I go."

Lon heard a muted explosion, then the rush of wind as the Shrike pilot blew his ejection capsule from the wounded fighter. The wind noise ended quickly as the pilot cleared the fuselage. The ejection capsule was gas-tight. There were times when a pilot might have to eject in vacuum.

"Major Osterman is homing in on him, Colonel," Captain Berger announced. He had a headset on to allow him to communicate without disturbing Lon. "They'll be over-head by the time the pilot gets to the ground."

"Stay with it until they have him," Lon said. That was all the attention he could spare. The fighting on the ground had started.

Sefer Kai's Charlie Company had formed up and started toward the raiders. He reported spotting at least twenty of the enemy. After the last pass by the Shrikes, the raiders had formed up again and started moving toward Erskeine, leaving two men to treat the wounded and tend to the dead.

"Get the men treating the wounded!" Lon yelled, interrupting Sefer's report. "They might have what we need, the antidote to keep the wounded alive."

"We'll try. We'll get whatever they're carrying," Kai said. "I'm leaving one platoon to handle that. We'll circle around to keep after the rest of the raiders. Need the angle anyway. Delta is only six hundred yards off."

The shooting started less than two minutes later. Lon listened to the traffic among the officers and noncoms of the two companies on the ground, concentrating, trying to follow the confusing babble of voices. There were at least three dozen raiders active. Maybe four dozen. Charlie Company counted, in passing, fifteen dead from the Shrike attacks, and found traces in the clearing that a shuttle had used it. But there was no shuttle there now. One of the men acting as a medical orderly resisted and was killed. The other had taken off, running. He had not been caught yet. A squad had been sent after him.

Delta Company got close enough to join in the firefight, stopping the raiders who had continued moving toward Erskeine. Now the remaining raiders were trying to move out of the middle, toward the northeast, over a hill that was too steep to allow them any easy route out.

The Shrike pilot was on the ground, reporting that he was safe, uninjured, and maybe a half mile from the clearing he had spotted. Someone aboard the command shuttle gave him a course. The shuttle was gliding in for a landing. One of the other Shrikes was overhead to provide cover in case there were more enemy assets in the area.

The first company of Bancrofter militia landed at Erskeine. The men debarked, and the shuttles took off to allow the other company to land. Contact had been made with the militia detachment and miners stationed at the camp. There had been no casualties there . . . except for the militiaman who had been shot by his commander. The start of the entire sequence.

"Sergeant Steesen is taking a fire team to meet the flier," Berger reported. "Should make contact in less than a minute."

Lon leaned back and rubbed at his eyes, then sucked in a deep breath. He was as keyed up as he might have been if he had been on the ground, physically part of the battle.

"Let me know when they have him aboard the shuttle," Lon said.

The firefight ended.

"We're still sorting things out," Sefer Kai reported. "There's a chance some raiders got away, but we're trying to make sure we've got security here, checking prisoners."

"You get that one medic?" Lon asked.

"Not alive. We've got all his gear, though. The other one is still on the loose. We won't do more than bandage the wounded prisoners, hope they stay alive long enough to be useful." Sefer did not sound particularly optimistic.

"Move them to the landing strip at Erskeine, Sefer," Lon said. "Bring them in."

"What about the raiders still on the loose?"

"We'll leave Delta to coordinate with the militia. It's your people carrying those tin cans on their backs. What kind of casualties on our side?"

"No dead—thank God—just two minor wounds. We got lucky."

This time, Lon thought. He closed his eyes in a wordless prayer of thanks. "It's about time we caught a little luck, Sefer," he said. "Good job. And pass that on to your men."

16

"The militiaman who was shot for trying to deactivate the snoops at Erskeine was from Miranda, not Lorenzo," Deputy Governor Daniel Henks said. He had come to Lon's office before nine o'clock in the morning. Lon had barely beat him to the office. Lon had decided to sleep in an extra couple of hours to make up for the sleep he had lost during the night.

"Miranda? That's a CHW world, isn't it?" Lon asked.

Henks nodded. "One of the original worlds that supported the breakaway Confederation on Union. And one of the largest populations."

"There aren't many CHW worlds that permit emigration," Lon said. "Except for punitive reasons."

Henks shrugged. "It expands the problem for us, however it came about. The first traitor came from a world that was in the process of joining the Second Commonwealth. The next comes from one of the core worlds of the Confederation. We have close to a hundred people on Bancroft who came from Miranda. Add in the other emigrants from Confederation worlds and the total must be more than six hundred."

"There probably wouldn't be many agents planted, Colonel," Lon said. "And there's a chance that some of them might have switched loyalties since coming here. Have you learned anything yet about these two men?"

"Nothing obvious," Henks said. "Nothing to point to

their contacts or confederates. Have you been able to get anything from the raiders who were captured during the night?"

"Only two of them made it back here alive, and neither is in any condition to talk yet. Since we can't treat their injuries without triggering whatever their bosses infected them with, we can't be certain either man will survive long enough to be questioned. Your people and one company of mine are still on the ground out there, trying to track the last of the raiding party."

"What about the items you took from their medic?"

"Still being analyzed." Lon hesitated. "If we find one of the fluids that doesn't measure up as a known medical treatment, we might try injecting one of the wounded men with it, then stick him in a trauma tube and see what happens." He shook his head. "I'm not particularly fond of that option. We could be killing the man to no point."

"No, you could be giving him his only chance to survive," Henks said.

For a time, Lon thought. Bancrofter justice would be less certain. "We should have some indication on what we have before much longer," he said. "If we'd been set up to do the analysis here, we might have it already, but I sent the samples up to *Long Snake*. Their lab is considerably more sophisticated."

"You'll keep me posted?" Henks asked, getting to his feet.

Lon stood as well. "Of course." He walked to the office door with the deputy governor, opened it, and then shook hands with Henks as he left. Lon stood in the open doorway until Henks left the building.

"We can't give you a one-hundred-percent guaranteed answer, Colonel Nolan," the chief lab technician aboard *Long Snake* said. "We would need much larger samples and a lot more time for that."

"What *can* you give me?" Lon asked.

"You sent us four samples. Samples two and three are identical and are normal first-response treatments—stabilizers and blood generators. We *believe* that samples one and four are identical to each other, but different from the others. We can't be certain what one and four actually are, or that they are indeed the same. So far we have been unable to complete any structural or functional analysis. The nanoagents in those two samples actively resist, attacking the probe nanoagents—with some success—and changing themselves in the process, apparently some sort of fail-safe device."

"Which means those samples are probably the ones we need to counteract whatever the raiders have been infected with to keep them from talking," Lon said.

"There's no way to be certain, Colonel, but that would be my guess. I must emphasize, though, that it is *only* a guess, not something I would care to bet my life on. For example, one of them could be the antidote you're looking for and the other could be the infecting agent."

"But we can rule out samples two and three?" Lon said.

"We have found nothing, ah, out of place in those samples," the technician said. "The analysis is not complete. We are still disassembling the active nanoagents. But there have been no surprises so far."

The two wounded prisoners were being held in the infirmary inside the militia base. It was a small facility attached to the headquarters building, four beds and four trauma tubes, added since the DMC's first contract on Bancroft. Lon went to the infirmary after ending his conversation with the lab technician aboard *Long Snake*. The battalion's senior medical technician, Sergeant Enos Carvel, was standing between the two occupied beds. He moved away from them, meeting Lon halfway to the door.

"How are they doing?" Lon asked.

Carvel shook his head, and moved farther from the two prisoners. Lon moved with him. "The one might die almost anytime if I can't get him into a trauma tube, Colonel. Frankly, I'm not certain a trauma tube can save him after this much time—even if we have the antidote to keep his own system from killing him. The other one, well, all I can really say is that he's not quite as bad off. Apparently his body's maintenance nanoagents stopped the internal bleeding and his major organs aren't affected, but he's running a fever and his system isn't keeping up with the infection."

"Is he conscious?"

"No. Any word on those vials we took off the dead raider medic?"

Lon gave him the short version of what *Long Snake* had said.

"If we don't take a chance," Carvel said, "at least one is going to die. Probably both of them. And since we don't know the proper dosage, or how long to wait between injecting the antidote and beginning standard treatment, we can't be certain that we'll save them even if we pick the right one."

"No chance at all without, minimal chance with?" Lon said.

"That's about the size of it, Colonel."

"Try one of them on the man who's in worse shape. Make your best guess on dosage and the waiting time. And save enough for the second man. I'll record the order to cover you," Lon said.

"Thank you, Colonel." Carvel hesitated, then said, "One thing: Even if we don't save the first man, we should be able to tell if we've got the right vial. Afterward."

"You mean if it doesn't leave the man the way the ones we treated before ended up," Lon said, and the medtech nodded.

"The sooner you start, the sooner you'll know," Lon

said. He went to the infirmary's main complink and keyed
in his order for the risky treatment, signed it, and displayed
the screen for Sergeant Carvel.

Lon waited while the medtech got the vial from which
the first sample had been taken and charged an injector.
Carvel talked through the process, for the complink, to
make certain there was a step-by-step record of what he
did, and the results.

"I have to assume," he said at one point, "that a medic
would carry enough of the antidote to treat the highest
estimate of possible casualties among the men under his
care, and that the delay between antidote and standard
treatment would be minimal. Otherwise, they could lose
people they didn't have to. That is, at least, how we would
handle the situation—in the unthinkable event that we
would intentionally poison our men to keep them from
talking if captured."

Carvel called two men in to help him move the treated
prisoner from bed to trauma tube. Lon helped as well. Carvel made the connections from tube to patient, then, standing with his hand over the contact that would turn the
medical apparatus on, he looked at Lon.

"Do it," Lon said, nodding.

The medtech touched the switch, then let his hand drop
away from it. Carvel watched the gauges at the head of
the trauma tube. Lon stared at the face of the man in it.

"It took several minutes before the first raiders we attempted to treat went bad," Carvel said after he had turned
on the trauma tube. There was nothing visible happening—
and wouldn't be, unless this patient's system turned on
him the way the earlier ones had. The man's open wounds
had been covered with bandages, so the two men watching
would not even see the wounds knit.

At the moment, the trauma tube reminded Lon of a glass
coffin, perhaps from some children's fairy tale. *There*

won't be any handsome prince to come along and save this poor bastard with a kiss, he thought.

"This is going to be borderline, even if we guessed right," Carvel said. Two minutes had passed since he started the trauma tube. "He lost so much blood the tube might not be able to replace enough in time. Heart, lungs, and kidneys were all near the point of failure. Brain waves are . . . depressed but still there." The whole time he talked, Carvel never looked away from the gauges on the trauma tube.

Lon scarcely dared to breathe, hardly blinked as he stared at the face of the man in the tube. Time seemed suspended, distorted beyond recognition of its passage. He was so focused that he might have been trying to heal the man by willpower alone. It had gone beyond the point of merely wanting a live enemy to question, it was the desire to see a man survive.

Live, damn you, live.

Five minutes. "No sign yet of his system trying to self-destruct," Sergeant Carvel said. "It was . . . about this long with the others. The medics who treated them couldn't say precisely how long. But when they went bad, they went in a hurry. Every organ in their bodies seemed to rupture or hemorrhage simultaneously, turned their insides to mush."

"I saw the bodies," Lon said.

"If we guessed right, I think he'll survive. This much time, the tube has had a chance to get the essentials covered. I wish we knew for certain how long it took for those other wounded to go bad. I'd sure like to know how much longer before I can breathe right again."

"We can breathe later," Lon said. "Let's be certain first."

Ten minutes. "It couldn't have been much longer than this, no matter how far off the medics were," Carvel said.

I think you're right, Lon thought, but he said, "Give it another five minutes to be certain. Maybe you should check your other patient."

Carvel started, visibly, as if he had completely forgotten that he had another patient in the infirmary. "Yes, of course," he said, looking around, then moving to the bed that held the other captive raider. He did not spend much time with the man, just long enough to check his heart rate and respiration—less than a minute.

"He's hanging in," Carvel said when he returned to his position at the head of the occupied trauma tube. "He can stand a few more minutes' waiting."

"Refresh my mind, Sergeant. Once the tube finishes working on this man, *any* foreign substances in his system should be flushed out and destroyed, right?"

"Yes, sir."

"Including any of these destructive nanoagents?"

"I can't see any way they could disguise themselves to avoid detection, Colonel. Either they act or they don't. And if they don't, they should be gone. What are you getting at?"

"Being able to question these men once they're out of danger," Lon said. "We need to know anything they can tell us about raider operations on Bancroft."

Carvel hesitated for a beat. "I don't see why they won't be fit for questioning—assuming they come out of the trauma tubes alive and fully repaired. This man, I think he may need more than four hours before the tube releases him. He was awfully close to gone." He looked at his watch. "It's been nearly thirteen minutes since I turned it on."

"Let's get the other man into a tube, ready for the injection of the antidote—the presumed antidote," Lon said. "Soon as we're sure of this one, you can start the other."

They waited past the fifteen-minute mark—closer to twenty—before Sergeant Carvel gave the second man a dose of the "sample one" fluid. Then Lon waited until ten minutes after the trauma tube had been activated for the second man.

"I think you've done it, Sergeant," Lon said, standing between the two trauma tubes.

"So far, Colonel," Carvel said.

"Just remember that they're prisoners. I'll make sure there are guards here before they can be a problem."

There was a noticeable pause before Carvel said, "Yes, sir. Of course. I hope you're not in *too* great a hurry to question them, Colonel. I'd like to give them at least a couple of hours after the tubes release them, time for a meal and some oral fluids, a chance for me to make absolutely sure."

It was Lon's turn to hesitate. Then he nodded. "At least two hours, Sergeant, but I won't guarantee a lot more than that."

17

By sunset, it was clear that the pursuit of the survivors of the failed raid on Erskeine was going nowhere. The miners had been evacuated from the camp. Lon had pulled the last of his men from it. Colonel Crampton had left one company of militia—on the long chance that the raiders might double back and try to make up for their failure—but pulled the rest back to Lincoln, including the detachment that had garrisoned the site.

"We have prisoners now," Lon reminded Crampton when the militia commander came in to share supper with him. "Before the evening is over, we should know everything those two prisoners know about raider operations here."

"I can hardly wait," Crampton said. "That also goes for the governor and deputy governor. I came here from Government House, and they're having difficulty containing themselves."

"As long as they keep the secret." Lon had explained to Sosa and Henks why it was necessary that no one else learn that they had prisoners who could—and would—talk. "We don't know what sources of information the raiders have."

"I haven't told anyone, not even my staff and company commanders, and they're all from old families," Crampton said. "Once we do question the prisoners, we're going to have to mount an operation in a hurry."

Lon nodded. "As quickly as we can without botching it. Plan first, then go in. Get the job done right."

"I've got no argument with that."

The two men were eating in Lon's office—Colonel Crampton's office before the arrival of the mercenaries. Lon ate with more appetite than he had since landing on Bancroft. Crampton had done little more than pick at his food. He was visibly excited by the prospect of learning the secrets of the raiders. Early on, he had pressed Lon about how soon they could start the interrogation. Crampton intended to be present for it.

"*If* we get enough information from the prisoners to allow us to do the job without more intelligence," Lon said.

Crampton had been lifting his glass. He stopped with his drink still a couple of inches from his mouth. "What do you mean by that? Why wouldn't we get enough?"

"First of all, we're assuming that there isn't a second level to the raider fail-safe nanoagents, that our equipment must have cleansed them completely from the men's systems. We *think* we have, but if we're underestimating the enemy's technology, injecting the prisoners with the truth drugs might still trigger a lethal reaction. Second, we can't be certain that the two men we captured will be able to give us enough information to locate the enemy's base camp and assess their strength."

"You think they blindfold their own men coming and going?" Crampton asked, setting his glass back on the table.

"As far as we know, we have a couple of privates, or the equivalent. Grunts. Maybe conscripts. We know they were treated with a lethal agent to keep them from talking to an enemy. But we don't know how much information the raiders share with the rank and file. If they're moved in and out of their base camp by air, there's not a reason in the world for their leaders to give them map coordinates."

Crampton simply stared at Lon.

"We can't let our hopes get too high," Lon said. "We should be able to get a lot of useful information, but we can't count on getting *everything* we want. Or need."

"I take it you didn't tell the governor that," Crampton said after letting out an audible sigh.

"I told him not to expect too much, but I didn't go into detail," Lon said. "I thought Dan Henks, at least, would figure it out once he had a little time to mull it over. Once the initial excitement faded. He's got the background in police and military affairs. We'd have to get one of their officers to expect anything really precise on locations. Maybe a noncom. And I don't think we got either."

"You certainly shot holes in *my* excitement," Crampton said. He sounded deflated. "Now I don't know whether to look forward to the questioning or dread it. Like a boy who wants Christmas to come but fears he won't get the gift he's set his heart on."

Lon smiled. "I've had trouble keeping my own expectations from getting too high," he said. "We'll learn what we learn. My adjutant and senior medical technician will handle the injections and the questioning. You and I will simply be spectators and advisers. We listen and, if we think there's a specific question that should be asked, we put it to Captain Berger, let *him* ask the prisoner. Having only one voice to deal with helps."

"Your Captain Berger knows what to ask?"

"We spent a couple of hours discussing lines of questioning. Torry is good. There's not much chance we'll have to interrupt to get him to ask something he hasn't thought of."

The room where the questioning would be conducted was adjacent to the infirmary—soundproof, without windows, illuminated to highlight the subject and obscure witnesses. The first prisoner—the second man treated that morning—

was wheeled in, strapped to his bed. A mild sedative had already been administered. Sergeant Carvel was one of the men moving the . . . patient. The medical orderly with him left the room and closed the door as soon as the bed was in position.

The two colonels were seated on the far side of the room from the bed, behind the lights, in shadows too deep to let the man on the bed make out their features. A table was in front of them, and each man had a portable complink. If they had questions for Captain Berger to ask, they would key them in on the complink; he would see them on a screen behind the prisoner's head. Sergeant Carvel stayed next to the bed; he would remain there throughout the session, administering drugs and observing the instruments that monitored the patient's vital signs.

"Is the patient ready?" Berger asked, standing just across the bed from the medtech.

"Vital signs are stable and proper," Carvel said.

"Administer the medication."

Carvel applied two med-patches to the prisoner's neck, one over the carotid artery, the other over the joint between two vertebrae. The man on the table was conscious, but just barely. His eyes were open no more than halfway, and he moved his head little, except as a direct result of Carvel's activities. The man did not, could not, resist.

"Three minutes," Carvel said after he had applied the second patch. Three minutes was how long the nanoagents in the patches would need to penetrate and work their way through to their "duty stations" in the prisoner's brain, ready to dispense minuscule doses of several drugs as necessary.

Torry Berger glanced at his watch, noting to the second when he would be able to begin questioning. Across the room, the two colonels each glanced at their watches, in perfect unison.

I'll never be comfortable with this, Lon thought. *It's too damned creepy.* It was only the fourth time he had directly witnessed an interrogation. The three minutes seemed to drag interminably. Lon found himself clenching his teeth and had to force himself to relax. He glanced to his left. Crampton was fidgeting visibly, crossing and uncrossing his legs, waiting for the questioning to begin.

Three minutes. Torry Berger leaned over the bed, until his face was eight inches above the face of the prisoner. "Tell me your name," Berger said, loud enough to make certain that he got the drugged prisoner's attention immediately.

The prisoner whispered something, too softly for Lon to hear, almost too softly for Berger. "Tell me again, louder," the captain ordered.

"Coffee. Brind Coffee."

Name. Age. Place of birth. Berger started the questioning gently, staying with personal questions, getting Coffee used to answering, weakening any mental reluctance, assisting the drugs.

Brind Coffee. Twenty-four years old. Calgary, North American Union, Earth.

He had worked for the Colonial Mining Cartel less than three years. Trained first as a security guard in West Africa, which included coursework on how to recognize and evaluate samples of minerals and metals. Selected then for additional training. *Military* training. Transferred to a permanent paramilitary unit; used to help put down a riot in a deep-water mining habitat; sent off-world then. The unit spent six months protecting a mine on Gardner. The unit was given two additional months of training, on the same world. Then they received orders to move again. They were not told the name of the world until after they landed.

Gradually Coffee's answers became less reticent, more coherent, plainer. Lon worked hard to conceal his impatience. He knew the reason for the lengthy prologue. It helped to have the subject used to answering questions like this, reliving his life, speaking of the routine, the common, the familiar. It helped to further submerge any notion of resistance once the important questions were put to him.

Thirty minutes into the session, Carvel replaced the patches on Coffee's neck. Berger was silent during that procedure, and while Carvel waited to check the gauges. It wasn't until the medtech nodded that Berger resumed his questioning.

Berger asked Coffee about his arrival on Bancroft, details of landing, setting up camp, and about the men with him. The questions were still not pointed, not directed toward anything that the mercenaries and their hosts could use. The ship that had brought Coffee and his comrades— *"How many?" "Six hundred"*—had parked in synchronous orbit on the far side of the world from the settled regions. The landers had operated only when it was dark on the colony side of the world, taking detachments in each night, needing nearly a week to get everyone to the ground with their supplies— *"And picking up the stuff that the first company had collected since they'd been here."*

Gradually Berger worked the more important questions in. Coffee wasn't certain how many troops the CMC had sent to Bancroft altogether. Six-hundred-odd in his ship. Fewer than that before. Each time a ship had come to take off the "goods" they had collected, a few more men were left behind—replacements and reinforcements. Coffee guessed that there might be more than a thousand of them now, even allowing for the casualties he knew about. They were not all stationed in the same place. He wasn't certain how many camps there were. He didn't know exactly where any of them were, not even his own, just that it was a system of caves, somewhere away from any of the settlements. They always moved out at night, marching to a clearing not too far from the cave. A shuttle picked them up, took them near their objective, and brought them back after they had finished.

Wes Crampton groaned softly. Lon frowned at him, but Coffee gave no indication that he had heard the sound.

Berger worked around the problem. He asked Coffee to describe the scenery he could see from outside the cave where he was stationed. *"Trees, hills, sky."* None of the men was allowed outside much during daylight hours, just a few on sentry duty. Coffee took his turns at that, but there was never much to see, certainly none of the enemy he was to watch for. He couldn't say what kind of trees there were, just a mix, not unlike trees he might have seen on Earth. The hills—a line that the caves were in, another to the west, several miles away; he knew it was west because of the sun.

There was another interruption in the questioning, another replacement of the med-patches. Sergeant Carvel gave Coffee a sip of water through a tube. Captain Berger moved out of the ring of light to get a longer drink himself. Fruit juice. He toweled the sweat from his face.

Wes Crampton leaned close to Lon. "I don't think we're going to get much more here," he whispered.

"Maybe not," Lon replied, "but we've got to go the whole route before we work on the other man. Tomorrow morning. There's no way to do it all tonight."

"Different people working the second man?" Crampton suggested.

"Best to let the same team do both. And these are the best I've got."

"We got more than I expected," Lon told Crampton after the session with Brind Coffee was over. They had returned to Lon's office. Someone had provided a pitcher of cold beer and two steins. Lon poured for both of them.

"What do you mean? We didn't get anything useful," Crampton complained as he reached for his glass. "Not one bleeding clue to where their camp—camps—are."

"We know they have more than one camp. We have a

better estimate of their total numbers than before. We know that one group at least, of about six hundred men, is living in a cave system, and that there's a clearing large enough for a shuttle close enough that the raiders can get from cave to clearing in an hour or less. We know they're using those little shuttles extensively, and no matter how good the stealth technology they have, we'll find a way to get around it."

Crampton shook his head. "I know you warned me not to expect much, but I thought we'd get *something* useful."

"We did." Lon held back a sigh. There was obviously going to be no pleasing Crampton. "We just didn't get an instant fix. In the morning we'll question the second man. We probably won't get anything startling from him either, but by comparing what the two men say, we might come a little closer to building our picture of raider operations."

"The governor isn't going to be very happy with tonight," Crampton said. He seemed to be talking more to himself than to Lon, so Lon didn't bother to answer. A few minutes later, Crampton excused himself and left. He still had to visit Government House before he could go to bed.

Phip Steesen came into the office as soon as Colonel Crampton had left. "You look all done in," Phip observed as he crossed to where Lon was sitting.

"I am. Help me with this beer. I hate to see it wasted."

Phip refilled the stein that Crampton had used, then took a long drink and smacked his lips in appreciation. "Major Osterman said there wasn't a whole lot in what the first prisoner said."

"Nothing we can use to mount an operation," Lon said.

"It was all recorded in CIC," Phip said. "The computers and analysts will be through it backwards and sideways by morning."

"We have a little more for the search," Lon said, yawning. "The physical description of what the man could see outside the cave. It's not much—a large cave system in a hill. Fairly broad valley to the west. Landing strip within a few miles."

"Seems to me we're not going to be able to do anything major unless CIC figures a way to track the shuttles the raiders use," Phip said. "Unless we manage to flush a group and follow them to their lair, the way we did the last time we were here."

Lon snorted. "If what Coffee said about how his group was moved for raids holds for the rest of their force, we won't do that. All we could do is track them to where they're supposed to be picked up by a shuttle after a raid. My guess is the raiders would abandon a detachment rather than risk having us get a shuttle or follow it to wherever it's going. Even if we manage to catch and wipe out every raiding party, it's not going to be a quick job. If they've got a thousand or more men here, it might take forty or fifty operations to get them all."

"And take a lot more than the three months this job is supposed to last," Phip said.

"We need a break." Lon pushed his beer mug away. "And I need to get some sleep. My head is starting to spin, and I haven't drunk enough of this to account for it."

For a time, getting into bed was too much of a chore to contemplate. Lon sat on the edge of it, arms resting on thighs, waiting to gather the energy to undress and slip between the sheets. Again. Over a period of several minutes, his only motion came when he yawned.

We need a break, he thought. *Something.* The job was supposed to be simple. Find the raiders and close them down, using whatever force might be needed. He had not suspected that finding the raiders would be so difficult. *We came prepared . . . for the last fight. Like so many other armies in the past.*

Lon got one boot off, then rested before attempting to remove the other. *I didn't make it all the way last night,* he remembered. Slept in his clothes. Didn't have a chance to shower and change until after the action was over at Erskeine.

He didn't remember getting the second boot off, didn't recall lying down. When his complink beeped to announce an urgent message, three hours later, the room lights were still on.

Captain Eldon Roim of *Long Snake* was on the link.

"An unidentified ship just emerged from Q-space," Roim announced when Lon clicked the accept key on his complink. "At its current speed, it's seventy-four hours from Bancroft. It's not broadcasting any standard ID codes."

"Have you challenged it?" Lon asked.

"I wanted to check with you first, Colonel."

"Do it," Lon said. "What kind of ship is it—civilian transport or military?"

"The profile we've picked up doesn't match any known military craft, but it's not a standard civilian transport either, none that I've come across."

"Will *Taranto* be able to intercept if it's hostile?"

"If they keep coming in, yes. But if they decide to make a run for it right away, probably not."

"Have *Taranto* start moving now," Lon said. "Give us all the leeway we can get."

"That will leave you without fighter cover, or just with the Shrikes on patrol now, if *Taranto* doesn't wait to recover them."

Lon's hesitation was minimal. "Have the Shrikes on patrol now land at Lincoln's spaceport when it's time. We'll service them on the ground and make do until Taranto gets back in position. If that ship is connected to the raiders, I want it disabled or destroyed."

"I'll pass the orders on," Roim said.

"And keep me posted. This might be a major break for us." Despite exhaustion, Lon had difficulty getting back to sleep.

18

It scarcely mattered that Lon was wakened again before reveille. He had slept only fitfully after being wakened the first time. Within ten minutes, he knew there would be no third try. He was up to stay.

The call that woke Lon was from Colonel Crampton. "The raiders have hit a dry hole, a mining camp known as Damron's Scar, due east of here, on the last ridge of hills before the coastal plain. The miners, garrison, and everything they had processed was lifted out yesterday. I've got two companies on the way. Maybe we can catch this batch."

"I'll get my alert company out as well," Lon said. "At least we don't have to worry about civilians on the ground."

When Lon made the call to send the alert company, he learned that the two Shrike fighters that had been patrolling when he sent *Taranto* to try to intercept the incoming ship had landed twenty minutes before, for refueling. The pilots were in the spaceport terminal, looking for a place to bed down for a few hours. That had to wait. Lon ordered them back up, as soon as their fighters could be readied.

Two minutes later, Colonel Crampton was back on the link. "Another raid, this one at Long Glen, forty miles northwest of here. They just hit. Colonel, Long Glen is a big village, maybe five hundred people live there—families. I'm diverting the shuttles I had going to Damron's

Scar and getting another company ready to move as quickly as the men can get to their shuttles. We have to protect those people."

"I'll divert our alert company as well," Lon said. "Get the next company out. Send them to Damron's Scar. We can't let the raiders think they can overwhelm us by hitting more than one place at a time."

By the time Lon finished issuing those orders, Captain Roim was waiting to talk with him.

"The intruder spotted us, altered course, and started accelerating," Roim reported. "If they keep going, there's no chance *Taranto* can intercept them before they can jump to Q-space again. Should I have *Taranto* abort the pursuit?"

Lon scarcely hesitated. Having *Taranto* close enough to use its fighters would be welcome, especially with two raids in progress. "Yes, abort. But keep an eye on that intruder. If they start decelerating again, look like they might try to come in, tell *Taranto* to be ready to head after them. I want all of the attack shuttles here as fast as you can get them to us. I'll send two companies to Long Glen and have a third ready to go to Damron's Scar if the militia needs help there. That puts the last company on alert in case the raiders hit somewhere else."

Let's put everything we can into this, Lon thought. *If we're going to have to take them piecemeal, best to get it started right now.* He allowed himself only a few seconds to rest. Then he got up and started moving. There was a lot of work to do, even if he was still tired.

Lon's office was on the west side of the headquarters building, so he did not have sunlight streaming in a window to announce the coming of day. Jeremy Howell brought breakfast in, and made pointed hints about eating when Lon started to push the tray aside. Lon picked at the food—a few mouthfuls of scrambled eggs, a couple of bites of toast. Coffee was different. He drank two cups quickly—on top of several he had already consumed since getting up.

Long Glen was only forty miles away. The alert company, Charlie, was on the ground there, engaging an enemy that appeared to be nearly its equal in strength. At the moment, Charlie was providing security for the landing strip to allow the two companies of militia to get down safely. It would be another twenty minutes before *Taranto* would be in position to launch additional Shrikes to help.

Lon had his staff busy, and all of the men were up as well—some to move out as soon as they could board shuttles, the last company going on alert status, ready to respond if the raiders staged a third attack. The command shuttle was on alert also, and Lon had notified his staff to be ready to leave immediately—*if* he decided to head toward one of the raids.

The raiders at Long Glen were not giving ground. A rocket hit one of the shuttles bringing in the militia, but the craft managed to land. There were a few minor casualties, but the men were able to disembark safely. The shuttle would need extensive repair work before it would be able to take off again, though, but in the meantime it would limit use of the landing strip.

"Shuttles can get in and out," Captain Kai reported, "but only one at a time, and there's absolutely no margin for error."

"There are two other clearings within five miles of you," Lon replied, scrolling his mapboard in for a closer view. "We're watching those for enemy shuttles. As soon as *Taranto* gets back in position, we'll have Shrikes covering both clearings."

"Why not put Delta on the ground, split between those two locations?" Kai asked. Delta was the other company moving toward Long Glen. Bravo was heading to Damron's Scar, leaving Alpha on alert in Lincoln. "We really don't need reinforcements here, and the way the landing strip is, putting them out like that might be a hell of a lot safer, and it gives us the option of closing in on the raiders from behind, no matter which way they go."

Lon spent a few seconds looking at his mapboard before he replied. "Good point, Sefer. I'll divert Delta as you suggest."

When he passed those orders to Captain Magnusson and the pilots of the shuttles carrying Delta Company, Lon made a point of mentioning that enemy shuttles might intend to use one or the other of the clearings. "Keep your eyes open and be ready for attack from the air," Lon warned.

His next call was to CIC on *Long Snake*. "Are you picking up that static from enemy electronics?" he asked.

"No, sir," the duty officer in CIC said.

"Any sign of enemy shuttle activity?"

"Not yet, Colonel. We're linking all our assets with new search frequencies and filters. Our hope here is that with the additions, and as many overlapping search vectors as possible, we'll be able to spot them in fairly short order, shuttles or men on the ground using active electronics."

In other words, Lon thought, *they still don't have the faintest idea whether they're going to be able to spot them at all.* He shook his head slowly. *I hope we get a chance to look over one of those shuttles before we get out of here, find out what makes their technology better than ours.* A coup like that would make the contract far sweeter than the payment Dirigent was receiving from the government of Bancroft.

"There's a good chance they won't be using the shuttles soon, though, Colonel," the man in CIC said. "Any stealth they have is only going to be really effective at night; and it's already light over both of the sites being raided. Daylight, they can be seen by the naked eye if they're low enough to be of any use."

"We don't assume that," Lon said. "They timed this raid too close to dawn to have expected to get out by shuttle before first light. What's the cloud cover over Long Glen and Damron's Scar?"

"Patchy over Damron's Scar; almost nonexistent over Long Glen, Colonel. We can see the shuttles on the ground at Long Glen in visible light from here."

Lon closed his eyes, trying to concentrate. *They've timed raids close to dawn before,* he reminded himself. *And it's cost them. Why stage two more at the same time when their men will be trapped on the ground for more than twelve hours? What are they trying to prove? What are they trying to get* us *to do?*

"I want a close scan for unidentified electronics, that fuzzy static, for an eight-mile radius around the two sites," he told CIC.

"We're already doing that, Colonel. You think they might be trying to draw us into a major battle?"

"I don't know what to think, but I want to be ready for any conceivable scenario. If they hope to sucker us into a trap, we need to be able to turn it back against them."

There was no fight at Damron's Scar. Before the DMC and BCM forces arrived, the raiders had left—empty-handed, since there had been neither miners nor metal at the site. Bravo Company was trying to find their track, with one company of militia. The Dirigenter shuttles were back in the air, helping with the search, ready to provide air cover if the men on the ground ran into an ambush.

"I don't know what to think," Lon said. He had Vel Osterman, Torry Berger, and Phip Steesen in the office. "Are they trying to draw us into a major battle, still feeling us out, or something else? They've shown they can be damned cunning, get in and out of a site if they have inside help. They didn't give themselves the cover of night this time, though, and that puzzles me. Maybe they didn't know Damron's Scar had been evacuated, but what about Long Glen? They couldn't have hoped to get in and out before we could respond, even if someone killed the snoops."

"As I recall, Colonel," Phip said, "the raiders didn't seem to act very logically the last time we were here."

"The operation is bigger now, and it's shown signs of being better organized and more coherent, not so damned haphazard. We have to assume that the raiders have some logical plan in mind."

"Maybe they were hoping to provide enough distractions on the ground to let that ship come in for a pickup," Vel suggested. "Or bring in reinforcements and supplies." He shrugged. "They can't count on getting munitions from the locals. Their rifles aren't the same caliber as the Bancrofters use. Any ammunition has to come from off-world, and fuel for their shuttles. I assume they must get most of their food and other supplies the same way, other than what they can gather raw materials for to use in replicators. And they're not doing their job if they can't get their loot out."

"That ship that came in, it's just sent an MR out," Torry Berger said. Message rockets were the fastest way to get information across interstellar space, other than taking a ship. Radio transmissions were limited by the speed of light. An MR—basically just a propulsion system and Nilssen generator, with minimal space for cargo, less than a cubic foot—made the same jumps a ship would.

"If they've sent an MR home, we can't assume that they're going to leave," Osterman said. "There'd be little point, unless they were afraid that the ship might be destroyed before it could jump to Q-space."

"Which means that we might be up to our butts in raiders in a month," Lon said. "If they choose to reinforce the assets they already have here. It would be nice if we could neutralize the raiders on the ground before any new-comers arrive."

"Colonel, I just thought of something else," Phip said. "This stuff today, drawing so much of our force away. Maybe the raiders figure on hitting Lincoln again, just to stir up the fear factor. Like they did before. Try to erode the support base among the civilians."

"Every raid contributes to that," Osterman said. "That's one of the reasons the government brought us in. They lose money and support every time a mining site is suc-cessfully raided—not to mention the people they've killed."

"They do stockpile all their export stuff here in Lin-coln," Berger said. "If the raiders were strong enough to hit the city in force, they could make one hell of a haul, especially if they had a transport coming in to pick it all up right away."

"How much of a haul?" Lon asked.

"The locals haven't given us precise figures, but I would guess perhaps as much as a ton of refined gold and plati-num, perhaps twice as much in other marketable elements and precious gems. Or more."

"There's no evidence that the raiders have the assets to attempt a *coup de main*," Major Osterman said. "If they did, they would have tried it before we arrived."

"Unless they were waiting for this new ship, and what-ever other units might be waiting to pop in," Berger said. "We don't know where that MR was headed. They might have a fleet one jump out. If that's the case, we could be in deep shit in a week."

"Vel, I want you to compile the data we have and get an MR of our own off to Dirigent," Lon said. "Apprise them of the situation in as much detail as possible, includ-ing a transcript of this meeting. I'll have my own report to add to the package. And make sure any outgoing mail gets out as well."

"How soon?" Osterman asked.

"We'll take a break now. Say an hour. That'll give me time to finish my report," Lon said. "Torry, you keep monitoring the action. Let me know if there's any significant change."

Phip hung back as the others left. When he was alone with Lon, Phip said, "You're really worried about this, aren't you?"

Lon nodded. "I have to be. I've got this nagging feeling that we're missing something important, maybe something vital. The raiders are being too damned cute. They have to have an ace in the hole, something we haven't figured out yet."

19

One Shrike was brought down by a surface-to-air missile at Long Glen just as Lon's staff reconvened. A barrage of SAMs were launched at the Dirigenter fighters and two shuttles that were in the air attacking the raider positions. None of the other craft were hit, but Lon decided to pull the shuttles out of action—they were less maneuverable and more vulnerable than the fighters. And Lon—pressed by his staff—decided to hold off on a personal visit to the scene.

Reports from the men on the ground kept revising the estimate of the number of raiders upward. By midafternoon the best guess was that there had to be at least two hundred raiders committed to the fight. The battle had turned mobile, but that brought no clear advantage to the Dirigenters and Bancrofters. The raiders were showing themselves to be more professional than the militiamen . . . and very nearly the equal of the mercenaries. *Maybe equal,* Lon allowed reluctantly. *The real test hasn't come yet.* It seemed clear that the raiders were better led, better organized, and better trained than the ones Lon's company had dealt with on Bancroft nine years before. Those had shown no solid organization at all.

"They learned. Have we?" Lon asked Phip Steesen. The two were alone in Lon's office. It was nearly time for supper, though Lon was having difficulty finding any appetite.

"Maybe that's the wrong question," Phip said. "Maybe we should be thinking more about *how* they learned from what happened here before. None of the prisoners taken in the last fight ever got back to Earth. There was at least one shuttle unaccounted for when we left, and who knows how many raiders we didn't bag. I know what the Bancrofters say, that they cleaned out the last pockets and that anyone left over must have eventually died out in the wilds, but I wouldn't make book on any of it."

"You don't think the survivors managed to hold together any kind of coherent group through the eight years before the new raiders showed up, do you?"

Phip shook his head vigorously. "Not for a minute. That wouldn't have helped. I think that some of them got back to Earth, or Mars, or wherever they were based. I think they carried back pretty good reports of our activities and how we defeated them. That shuttle we didn't find, and however many other shuttles we might not have known about—I think they took the survivors off the next time a ship came in to pick up booty."

"I can't argue against the possibility," Lon conceded. "That would tell them a lot about how we operate, and since we trained the first thousand members of the BCM, it would tell the raiders how the locals operate as well."

"It tells them how *you* operate, Lon," Phip said, lowering his voice. "We got picked for this because the locals wanted the same man. Maybe it would have been better if someone else had come, someone who thinks differently, who commands differently."

"Too bad you didn't come up with that argument before we left Dirigent. We might still be home with our families."

"Yeah, well, you know how it is. Give me enough time and I can fumble through and find the answer to anything. You got any idea who it was put the idea of getting the same troops here? I know it sounds kind of logical, but did the governor think it up on his own? Or Henks? Or somebody else, maybe one of the immigrants working in Government House?"

"And I thought *I* was cynical. You look under your bed before you climb in at night?"

"I'm a bit older, and I've been in this outfit longer." Phip grinned. "Let's go eat, and maybe have a beer. All this thinking is giving me one hell of a headache."

Four hundred Dirigenters and six hundred Bancrofters were involved in the engagement near Long Glen. Two hundred of each were pursuing the raiders who had hit the empty mining camp at Damron's Scar. Before he could go to supper, Lon argued with Colonel Crampton over the second force. Crampton had showed up at Lon's office as Lon and Phip were leaving. Lon wanted to bring the men at Damron's Scar back to Lincoln, ready to deal with more serious threats. Crampton wanted to continue looking for the raiders who had triggered the snoops in the abandoned mining camp.

"We need to get rid of *all* the enemy," Crampton insisted. "Letting some get away doesn't do it."

"We're wasting resources there," Lon repeated—for the third time. "The chances of finding those raiders is too small to be worth the effort. We're better off having those companies here, where they can respond quickly to any new threats."

At the end, because Lon insisted, Crampton agreed to pull the men in the morning, if they hadn't found the raiders yet.

"He's as stubborn as you," Phip whispered after the militia commander left.

"I can see his point. His worries aren't quite identical to ours," Lon said.

"You just could have told him you were going to pull our company out of that place and let him worry about keeping his own people there without us," Phip suggested.

Lon started walking again. "For a second, I considered it," he admitted. "But it's better to do it this way. Consulting rather than commanding."

"Load of bull crap," Phip said.

Supper sat like lead in Lon's stomach. After he ate, he spent an hour conferring with CIC and with his company commanders at Long Glen and Damron's Scar. The fighting was intermittent near Long Glen now, occasional skirmishes moving gradually farther from the village. North of Damron's Scar, traces of the enemy's path had been found, lost, then found again. And lost again after dark.

"Don't push your men too hard tonight, Brock," Lon told Bravo Company's commander. "We'll guide you toward a suitable LZ in the morning, get the shuttles in to bring you back here . . . unless you run into something before then. And from what you've told me, I don't expect that."

"I think they're playing hide-and-seek with us," Captain Carlin said. "Just showing enough trail to keep us interested, if you know what I mean. I've got my scouts looking for any hint of ambush."

"They're capable of it," Lon said. "Watch your back, Brock."

Sefer Kai and Ron Magnusson had similar impressions—that they were being drawn intentionally by the raiders. "They hit Long Glen hard, but they started withdrawing, fighting in good order, stepping lively enough to keep from being surrounded," Captain Kai said. "Then, just when it seems that they've managed to break contact, something happens. They send a patrol to ambush our scouts, hit us on a flank . . . *something*."

"Colonel, if we didn't have near a thousand men here, I'd swear they were trying to draw us into a fight-to-the-finish battle on their ground. They don't want to lose us,"

Captain Magnusson added. "Like kids, one daring the other to cross a line, over and over."

"You know to watch out for whatever tricks they've got up their sleeves. You having any trouble with the BCM commanders?"

"They're a little too eager, Colonel," Magnusson said. "They want to press on full speed, all the time, force the engagement right this second, and damn the consequences."

"Hold them in as best you can," Lon said.

Lon went to his room, undressed, then took a long, hot shower. It eased some of his tension, left him feeling sleepy, ready for bed. He made one last call to the duty officer, to make sure that nothing new had come up in the past fifteen minutes, then turned out the light and climbed into bed. The timeline on the complink next to the head of the bed said 2127 when he closed his eyes.

It was 2317 when Lon opened his eyes again. For a few seconds, he thought that the sounds of explosions he had heard had been part of a dream. Nightmare. Then he heard another explosion, and the stutter of a rapid-fire cannon, and he knew that it was no dream. Then the siren sounded to call the men out of barracks, ready to respond to . . . whatever.

Lon got out of bed, leaping to his feet, just as the glare of a secondary explosion lit up the scene outside his window. The sound of this blast took a second to reach him—extremely loud, and close. The room seemed to tremble at the concussion.

"What the hell was that?" Lon demanded, hitting the switch on his complink that connected him to the duty officer.

It was all of ten seconds before the duty officer, Harley Stossberg, answered. "That was your shuttle, Colonel, blown up where it sat. Air raid. Looks like two raider shuttles."

"Was the crew aboard?" Lon asked.

"No, sir. In barracks."

Lon had already started pulling clothes on, beginning with his battle helmet. He switched to the radio circuits in that. "I'll be down in two minutes, Harley. Get on to CIC and get all the Shrikes in we can. And get the crews into the shuttles on the ground, ready to take off. Give us something to fight back with."

"In the works, Colonel," Harley said.

Reports came in about the air attack. Two raider shuttles had come in from the west, attacking the Dirigenter craft on the ground just south of the palisaded walls, strafing the compound, then moving on to launch rockets and fire cannons as it passed over the main boulevard of Lincoln toward Government House at the far side of town. By the time Lon had his boots fastened, he knew that Government House had taken one rocket hit. The north wing—where the governor's office was—had started to burn. There was no word on casualties. The governor and his family lived in the mansion, and there was considerable staff and security on duty there, around the clock.

Lon strapped on his pistol belt and picked up his rifle. He ran to the stairs and down to the duty office on the floor below. His staff, in various degrees of dress, were already working the complinks. A half-dozen different conversations were in progress. Lon stopped just inside the doorway and listened. It was hard to make sense of anything in the seeming confusion.

Major Osterman concluded one discussion, then crossed to Lon. "We're less than a minute from having two Shrikes here, Lon," he started. "The two that were patrolling over our people north of Long Glen. *Taranto* has launched another four. They'll need seventeen minutes to get here. We have three wounded men in the compound. The command shuttle looks like a total write-off. No word yet from Government House or from in town. I looked out that way. Three or four fires started in buildings facing the boulevard between here and Government House. It's late, so—with a little luck—there won't be any civilian casualties in town. Not much nightlife here." He stopped just long enough to take a breath. "Alpha Company is outside the walls, and we've got eight men with SAMs waiting for a shot at those shuttles if they make another pass."

"Any enemy activity on the ground?" Lon asked when Vel stopped his rapid recitation again.

"No evidence of ground forces yet. They haven't tripped any of our snoops, and CIC hasn't picked up any of that static, except . . ." He stopped and shook his head.

"Except what?" Lon asked.

"This isn't certain yet, but CIC *thinks* that—just maybe—they've come up with a way to get around the stealth capabilities of the enemy shuttles. We had about seven seconds' warning before they opened fire—not enough to allow us to do anything, but enough to lend some credence to what CIC told me."

"Either they do or they don't, Vel. Did they say 'shuttles headed in' or not?"

Osterman closed his eyes for a couple of seconds. "What they said was, 'There appear to be two objects moving toward Lincoln at high speed from the west-northwest. We think—' That was when the first rocket exploded and Harley missed the end of the sentence."

"Something iffy?" Lon asked.

"I haven't had time to go over it with CIC," Osterman said. "That would be my guess, though. Maybe they'll be able to hone it a little better now that they know they're on the right vector."

"Any new activity with our people in the field?"

"Torry's checking that now," Osterman said, turning toward the complink where Captain Berger was seated.

Before they could move close enough to ask Berger what he had learned, Corporal Howell shouted for Lon from the next complink. "Colonel! *Long Snake* reports a new pattern of static on the ground near Long Glen— behind our people!"

"Warn Captains Kai and Magnusson, Jerry!" Lon shouted back. "You have details on just where this new static is?"

"Yes, sir, between our companies and the village, closer to the village."

"Go on, get the word out." Lon turned to Osterman again. "That's what they've had up their sleeves."

"Which? Putting us in the middle of two forces, or luring us away so this new batch can hit Long Glen?" Osterman asked.

"Either way, it stinks," Lon said. "Get on to Brock and get Bravo Company headed toward the nearest clearing where their shuttles can get in and out. I'll call Colonel Crampton and advise him to do the same with his militia companies there."

"We bring them back here or send them to Long Glen?" Osterman asked.

Lon shook his head. "We'll hold our options open for now, decide when they're ready to get airborne."

Lon moved toward his desk as he initiated the call to Colonel Crampton, using his helmet radio. Crampton did not argue with the decision to pull everyone away from the hunt north of Damron's Scar now. His voice was more than a little shaky.

"I just heard that the governor and his family are unhurt," Crampton said after agreeing to Lon's suggestion. "But several members of the staff are either hurt or dead."

"You getting the fires under control?" Lon asked.

"We're just now getting the fire brigade out, and there are too many fires for them to get to all of them at once. I'm sending two platoons of my men to help, calling for garden hoses and civilians as well. Are those shuttles coming back?"

"Hang on. I'll see if we've got a tag on them yet."

It took nearly a minute. "They banked around toward the north and headed west," Lon reported. "Then CIC lost the faint track they had. We've got a good vector, though, and we'll send Shrikes to check it out. They'll be available in a little more than ten minutes. I'm keeping two over Lincoln for defensive purposes, though. By the way, the raiders have brought a second batch of men in, between Long Glen and our people. We've already warned them that they've got trouble behind them."

Damage reports. Manning reports. Casualty reports. Action reports. Slowly, Lon's staff brought order to the confusion. The two Dirigenter companies near Long Glen had started moving, circling to try to catch the new raider force on the flank. Half of the Bancrofter militia were circling the other way, leaving the rest in place between the two enemy units. Bravo Company and the militia companies with it were moving toward a landing zone. They would need another hour to reach the LZ and secure it for the shuttles that would come in to pick them up.

Lon got behind his desk and took off his helmet. There seemed to be no imminent danger of a ground assault on Lincoln, and there was no sight of the enemy aircraft. He was just beginning to relax when he had a call from Captain Roim.

"That unidentified ship has made a series of course changes over the last thirty minutes," Roim reported. "It looks as if they might be coming in toward Bancroft again."

"Even if they are, what'll it take them, another couple of days?" Lon asked.

"The earliest they could reach our positions is forty-three hours, Colonel. Should I send *Taranto* after them again?"

"No, we can't afford to play cat and mouse with that ship right now. If it wants to come in, let it. Let them do the traveling. We can hit them later. Just keep alert for the possibility of more potentially hostile ships coming in-system."

"We always do that, Colonel," Roim said.

It was 11:37 P.M., 2337 hours in military time.

Coffee and chocolate bars. Vel Osterman lit a cigar but, after a couple of puffs, set it aside and let it go out. Reports continued to come in, but not as frequently, not as urgently, as in the first minutes after the air raid. There were soft discussions among members of Lon's staff, men looking for proper countermeasures, new angles on the problems of Bancroft.

Midnight. Twelve-thirty.

"Colonel, Charlie Company and the militia unit with them will reach the LZ in approximately twenty minutes," Captain Berger reported. "Have you decided whether to bring them here or send them to Long Glen?"

Lon closed his eyes briefly before he replied. "Bring Charlie back here. I'll advise Colonel Crampton to do the same with his people. Charlie's been out. We'll try to give them time to get cleaned up and get some sleep. Alert Alpha to move to Long Glen as soon as Charlie gets in."

After talking to Colonel Crampton, Lon called Captain Kai and told him the arrangements. "Your men might go back in, somewhere, almost anytime, Sefer. Make sure the rocket packs are charged and serviceable."

He cut Kai's reply short to take a call from CIC.

"Colonel, we've got a report from one of the Shrike pilots who tried to follow the raider shuttles. He thinks he might have spotted where one or both of them landed. *Thinks*," the duty officer said. "It's marked on the mapping computer, and we're going to keep something in the air over that location all night."

Lon almost leaped to his feet. "Torry!" he shouted. "When you get Alpha assembled, they're not going to Long Glen. We may have found where the enemy parks their shuttles. I'll take Alpha as close as we can get. Have Bravo ready to follow us in after they've had a chance to get a few hours' sleep."

"You'll take them in?" Major Osterman asked.

Lon nodded. "I'll take them in."

20

Osterman would not argue in front of the rest of the staff, but he followed Lon out of the office to make his case. "It's hardly protocol. You have the entire contract to administer, not just one company to go chasing through the woods."

"This might *be* the entire contract, Vel," Lon said. "If we can cripple their transportation, the rest of it gets simpler—tedious, perhaps, but simpler. I need to be on the ground, where I can see what's going on firsthand, not back here trying to coordinate through secondhand reports. I'll be with my old company, and there are enough people still in Alpha who have worked with me for years."

"I hate to say this, but you've been away from that kind of action a long time as well, staff assignments in garrison and more than half a year on that intelligence lark to Earth."

Lon smiled. "I'm not that far out of shape. The Corps has no use for deskbound officers. If I can't cut it out there, it's time for me to take up bartending as a trade."

Osterman chuckled. He knew about the pub Lon's in-laws ran. "Okay, you've made your point. Just don't take silly chances. The reason we got picked for this contract was the locals want your brain and experience behind the whole operation. Don't make them have to be satisfied with the second string."

"You'll have my full cooperation. I want you here to

coordinate getting people where they need to be. If the
raiders do have their shuttles parked where we think they
do, they've probably got most of their men fairly close as
well, so this operation might turn into an all-hands affair
in short order."

"I'd say that's another reason for you to stay here and
leave this expedition to Captain Girana—or me, if you
think it demands higher supervision on the spot," Osterman said.

"Maybe next time, Vel. You'd better get back inside,
stay on top of things here. I'll leave Phip with you, though
we might have to chain him to the desk for me to get away
without him. Get on to Colonel Crampton and make sure
he's ready to pour as many men as possible in on this as
well. Now I need a few minutes to get ready to catch my
ride."

I am back in shape, Lon told himself as he climbed the
stairs to his room. *Almost all the way.* He had been pushing
himself hard, to make up for the months he had been unable to maintain his normal training regimen. He was still
five pounds heavier than he wanted to be, and the workouts
were still a bit more difficult than they used to be, but he
was fit enough to pass an annual fitness test with points to
spare.

He needed only five minutes to get his combat pack and
gear. Corporal Howell kept his boss's things in good order.
Rifle, pistol, ammunition. Lon refilled his canteen, adding
a single drop of lemon concentrate. He no longer recalled
where he had picked up that trick. It helped keep water
"fresher."

When Lon left his room, ready to leave, Howell was
standing in the corridor, similarly attired. "My job to go
with you, Colonel," he said.

"Haven't you learned not to volunteer for anything yet,
Jerry?" Lon asked.

"I don't want to stay here and listen to Lead Sergeant Steesen rant about being left behind, sir. He hurts my ears when he screams."

Lon chuckled. "He *can* get shrill. Okay, let's go."

"Alpha Company is already moving out to the shuttles, sir. Captain Girana knows we're coming along."

"Then we'd better hurry." Lon moved past Howell, toward the stairs. The corporal had to scramble to stay with his boss.

Captain Girana had already given the order for his men to board the two shuttles that would take them to Long Glen. The files of men were moving into the craft when Lon and Corporal Howell reached them.

"Getting bored riding a desk?" Girana asked.

"Got to get out once in a while, Tebba," Lon responded. They talked over a private radio frequency, even though they were only a foot apart, to ensure that the conversation remained confidential. "This could turn into the main event."

"I thought it might," Tebba said. "They're not going to leave their transport far from protection. We find where the birds are, we're apt to find most of their foot soldiers."

"Very possible," Lon said.

They moved aboard one of the shuttles together.

"You might want to keep a special eye on Harley this time around," Tebba said as the shuttle took off.

"A problem?" Lon asked.

"No, I just want your evaluation. Look, I know we haven't talked about this before, but this isn't a whim. I've been thinking it's about time for me to hang up my boots. Get out and do something else. I've got nearly forty years in the Corps. Soon as Harley's ready to take over the company, I'm out."

Personnel turnover was slower in the DMC than in many planetary or national armies, certainly slower than in armies of even two centuries before, but it was just as inexorable. There were, inevitably, fatalities. The business of the DMC was war, and war always exacts its price. Medical retirements were rare—trauma tubes and the extensive regenerative therapies available had almost totally eliminated the need to invalid soldiers out. Transfers between units did occur, but with minimal frequency. Ninety-five percent of all soldiers in the DMC remained within the same regiment throughout their careers; 80 percent stayed within the same battalion; 60 percent never left the company they reported to after completing recruit training. But men aged. Their priorities changed. There were no minimum enlistments: The DMC had no use for reluctant soldiers. Except on contract, a man could get his release from the Corps on seventy-two hours' notice. Many served for ten years or less. A Dirigenter could take full retirement after twenty-five years. Fewer than one in a hundred stayed longer than thirty-five years, and in the enlisted ranks, the rate was little more than half that.

"Do *you* think Harley's ready to handle the company?" Lon asked after several seconds of silence.

"I think this contract will tell the tale," Tebba said. "It's been quite a while since we had a really hot combat contract. The rest, no question. Harley can handle garrison duty and training contracts. But that's not enough. He has to be able to shine in combat before he can take over a company. If he handles himself well here, that should remove any doubt."

"I'll keep my eyes open, Tebba. Now, about this little expedition . . ."

Lon spent the rest of the flight briefing Tebba and his two lieutenants, Harley Stossberg and Min Jason. Jason had been with Alpha nearly two years—had won his lieutenant's pips as an officer-cadet in the company, on a one-company combat contract. Jason was blond, thin, and deceptively slight in build. It seemed impossible that he could march all day carrying full combat kit, but he could, without complaint. The talk in battalion headquarters was that Min Jason was a goer, likely to progress far and fast in the Corps . . . if he survived and didn't make any serious mistakes. His intelligence test scores were in the top percentile in the regiment. "He'll go far, Lon," Matt Orlis had said more than a year before. "If he lasts, that boy will be General someday, and might set records getting there."

If he lasts. For a soldier, there always had to be that qualification.

The landing zone CIC had found for Alpha Company was seven miles from the suspected position of the two raider shuttles, just east of north, across one of the lower ridges in the mountain range, with the peaks little more than four hundred feet above the flanking valleys. The shuttles circled around to land from the north-northwest, cutting engines as far as possible to minimize the noise of the aircraft.

Lon hung back, letting the men of A Company deploy into an initial perimeter. He and Corporal Howell were the last men off the shuttles, staying out of the way during the critical first minute on the ground. As soon as the company was in position, away from the shuttles, both of those craft got back into the air, heading north again, to circle above ten thousand feet—high enough to be out of immediate range of any enemy on the ground, but close enough to provide close air support on less than a minute's notice.

"Looks like this valley's been burned over in the past year or two," Tebba said when he reported to Lon that his men were ready to move. "All new growth. A lot of fallen trees."

"I noticed," Lon replied. "Get a heading for the clearing where that pilot thinks the enemy shuttles are. We'll take the most direct route that's practical."

"Already working. I've got a squad moving now. The

rest of first platoon will follow as soon as the point squad is a hundred yards out. Main body after that, along with a squad on each flank. Fourth platoon will provide the flankers and rear guard."

"Jerry and I will stay with the main body for now, Tebba," Lon said. "Keep a few squads between us and you."

Orders were passed by radio, but once the company was on the move, talk over the radio was kept to an absolute minimum, and limited to officers and noncoms, to cut down on the chances that the electronic emissions might be detected by the enemy. When possible, hand signals substituted. Every man in the company knew the routine signs.

The plan of attack, sketchy though it was, called for Alpha to be in position near the suspected enemy position before first light. That gave them a little more than three hours to cover seven miles . . . virtually none of it level. Lon did not expect time to be a problem. The terrain was not terribly severe, even with a hill to cross.

Lon fell into the routine of the march without conscious effort, keeping a watch on both flanks, keeping track of the man in front of him, listening for any hint of danger on either side of the column. He kept his rifle at the ready, safety off, selector switch set to automatic, but he kept his finger outside the trigger guard, so there would be no accidental discharge. Lon and Jeremy were in the center of the main body, between the company's second and third platoons. Lon monitored the radio frequencies used by the officers and noncoms but did not interfere—did not violate sound discipline. When a call came in for him from headquarters, he kept his replies minimal, just a click of acknowledgment when possible. Charlie Company would be ready to move on short notice. Extra shuttles had been brought down from *Long Snake* to make it possible to bring the two companies at Long Glen in on little more notice. Colonel Crampton was ready to move six hundred men, almost as quickly as Charlie Company could be delivered to the scene.

After an hour, Tebba Girana called for a ten-minute break. The point squad took slightly less. While the company was stopped, the men mostly just sat or squatted where they were, taking a drink of water and a bite from an energy bar while they remained alert, watching either side.

When the point squad reached the ridge, there was another short stop, while the first dozen men up scanned the next valley with binoculars and infrared sensors, looking for any indication of an enemy presence. They concentrated on the area of the clearing but did not exclude the terrain around it, or the slope on the opposite side of the valley. That was nearly fifteen miles away, too far for the soldiers to expect to tell much.

There has to be something *down there,* Lon thought after hearing the negative report from the point squad's sergeant. *That pilot couldn't have been completely wrong.* Lon wasn't certain if that was simply wishful thinking. He was uncertain whether enough time had passed for the thermal signature of well-shielded engines to cool off sufficiently to be invisible. He did not have the math in his head for the calculation, and since he didn't know how much better the raiders' stealth technology was than what the Corps possessed, he couldn't have done the calculation anyway. But that could not stop him from puzzling over it from time to time.

As the main body neared the ridgeline, Tebba Girana stepped out of line and waited until Lon reached him. The two men lifted the faceplates of their helmets, switched off transmitters, and whispered.

"I think we ought to fan the point squad out, maybe add a second squad, give us a broader sweep moving in," Tebba said. "That'll give us a better chance to spot any snoops, boobytraps, or sentries, and maybe spot signs of people where there shouldn't be any."

"Go ahead," Lon replied. "Maybe increase the separation between the point and the rest just a little?" He made it a question, willing to defer to Tebba's technical judgment.

"A little, I think, not much. If they run into trouble, I want us to be close enough to reinforce them in a hurry."

Lon nodded.

"How close to the coordinates do we go?" Tebba asked. "We've still got a little time in hand. Should we go in to try to confirm the presence of those shuttles, or wait until reinforcements are in the air, ready to come in?"

"We stick with the plan I laid out before," Lon replied. "I'm not going to bring everyone in until we know the enemy is here. We get confirmation first. When we get on the slope going down into the next valley, have your men keep their eyes open for any hint of caves as well. If those prisoners had it right, the enemy's base could be under this ridge, not too damned far away."

"Yeah," Tebba said, and he hesitated a beat before he added, "I thought about that."

"We'll find a decent spot maybe halfway down the western slope and send one platoon ahead to scout out the coordinates that pilot provided," Lon said. "Wait until we get word from them, one way or the other."

"That's going to put us three miles back, Lon. That platoon gets in trouble, we might not be able to get to them fast enough to make a difference."

"Unless the raiders have a major ambush sitting in place waiting for us, we'll have time. Just tell the platoon leader you send to back off at the first hint of trouble."

"I'll send Harley, with fourth platoon," Tebba said after another hesitation. "Fourth used to be Wil Nace's platoon. Right now, it might be the best one I've got for this job."

• • •

I hope we're not losing sleep for nothing, Lon thought as he waited for fourth platoon to complete its scouting mission. The rest of the company was in position just below the ridgeline, with half a company on the reverse slope, securing the rear. Lon had changed his mind after looking over the valley from the ridge, deciding that altitude would give more advantage than a few dozen extra yards to the west. No foxholes or trenches had been dug, but most of the men had improved their positions as best they could without a lot of effort and noise, moving rocks, scooping out shallow depressions in the rocky soil—whatever was possible and quick.

Fourth platoon had been out less than twenty minutes. There was no radio traffic from them, or within the platoon. Lon did not expect any, unless they ran into problems, and then he knew he might hear the trouble before Harley or Wil could report it.

It shouldn't take more than another half hour, Lon decided, noting the time on his helmet's head-up display. *That'll give them time to get right in the middle of the enemy, if they're there.* Earlier, it had been easy to think that the Shrike pilot couldn't be mistaken, that there had to be *something* out of place in or near that clearing, but Lon was no longer so confident. *Ghosts in the night.* He shook his head. *Some things never change.* But some did. Cold, hard ground felt colder and harder, more uncomfortable than it had twenty years before, when he was young, when it was all *new.*

He wasn't certain what brought Lon, Junior, to mind just then, but Lon could almost see him lying on the hillside in camouflage battledress, looking over the barrel of a rifle, waiting for some enemy to attack, fidgeting impatiently, anxious for the fight to start. Another image flashed quickly through his brain, sending a shiver of momentary terror down his spine. He was looking at his son in uniform head on, and could see a bullet hole through the center of Junior's forehead.

Lon lifted his faceplate halfway and reached in and rubbed at his eyes, hard enough to bring spots of color to his vision, trying to banish the waking nightmare. The image was already gone, but it left a knotted lump in Lon's stomach. *Come on, Harley, find the enemy.* Anything to end the thinking time.

Thirty minutes. Forty-five. Lon found it difficult to avoid staring at the timeline at the top of his faceplate. He had an itch to call Harley to ask for a report, but he did not scratch. Harley would report when—if—there was anything to report. Calling would be an unnecessary distraction for Harley, a poor example, and a sure way to telegraph his own nervousness—never the best course for a commander.

Charlie Company boarded its shuttles in Lincoln. The men had their rocket packs. If needed, they could reach the site in less than ten minutes and jump in wherever Lon thought they might do the most good. *If* Alpha's fourth platoon found the enemy shuttles or flushed an enemy force.

Lon scanned the valley floor with his binoculars. He checked his head-up display for the green blips that indicated the positions of Harley Stossberg and fourth platoon's noncoms. They were very nearly to the location the Shrike pilot had given—where he thought the two enemy shuttles had gone to ground.

Any second now, Lon thought.

When the gunfire began, it still startled him.

21

Gunfire, then the first report from Harley: "We missed a sentry, dug in and camouflaged." His voice showed the excitement of the moment, the adrenaline rush of sudden action, but he did not seem unduly flustered or emotional. "At least two or three more sentries. Enemy electronics going active—close, very close. It was like we just walked into range. I've got one man down, vital signs weak but still present."

"What about the shuttles?" Tebba asked as soon as Harley paused in his report.

"No . . . *Yes.* There's one. Two. I see them, Tebba. Under thermal camouflage rigging. Sandbags on the sides, about three feet high. And something beyond the shuttles. I can't tell what that is yet, something fairly large."

"Take the shuttles out before they turn their guns on you," Lon said, breaking into the conversation he had simply been monitoring before. "Blow those suckers."

Harley did not have time to acknowledge the order, let alone give orders before Lon saw first one and then a second rocket trail, bright streamers through gaps in the forest. There were two quick explosions.

"Good work, Harley," Lon said. *I like prompt results,* he thought with a grin.

Then there was a third explosion, larger than the first two. A fireball erupted through the forest canopy and cast arcs of burning material up and out, scattering fiery blobs

over more than an acre of ground. Lon heard a few excla-
mations of surprise, even a couple of curses, before Harley
came back on to report.

"That third object. It was a fuel tank. We've got a
damned inferno in here. The enemy has stopped shooting,
for the moment, anyway. I still can't tell how many we're
facing, but they've got to have more people close, and
they'll be all over us now."

"Pull back, Harley," Lon said. "You've done your job.
Get that platoon out of the way as fast as you can. We're
set to provide covering fire if the raiders get their act together too soon."

"On our way," Harley said.

Ten seconds later, gunfire erupted again. Even at a distance, Lon could tell the difference between the raiders'
weapons and those the DMC used. The sounds were dis-
tinct, difficult to confuse.

"Tebba, that sounds like more than a few sentries," Lon
said, switching channels to talk just to Girana.

"It does," Tebba said. "At least a platoon, maybe more.
Should we move to reinforce fourth platoon?"

"Not yet," Lon said after a short hesitation. "Let's see
what Harley needs. Just have your men ready to put covering fire in over their heads."

"That blaze could make things difficult," Tebba said.
"Plays hell with the night-vision gear anywhere close to
it. And that smoke is getting thick."

At least a score of smaller blazes had started around the
major fires, bright points topped by billowing smoke as
trees and the new foliage of spring started to burn. Burning
wood crackled. Some of those sounds were almost like
gunshots.

"We're pulling back in good order," Harley reported
nearly two minutes after his previous transmission. "I've
got a couple of men with minor burns, still fit enough to
move on their own and fight. I make the opposition at least

equal to our own strength. We're making headway, though. They're wasting time moving around, trying to avoid being backlighted by the flames."

"Get men out ahead of you on this side, Harley," Tebba said. "If they've got men in caves somewhere under this ridge, they could be between us."

"I hope there's more eyes than we have watching for that, Tebba," Harley said. "We're a little busy just now."

"Doing what we can, Harley." Tebba switched channels again. "Lon, you going to bring in Charlie now? Even if no extra raiders show their heads, we're going to have to give this area a close search and see what else is around."

"They'll be in the air in fifteen seconds, Tebba," Lon said. He had just finished giving the order. "I'd like to have a better idea where to set them down before they get here. I'm not going to give drop coordinates until the last minute."

More waiting. Lon played with the idea of sending another of Alpha's platoons out, to try to flank the raiders who were chasing the platoon Harley was with, but he decided to wait. The three platoons on the ridge might not be compromised yet. The raiders might not have any idea that there were more soldiers that close. *Keep the aces facedown as long as possible,* Lon told himself. *If they don't know how many we are, we still don't know how many they are either.*

Lon spent several minutes talking with Vel Osterman in Lincoln. The engagement near Long Glen had joined again, with Bravo and Delta Companies moving back toward the mining village and the new raider force that had landed there. There had been several skirmishes, with the raiders hitting and moving, drawing the pursuit toward and then around the village. The Bancrofter militiamen were positioning themselves to keep the first raider force from doubling back. That entire operation was so fluid that it was difficult to be certain of much. The raiders were operating in small teams now, splitting apart, but still apparently working in concert, harassing, sniping.

As far as he could, Lon tried to put Long Glen out of his immediate thoughts. He had his own situation to concentrate on. Two shuttles carrying Charlie Company were in the air. Colonel Crampton reported that he had four companies of militia in shuttles ready to lift off as soon as Lon called for them.

The sky was beginning to show the approach of morning. Lon and the three platoons on the slope below the ridgeline were still in shadow, but that line behind them was more clearly etched now. Stars were fading from view. Sunrise was no more than twenty minutes away.

"Tebba, I'm going to bring Charlie down well on the other side of the fight," Lon said, glancing into the eastern sky. "They're going to be visible jumping in, so we've got to give them some space. We need to let them get down and organized before they get sucked into a firefight."

"Where's that Shrike that was stooging around?" Tebba asked.

"Just waiting for my go-ahead," Lon said. "I want to make sure we've got clear separation between fourth platoon and the enemy before I have him come in—unless things get too hot for Harley."

"He's got more than a hundred yards' separation between his people and the enemy now, Lon. Maybe one-twenty. It's not going to get much wider than that."

Lon switched channels. "Harley, link to the Shrike pilot. Lead him in for a strike on the raiders coming your way. Be careful. Give him the right coordinates."

"Don't worry, I'm not about to screw up and order my own ass shot off, Colonel," Harley said. "Switching channels now."

"Tebba, Charlie will drop right after the Shrike makes its second pass," Lon said after he also switched channels. "I'm going to bring them in one mile due west of the explosions. And I'm going to have Colonel Crampton send two companies in the same place we landed."

"If you bring them in right away, we won't have time to get a detachment back there to secure the LZ," Tebba said.

"No help for that. I don't want to weaken our position here. Any luck at all, there shouldn't be any raiders behind us. I'll tell Crampton we don't have anyone there, to treat it as if the enemy might be waiting."

The second raider force revealed itself as the Shrike made its attack on the first force. Two surface-to-air missiles streaked toward the Shrike, launched below and left—south—of the line Lon and the three platoons were holding high on the hillside. The first missile veered farther left, missing the Shrike by a wide margin, but the second caught it near the tail, blowing the tail control surfaces away. The Shrike spiraled into the ground, exploding on contact, no more than fifty yards from where the craft on the ground had been destroyed. The pilot never had a chance to eject.

Lon called Captain Kai. "Sefer, switch your drop zone. Half a mile west of the main fires instead of a full mile. We've got more bogeys on the ground, no count on them yet. I need your men sooner rather than later."

"Half the distance," Kai said. "I'll pass that to the pilots now, Colonel."

Charlie Company jumped from its shuttles less than two minutes later. The jumpers were not invisible. Thin tails of pale blue marked the exhausts on their rocket packs, and sunrise was close. There was some light. To cover the jump, Lon ordered the rest of Alpha Company to take the raiders near the base of the hill under fire, even though they did not have a good read on the exact position or number of the enemy there—only the spots from which the two missiles had been fired. Rifles and rocket-propelled grenades. The grenades offered more hope of hits than the rifles, though the range was extreme.

The enemy reacted quickly, turning to respond to the gunfire from near the ridge. After thirty seconds, Lon estimated that there might be a full company of raiders below—three hundred feet lower and twice that distance to the south-southeast, at the base of the line of hills.

The second Shrike made a fast pass across the enemy positions, too high and too fast to use its cannon. It scattered three missiles along the enemy line, then climbed out of harm's way as quickly as possible, almost straight into the sky. It didn't level off to circle around until it was above fifteen thousand feet.

Lon rested in the most solid firing position he could manage. The range and angle made accurate rifle fire difficult, even with his helmet's optics linked to the rifle's sights, but he got off several three-shot bursts, waiting until he saw the muzzle flashes of enemy rifles and targeting them. No one in the company was firing on full automatic. Dirigenters were taught not to waste ammunition. For the same reason, Lon's men were being extremely sparing with their rocket-propelled grenades. The range was near the maximum effective for the weapons.

Charlie Company hit the ground and got organized. Jumping into a wooded area, there had been some inevitable dispersal as men maneuvered to find clear routes among the trees. Squad leaders and platoon sergeants were busy gathering their men and checking to make certain that there had been no serious injuries on the jump. It took several minutes for Lon to get the report: Three men had minor injuries—sprained ankles or knees; several others had cuts suffered coming through the foliage.

"Move toward your right, Sefer," Lon told Captain Kai. "We want to put the raiders at the foot of this ridge between us. Move carefully, though. They might have a lot more men underground anywhere along here."

"In other words, while we're trying to flank them, they might be flanking us farther down the line," Kai replied.

"We've got more men coming in, Sefer. The sooner we know the size of the opposition here, the better."

"That's easy for you to say, Colonel. We'll do what we can. Just remember, there's not enough juice left in the rocket packs to take us back up to the shuttles."

"I'll keep it in mind," Lon said, suppressing a chuckle. A year earlier, Sefer Kai had startled a regimental officers' conference by suggesting that the rocket pack system might be upgraded to permit extraction as well as insertion, glossing over the considerable difficulties of having two hundred men attempt to rendezvous with shuttles traveling a minimum of 180 miles per hour.

I wish we could close off the trouble at Long Glen so I could bring the rest of the battalion here, Lon thought. Having two major engagements going at once was not the way he wanted to handle the raiders. And if the raiders were able to stage a third raid at the same time, the Dirigenters and their hosts would have trouble responding to that at all.

Daylight. They probably won't try any new raids before sunset, Lon thought . . . hoped. *With a little luck we can clean up one or the other of our operations before then.* It was too soon to make any serious plans for consolidating forces to concentrate on one site or the other. The people of Long Glen couldn't be left unprotected until the immediate threat there was over. And this nameless site couldn't be abandoned until Lon's men could determine whether there was a major raider base concealed nearby. That might take days, even if the raiders engaging them were all neutralized quickly—killed or captured.

"Tebba, did you mark where the first firing started below us?" Lon asked,

"Not precisely. I think we can narrow it down to within twenty or thirty yards, though."

"That should be close enough. We get this firefight ended, that's where we'll need to start looking for a cave entrance."

"I don't think they'll be anywhere with only one exit, Lon," Girana said. "You remember last time. That cave had more ways out than an illegal whorehouse."

"Yeah, I've been thinking about that. When those militiamen get here, I'm going to have them covering the ground behind us and around to the south from here, looking for holes as well as raiders."

"Going to be midday or later before they can do much good at that," Tebba said. "I've already got men putting snoops out behind us and past the ends of our line here."

"We're getting close monitoring from overhead as well," Lon said. "But we can't do any real probing for caves on the ground until this firefight ends."

Real guerrilla warfare, Lon thought. *It's hard to keep thinking of this as just simple raiding. It might not be enough to deal with the men Earth has put on the ground here. Unless the Bancrofters can keep more of them from coming in after we leave, they could find themselves faced with the same thing, again and again.* He shook his head. It was starting to look more and more as if Earth had more final intentions toward Bancroft, destabilizing the government and then taking over the world directly.

What's that unidentified ship doing now? Lon wondered, and he called Vel to have him check with CIC again. *I feel as if I'm juggling ten-pound razor blades,* he thought while he waited for Osterman to radio back. *If I'm not careful I could miss a blade and slice my head off.*

"Action coming from the south!" Tebba shouted over his link to Lon. "One of the snoops picked up movement, two hundred yards out, just on the other side of the ridge. They're trying to sneak in behind us."

"How many?" Lon asked.

"Can't be sure, but it looks like just a couple of squads . . .

so far," Tebba said. "Might be more behind the ones the snoop can see."

"I'll take a squad and have a look," Lon said. "Okay if I grab the squad closest to me?"

"You're the boss."

Lon signaled to the leader of the squad that was closest, Dominic Schwartz, a newly promoted corporal, and quickly briefed him on what they were going to do, cutting into the squad's operational channel so that everyone would hear the plan.

Schwartz put his point man out, and Lon got into the squad's line in the middle of the first fire team—and Jeremy Howell followed right along, though Lon had not "invited" him.

"More volunteering?" Lon asked softly.

"Hard to break the habit, sir," Howell said. "My mama always said bad habits would be the death of me."

"Not today, okay?"

"Fine by me, sir."

"Stick close to me and keep your head down," Lon said.

There was no elegant plan. Lon merely planned to take the squad along the western side of the ridge until they were behind the raiders moving on the eastern side—then cross over and take them from the crest and behind. Tebba would have men watching the crest farther north, to make certain the raiders weren't able to sneak up on the rest of the company.

Walking silently across the steeply pitched slope required concentration. There was loose rock in among the roots and a very thin layer of soil that was all the hill offered to anchor the few short, scrawny trees, sparse bushes, and grass that managed to grow so near the summit. The trees would offer little cover. This high up spring was just beginning to sprout new leaves.

Four minutes. Lon estimated that they should be just opposite the raiders, separated only by the top thirty feet of the ridge, less than fifty yards apart laterally. *As long as they don't peak over the crest too soon,* Lon thought, glancing that way himself. Every man in the squad with him was thinking similar thoughts.

Tebba reported that there had been no additional warnings from the snoop on the other side of the ridge. "It counted twenty-two men moving past," Tebba reported. "From your blips, you should be twenty yards or so beyond the end of the raider column."

"Too bad we can't see blips for the raiders," Lon whispered back. "I think we'll give them a little more space before we turn."

"Your call," Tebba said. "You're the one on the scene."

Two minutes. An extra thirty yards. Then Lon told Corporal Schwartz that it was time to turn left. The squad turned, moving from column to skirmish line, with two to four yards' separation between men as they started climbing toward the crest of the ridge. The distances between men varied considerably over the next few minutes because the terrain did not always permit straight movement. The ridgeline was irregular, the last stretch of the climb was steeper, and there were places where men would have needed ropes and climbing gear to hold their relative positions. Schwartz halted his men just below the crest and dressed the line as best he could, making certain the men were not bunched too tightly. Then he had the man at the far end of the line—presumably the man farthest from the raiders—edge up; he would be the first to look across for any sign of the enemy.

"Be ready for anything," Schwartz warned the rest of his squad. "We could be within spitting distance of them if we've guessed wrong or they quit moving."

Lon did not interfere. The corporal would know his men better than Lon could. Every private in this squad was new since Lon had last gone into combat with it. Only Schwartz and the lance corporal commanding the squad's second fire team had been with it before Lon had transferred to battalion from A Company.

"Colonel, you ready?" Schwartz asked.

"Whenever you are, Corporal," Lon replied. "Just think of Corporal Howell and me as two extra rifles in the squad. I'll leave the operation to you if possible."

"Thank you, sir. Ten seconds."

Lon could not avoid a silent countdown. Schwartz gave his point man the order to look over the crest. Lon kept counting seconds in his head until the man reported.

"Nothing within fifty yards of us, Corp. More like seventy yards. Looks like they haven't started moving up toward the crest themselves. I can see fifteen men. There might be more farther on, though."

"When I give the word," Schwartz said, "you and Maguire go over and get into what cover you can find." Maguire was the next man in line, and he carried one of the squad's two grenade launchers. "We'll get in position and open up on them together. Wait for the order," the corporal repeated.

Lon adjusted his footing and checked to make certain that his rifle's safety was off. His head was two feet below the crest; he was lying against the rock at nearly a fifty-degree angle. There was another narrow ledge pressing against his thighs, just above his knees. When Corporal Schwartz gave the order to start the action, Lon would move up to that last ledge to give himself an angle of fire along the crest.

Schwartz gave the first order, and the two men farthest south rolled over the crest and slid into position several yards down the slope on the other side. As soon as they reported that they were ready, the corporal alerted the rest of the squad, then checked with Lon.

"You give the word," Lon told him.

Schwartz switched back to his squad frequency to give it. "Go!"

Lon stepped up to the firing position he had marked, getting his rifle across the top and tracking for targets. He had just started to squeeze the trigger when he heard the sound of the first grenades being launched. He got off three bursts with his rifle before those grenades exploded. Both grenadiers followed up with three more shots apiece, scattering their grenades along the line of the enemy squads.

The raiders under the barrage did not get off a single shot in return.

"We'll check 'em out, Colonel," Schwartz said. "I'd feel a lot better if you was to stay put for a couple of minutes, sir. Make it easier on my boys."

"We'll start back on this side of the ridge, Corporal," Lon said. "Good work. Tell your men I said so. And be careful checking out those raiders."

One little bit of this finished nicely, Lon thought. *If the rest would just go the same way.*

22

Harley Stossberg and fourth platoon worked their way back toward the line of hills, angling slightly toward the north, pulling out of contact with the raider force that had been protecting the shuttles and fuel supply. They left several mines to complicate the enemy's pursuit.

Charlie Company was moving south of the now smoldering remains of the two raider shuttles and the trees and ground cover that had been ignited by the explosions. Even the fuel in the storage tank had mostly burned out, leaving only a few trickles of flame centered in the ashes of the larger blazes. The morning air was thick with smoke trapped by the trees, and the odors of fire still clung, irritating noses and throats.

Captain Kai detached one squad to investigate the remains of the shuttles. The patrol was almost to the central blackened area when the point man tripped a mine that had somehow survived the earlier explosions and fire. Attached to the underside of a large branch, near the trunk of the tree, the mine's blast was focused toward the ground. The squad's point man was killed. The next man in line suffered major injuries from shrapnel, and the third man caught several large splinters of wood from the tree. The remaining men first went prone—a reflex—then moved to care for their casualties.

Two hundred yards away, Captain Kai halted the rest of his men, waiting for word on the results of the explosion.

His men watched their perimeter more intently than usual, in case the blast was the prelude to an ambush that might also include them. As soon as Kai heard from the leader of the detached squad, he passed the results to Lon.

"Lozzet needs a trauma tube, but Baukir's condition is okay; med-patches and bandages will do for him." Lozzet was the man who had taken the shrapnel.

"How critical is Lozzet?" Lon asked.

"The medic says he needs to be in a tube as soon as we can manage, no more than thirty minutes," Kai said.

On the ridge, Lon squeezed his eyes shut, just for an instant, while he tried to decide among risky options. Thirty minutes was going to be difficult. Coming in on rocket packs, Charlie Company had not brought a trauma tube along.

"We can't bring a shuttle into that clearing without securing the entire area first," Lon said. "Too easy for the raiders to bring it down. The medics up here have a portable tube, so either your men will have to carry Lozzet here, or the medics will have to carry the tube down to where he is." Lon's pause was minimal. "Have his squad carry him toward the ridge. Use the rest of your company to run interference, angle over and try to put a wedge around them. I'll have Tebba detail two squads to escort a medic and the tube toward the bottom of the slope, to meet you partway."

"We'll get him there," Kai said.

"Sefer, don't get careless. Don't make a lot more casualties to get one man to treatment. We've only got the one trauma tube on the ground." Lon felt his throat tighten, as if it didn't want to let those words out. *Take care of your casualties. Get them to help as quickly as possible. Never abandon a man while there's any hope at all for him.* But, too often, that led only to the creation of more casualties—often without saving the man whose rescue occasioned them. It wasn't always easy to act prudently, though. The pull of emotion, the dedication of comrades to each other, made that difficult. The gamble was accepted more often than it was declined.

Lon switched radio channels and told Tebba what was needed. "We've got to give those men all the cover we can."

"We'll do what we can," Tebba said.

There were two groups of raiders operating openly—known to Lon and his men. One group was on the valley floor, still harassing the platoon of Alpha Company that had been sent to look for the shuttles and their defenders, but losing ground, finding it difficult to regain contact with Harley and his men. The other group was on the side of the valley and on the lower slopes of the line of hills that bordered the valley on the east. The intensity of the fighting had declined over the last several minutes, and it was slow to build again as Charlie Company moved to get its casualties to help.

On the slope, Lon and Tebba readjusted the lines, moving the center farther downhill to put Alpha Company in a wedge-shaped deployment, with only a single fire team at the top of the wedge to guard the rear. Attempting to cover the movement of Charlie Company and the men carrying the one seriously wounded man, both platoons were free in their use of rocket-propelled grenades and almost profligate with rifle ammunition—more concerned now with suppressing hostile fire and movement than in causing enemy casualties.

Lon contributed to the covering fire, interrupting his shooting only for essential radio conversations. The three companies of Bancrofter militia were nearly all on the ground. The first company had already started moving toward the action. *Taranto* had sent down two more Shrikes, to replace the one that had been shot down and to relieve the other one on station. Four other Shrikes were on alert in case one of the firefights escalated. At Long Glen, Lon's men were boarding shuttles to join this new fight, leaving the village's defense to the militia. Aboard *Long Snake,* a shuttle was being loaded with ammunition and other supplies for the Dirigenters on the ground. That lander would come in at the same time Bravo and Delta Companies did, and those mercenaries would transport the load to the rest of the battalion.

The rendezvous of wounded soldier and trauma tube took more than twenty minutes. Without time to move them to a more secure location, a perimeter had to be set up around the rendezvous point. Charlie Company set that up initially, only linking up with Alpha Company after the fact—as Harley Stossberg and Alpha's fourth platoon returned to the rest of the company. That platoon had several men with minor injuries, but nothing requiring a trauma tube.

"We're too spread out," Lon said on a circuit that connected him with both Kai and Girana. "We need to set up a better defensive perimeter here on the slope until our reinforcements arrive."

"We can carry the trauma tube," Captain Kai said, "but we'll have to move slowly with Lozzet in it. Where do you want us?"

"Move toward your left, Sefer," Lon said. "As you get into position on the slope, you'll take the north half of the perimeter. Alpha will move around the circle and take the south half. We'll adjust our spacing later. Right now I just want to get everyone pulled in together. It's going to be at least another ninety minutes before the militia starts to arrive."

"When do the rest of our people get here?" Kai asked.

"It's going to be at least four hours, unless I have to bring them in on this side, and I don't want to do that," Lon said. "Unless we're up to our armpits in crap, I won't risk shuttles and the men in them this close to the enemy."

"You still bringing the militia around on the south?" Girana asked.

"That's the plan. Two companies of them, at least. I think I'll bring the last one straight over the ridge the way we came. Put them in on the north end of our position and on the crest."

Waiting. The raiders were doing only occasional sniping now. They appeared to be moving, but Lon could not be certain where they were moving to. It was rare for any of his men to spot any of the enemy, and they were not intercepting any enemy electronics, so the Dirigenters held their fire as well, simply targeting the snipers when they spotted the location of one of them.

Lon had Alpha and Charlie gradually expand their perimeter on the hillside, arranging better defensive positions. Men worked at scooping out shallow depressions for themselves, where there was soil over the rock of the hill. Others moved stones and branches—anything to give themselves even a little better cover against enemy gunfire.

If they know how we dealt with their people nine years ago, they won't let themselves get boxed up in their caves this time, Lon thought—certainly not for the first time. From what had happened so far on Bancroft, he felt he had to assume that these raiders knew about the fate of their predecessors. *They'll come out, take their chances in the open. They must have contingency plans. Even if they didn't know we would be here, they'd know that the Bancrofters would be after them sooner or later.*

Lon rolled over onto his side and looked into the sky. Two enemy shuttles had been destroyed on the ground, but it seemed certain that the soldiers of the Colonial Mining Cartel must have more aircraft available—somewhere. They had moved men into Long Glen after the two here had been spotted and were under surveillance. And the abandoned mining camp. *They won't come out in daylight,* Lon thought, *not without heavy cloud cover to hide them.*

But after dark, that's another story. They could use whatever resources they have to move troops or just to attack us. Maybe. Would they risk whatever air resources they still had, knowing that the Dirigenters would be watching for them? "I wouldn't," Lon mumbled, after checking to make sure his transmitter was off, "not unless the situation were desperate."

Was it? For the raiders? How would they view their position? They were being hit hard, whenever they exposed themselves, in significant numbers. Most of their raids were being frustrated, and they were losing men and equipment.

That unidentified ship was still in the system, edging closer to Bancroft but maintaining fleeing room, keeping the planet between itself and the Dirigenter vessels. *Taranto* was not moving after the intruder, but staying in position to support 2nd Battalion's operations on the ground and to protect *Long Snake* and *Tyre*. *It can't just be a transport coming to pick up what the raiders have grabbed,* Lon thought. *I don't think they would have stayed around with so much opposition. They must have extra men or critical supplies, maybe more shuttles.*

It was all guesswork, deduction from insufficient data. Trying to juggle all the maybes and what-ifs was starting to give Lon a headache. *One step at a time,* he thought. *Worry about the enemy below you, the ones you know about. Worry about the rest after you take care of these.*

He rolled back over, looking over the barrel of his rifle into the valley. It had been several minutes since he had heard a gunshot, from either side. The raiders might be withdrawing from the area as fast as caution would permit. By the time Colonel Crampton's three militia companies arrived, there might not be any raiders within shooting distance . . . or they might have the equivalent of a DMC battalion lying in wait, ready to spring a massive ambush.

"Tebba, we need to put some feelers out, find out where

the raiders are," Lon said, opening his channel to Girana. "I need to know if they're still close and what they're doing, before the militia companies walk into something big."

"I've been thinking about that, too," Tebba said. "The raiders have gotten too quiet for my liking."

"Maybe one fire team south along the ridge, another probing into the valley," Lon said. "They're to avoid getting caught in an exchange of fire if at all possible. I just want to know where the enemy is, not start the shooting again. I'll have Sefer put out probes on his side." As soon as Girana acknowledged, Lon called Captain Kai and gave him his orders.

Stealth was second nature to Dirigenters, something they trained hard at, but it made for slow patrols. At night, Lon's men might even have been able to infiltrate a strongly held line without being observed. In daylight they might be able to come within thirty yards of the enemy without giving themselves away—except by wildest chance. The camouflage battledress they wore had been designed specifically for conditions on Bancroft. Each fire team—six men at full complement, half a squad—could operate with the assurance of scores, often hundreds, of hours training together, at just this sort of maneuver.

Lon set his helmet to monitor the radio frequencies that the patrols would use, but did not expect to hear anything unless one of them ran into trouble. Part of stealth was not using active electronics that could be monitored by an enemy. The lead company of militiamen was also observing electronic silence, and the other two companies had already reduced transmissions to a minimum. Lon noted that with approval. The BCM had maintained the level of training the mercenaries had established for them on their previous visit to the world.

But the raiders were also observing strict electronic silence. No emissions were being detected by the battle helmets of the Dirigenters or by the Shrikes and shuttles in the air—all of which were monitoring the area around the two companies of 2nd Battalion. Had they picked up anything, even the vague static that was not quite an intercept, the information would have been linked through to Lon immediately.

Vel Osterman relayed a report from the militia commander on the scene at Long Glen. The raiders there had broken off the engagement, disappearing into the forest. The militia was not pursuing, but maintaining its defensive perimeter around the village.

Wait. Lon talked with Colonel Crampton, who was moving with the third company of militia on its way to reinforce Lon's two companies. Lon laid out his suggested deployment for the militia, and asked Crampton to put out patrols along the eastern side of the line of hills, especially to the north. "That's the section we've given least thought to," Lon said. "The raiders have kept our attention focused west and south, which makes looking the other way seem very desirable just now."

It was past noon before the first militia company started crossing the line of hills through a pass 2½ miles south of the mercenaries. They would put patrols out farther south, but the bulk of the first two companies would work their way north, spreading out to cover both the flank of the ridge and the section of valley between it and the wreckage of the raider shuttles—looking for contact with the enemy.

They knew to look for cave entrances.

Bravo and Delta Companies of 2nd Battalion were on the ground, at the landing zone in the next valley east. The supply shuttle was also on the ground. It would take a solid three hours—and then some—for those two companies to reach the rest of the battalion and get into position. Lon had not given the commanders of those two companies orders for the disposition of their men yet; he wanted to hold off as long as possible on that, in case the fight started up again before they arrived.

Lon took his mapboard out of its pocket on the leg of his battledress trousers and unfolded it. The screen activated, with the map centered on Lon's position. He scrolled and increased the magnification until he was looking at the area between the ridge and the site of the wrecked shuttles—about twelve hundred yards. The direct line between Lon and the wreckage was two-thirds of the way up on the screen. It was still little more than a vague hunch, but Lon thought that the enemy was probably concentrated more to the south of Alpha's positions, near the base of the line of hills, though there were some raiders— from the group that had been defending their shuttles— who were definitely north of that direct line.

Data on the mapboard were compiled from cameras and other sensors on all of the Dirigenter assets with line-of-sight view of the coverage area—ships in space, Shrikes and shuttles in the air, and even video feed from the helmets of Lon's officers and noncoms. CIC's computers on *Long Snake* processed the information in real time, with less than twenty seconds' lag. The resolution available on a mapboard or portable complink was good enough that humans in the open would be visible on the photographic overlay, even if the camera angle caught only head and shoulders.

Lon scanned his mapboard systematically. He had years of practice and knew what to look for. His men were shown by bright blue blips on the screen. The formation was just what Lon had called for. The arriving militiamen were shown in yellow—to provide contrast against the primarily green of the terrain. In ten minutes of searching the screen, Lon found a few figures that weren't identified by blips of either color and tagged them so they would stand out on the mapboards of his officers and noncoms.

"If any of the men with beamers can target those men,

take them out," Lon told Tebba. One man in each fire team carried a beamer, an energy rifle: silent, striking at the speed of light.

Then Lon switched to an infrared overlay that painted the terrain by temperature. Out in the open, it was only sixty-four degrees Fahrenheit, cooler in the shadows. Infrared resolution was not as precise as visible light, but Lon was only looking for anomalies, evidence of an unusually cool location—which might mark a cave entrance emitting a breeze. It was an imperfect search method, dependent on too many variables, but it did offer a chance of discovering entrances to the caves he assumed were under the line of hills.

This might work better in the middle of summer, he thought, *when outside temperatures are twenty or twenty-five degrees hotter than they are now. Or in the dead of winter.* The temperature inside an extensive cave system would be a steady fifty-eight degrees. The greater the difference between inside and outside, the better the chance of spotting an opening. With little more than ten degrees' difference, and foliage intervening, Lon had no success. After reducing the magnification to give himself a broader view of the area, Lon finally folded the mapboard and put it away.

Several gunshots sounded, close together, coming from near the location of one of the men Lon had spotted. He guessed that one of the men with a beamer had hit a target, and the men around the victim were firing back. A few seconds later he received confirmation from Tebba that one of the targets had been dropped.

"They haven't all just hit the trail," Tebba said. "They're down there, somewhere, waiting for whatever."

"Maybe waiting for dark, the way we might in similar circumstances," Lon replied. Despite sophisticated night-vision systems, the dark remained the infantryman's friend. Not even the best system, such as that incorporated in Dirigenter battle helmets, provided vision equal to what unaided eyes could see in clear daylight. Depth perception was reduced, and thermal insulation could reduce the visibility of a target drastically. In theory, the Dirigenter system provided 80 to 90 percent of daylight vision. In practice, it could be somewhat less than that.

"Waiting to fight, or waiting to escape?" Tebba asked, and Lon had no answer.

A private in Charlie Company's third platoon was killed by a sniper eighty minutes later—one shot that caught its victim just under the bottom of his helmet's faceplate and angled up through the brain. The man died almost instantly, before his squadmates to either side could even react to the gunshot. No one marked the direction the shot had come from. The squad laid down a few dozen rounds of rifle fire across a thirty-degree arc, with no way to tell if any of those shots found a target.

The last of the three militia companies moved into position. Lon's Bravo and Delta Companies were approaching the eastern base of the line of hills, more than a mile apart. Bravo would arrive in a little over an hour, Delta thirty minutes after that.

Colonel Crampton and a younger militia officer worked their way to Lon's position and settled in behind what cover was available. "Colonel," Crampton said, "this is my son, Lieutenant Wilson Crampton. He commands 2nd Company."

Lon nodded. "Lieutenant." The younger Crampton nodded back. They were separated by his father, and since all three men were nearly prone, there was no question of handshaking.

"Do you think you've located the main body of the raiders?" Colonel Crampton asked.

"I'm not sure what to think," Lon replied. "We have *some* raiders, and we certainly took care of two of their shuttles and a large fuel tank. The last few hours, there's been nothing but occasional sniping back and forth. I wanted to wait until we had as many men here as possible, just in case we are sitting on their main force. I'm not sure what the raiders are waiting for—probably nightfall."

"You plan to move against them before then?"

"We're already moving. With two companies of your men moving in on their flank, they've got to do something."

"Well, I've deployed those companies the way you suggested, leaving two platoons to cover their rear, in case the raiders have cave exits south of where we crossed the ridge," Colonel Crampton said. "And Wilson's company is on the reverse slope, above us." He gestured over his shoulder.

"If the raiders don't engage before then, we'll start pressing as soon as my last two companies get in position," Lon said. "About ninety minutes from now."

"When the last of your men get here, we should have nearly fourteen hundred altogether. That should be enough to handle anything the raiders can put against us." The militia commander's voice did not sound as confident as his words.

23

There were several small skirmishes while Lon waited for the rest of his troops to arrive and move into position. The raiders clashed with the militia companies moving in, but none of the actions seemed to involve more than a single squad of raiders—patrols or a rear guard covering the withdrawal of the rest of their force. It was impossible to be certain which.

Lon set up a commanders' conference on the radio, with Colonel Crampton and all of the commanders from the DMC and the BCM, going over the plan he had devised. On the south, two militia companies would press west, beyond the burned-over area and the clearing that the raiders had used for a landing strip. On the north, three of Lon's companies would push west. The two forces would curve in toward a rendezvous a mile beyond the clearing. Alpha Company and the militia's 2nd Company would hold positions along the ridge to complete the circle.

Lon hoped to trap the raiders within that circle. Once it was complete, mercenaries and militiamen would draw it tighter, aiming to force combat and neutralize this raider force. Once armed opposition ended, they could turn to searching the line of hills for the cave system Lon suspected had to be there, serving as a base for the raiders. If the raiders had already withdrawn the men who had been in the area, the combined force of Dirigenters and Bancrofters would establish a solid perimeter, then go to work searching for the caves. They would cover as much of this line of hills as necessary to find those caves . . . or be certain they did not exist.

"What if their main force is here and we get more than you seem to be bargaining for?" Colonel Crampton asked after Lon had laid out the essentials.

"We're *hoping* to draw their main force into battle, Colonel," Lon replied. "I'll have six Shrike fighters to provide close ground support, as well as the guns and rockets of four of our attack shuttles, once we can cut down on the odds of the raiders using SAMs to bring the aircraft down. My guess is that the raiders will offer combat early once we start pressing—if their main force is concealed in caves here—rather than risk having the same thing happen to them that happened to the raiders nine years back."

"You really think they *know* what happened then?" Colonel Crampton asked, clearly skeptical.

"It's virtually certain, Colonel," Lon said. "My best estimate is that they knew about it before this new incursion was launched, a year ago. That knowledge most likely influenced their planning for this new attack on Bancroft."

Crampton hesitated before he said, "I must confess I still have my doubts about that, but I can see that we have to proceed on the assumption that it's possible."

Bravo Company arrived, carrying part of the resupply for Alpha and Charlie. Ammunition and food packs were distributed. Men ate while they could. Bravo and Charlie started shifting into position for their thrust westward. Delta Company was climbing the eastern slope of the ridge. The extra supplies they carried would be left with Alpha and 2nd Companies. Colonel Crampton's other two companies had gone into a temporary defensive perimeter, waiting for the attacking force to be complete. Company commanders briefed their platoon leaders and noncoms. Sergeants briefed platoons and squads.

"Colonel, I've never been in a fight as big as this one looks to be," Corporal Howell said. He had kept busy through the afternoon, passing messages both ways, assisting Lon as he normally did.

"You starting to think better about your choice to come along?" Lon asked, turning his head toward Howell.

"This *is* where I should be," Howell said, "but I think my stomach's tied itself in about three knots."

"I know the feeling." Lon closed his eyes for an instant. *Even if we get slammed completely here, there'll at least be a few people back in Lincoln to get the message out.* Vel, Phip, and most of the headquarters detachment were still there. And the ships overhead. News would get home. *I don't want to go down in the history of the Corps as the commander of the worst defeat since 9th Regiment was destroyed on Wellman,* Lon thought. The 9th had never been re-formed. The Corps consisted of fourteen regiments, but there was no number nine—and never would be again.

Gloomy thoughts had often plagued Lon before action. After two decades as a professional soldier there was still a part of his mind that recoiled at what combat offered—*threatened*—*promised*—fear, injury, death. Why would anyone risk that? Duty. Dedication. Patriotism. The men of the DMC might be mercenaries, but serving in the Corps was still an act of service to their world. Soldiers and military matériel were the stock in trade of Dirigent. It did not have significant deposits of rare metals and minerals to offer. At times it had to import the products of better-endowed planets. Like Bancroft. Without the Corps and the munitions industry that had grown up beside it, Dirigent would still be an agricultural world, a small colony with perhaps no more than 10 percent of its current population—vulnerable, prey to any predator that came around.

With all that, how can I possibly keep Junior from join-

ing the Corps when he's old enough? Lon wondered, and the intrusion of that old worry shook him from his morose meandering. Colonel Crampton had a son as well, and the younger Crampton was clearly following in his father's professional footsteps.

There's no reason to think this will go that badly, Lon told himself. *We've got the manpower and heavy weapons overhead. Even if we were outnumbered, we ought to be able to hold our own.*

Delta arrived. Lon told Captain Magnusson to give his men fifteen minutes to rest and eat before moving down the western side of the hill to join Bravo Company for the push. Then Lon alerted Colonel Crampton and all of the company commanders in the combined force that they would be beginning their push in forty-five minutes. Lon ate a quick meal himself, forcing the food in. His mouth was dry. The food needed a lot of water to wash it down. There was nothing novel in that, either. The best food in the galaxy would have been hard to eat just then.

Lon took the magazine from his rifle, jacked the cartridge out of the chamber, and looked down the barrel to make sure it wasn't plugged—an inspection instigated by nerves. He put a full magazine in and ran the rifle's bolt to put a shell back into the firing chamber, then looked to make certain the rifle's safety was on. He took his pistol from its holster and ran a similar check. The handgun's magazine was full, so he merely put it back in. He was ready.

Twenty-five minutes remained before his force started trying to close the horns around the raiders in the valley.

Ten minutes before the designated time, Lon's palms were sweating enough to annoy him. He wiped them on his trouser legs. Although he would remain in place, far from the greatest danger, he was at least as nervous as he would have been had he been in the spearhead, walking point toward an expected ambush.

The patrols he had sent out earlier had pinpointed the location of several small raider groups, but nothing that looked as if it might be the main body. "Looks like they left outposts," Tebba said when he passed the reports to Lon. Girana was acting as Lon's second-in-command in the field. "No more than a squad each place, with snoops and mines planted to give them warning of anyone approaching. We were lucky not to trip any of the mines."

"What about their snoops?" Lon asked. "Our patrols give themselves away?"

Tebba was too far away for Lon to see him shrug. "Probably, but we didn't pick up any emissions from the snoops our patrols spotted."

"If we get a chance to do it safely later, I want one or two of those snoops," Lon said. "Give the labs back home something to play with. Maybe they can pick up something to improve our gear." "Safely" was the key word. A man couldn't simply pluck an enemy snoop from the ground and stick it in his pack. The odds were at least even that it would be booby-trapped.

"I want those outposts targeted," Lon said. "We drop a couple of grenades on top of each of them right as we kick off the operation."

"Already coordinated that, on both ends, Lon," Tebba said.

Lon changed channels to speak with Colonel Crampton. "Sixty seconds, Colonel. Your men ready to move?"

"Ready."

Again, Lon switched channels to connect to all of his company commanders. He was watching the timeline on his visor's head-up display. "Thirty seconds."

When those seconds had elapsed, Lon's order went to Colonel Crampton and all of the company commanders in both units: "Go!"

•   •   •

From Lon's position, there was no immediate sign of movement. It might take several minutes before he would see blips moving on his mapboard or on the overlay of position blips he could cycle onto his head-up display. The first clear indications he had of action were the sounds of grenade launchers firing RPGs, and the whistles of the projectiles as they arced toward their targets. The explosions came in a tightly grouped series of explosions—the flash of blasts, the noise of detonation, the ripping of shrapnel, occasionally the cracking of a tree limb, small clouds of whitish smoke. A second volley of grenades sounded more ragged. The explosions were not as closely spaced as the first.

Scattered gunshots—the heavier-caliber weapons that the raiders used—sounded. The reply sounded uncoordinated, and there were not many shots.

Lon shook his head as he scanned the valley. *I've got a feeling most of them pulled out,* he thought, *that they just left enough men behind to keep us occupied. If they hit somewhere else tonight while I've got all my men and a third of the militia tied up here, we could have trouble responding quickly enough.* He had discussed that possibility with Colonel Crampton before committing so many men to this operation, and Crampton had been even more convinced than Lon that they had to do it.

"Looks like the best chance we've had to do a significant number of the bastards" was how Crampton had put it.

Lon heard the deeper explosion of a land mine to the south. A militia squad had tripped it, though it was nearly five minutes later before Corporal Howell could relay details to Lon. Three men had been killed and five wounded by the blast. That squad and several medics stayed where they were while the next squad took over the point and kept moving—a little more slowly, far more cautiously.

On the north, the advance stopped for two minutes while the point squad used hand grenades to trip a mine they had spotted. It took several attempts to set it off.

Flanking patrols on both sides ranged farther from the main advances, looking for any indication that the raiders had pulled out along the valley. They left electronic snoops every hundred yards or so to leave a warning system in place. Extra snoops had been among the supplies brought in by Bravo and Delta Companies.

Half an hour after the start of the advance, the leading company on the north came under fire—a barrage of RPGs accompanied by rifle fire that was intense for several minutes . . . and then ended completely as the raider patrol that had launched the attack disengaged. Casualties in Charlie Company were light, but two men were dead. The attack was enough to slow the advance. It was all too possible that the raiders would set up a second ambush.

Lon linked to Tebba Girana and Lieutenant Crampton. "Let's start moving down the slope," Lon said. "No rush. Make sure your men are paying attention to any holes that might lead into a cave system here. We find anything like that, we stay above it, make sure the raiders can't come out behind us."

One platoon from Alpha Company and one platoon from Lieutenant Crampton's 2nd Company would remain near the ridgeline as a rear guard.

Lon's knees felt stiff from lying almost motionless for so long. His first few steps were awkward, almost painful. He stumbled and slid, but Jeremy Howell was close enough to steady his boss. Lon nodded his thanks.

"You're too close to me, Jerry. You forgotten everything about proper spacing?" Lon said, as gently as he could.

"Yes, sir, I guess I have," Howell said, the tinted faceplate of his helmet masking his grin. He moved to the side a couple of paces, but before they had gone ten yards, he had cut that separation in half. Lon noticed but said nothing.

Halfway down the slope, Lon halted the movement of his men to allow the militia company to catch up. The lower half of the hill was more thickly wooded, with taller, thicker trees and fuller greenery. The line was still above the valley canopy, but looking out through trunks and foliage around them. With limbs and leaves overhead, the temperature felt several degrees cooler—a relief after lying in the sun for so many hours.

It took 2nd Company five minutes to get back into position. Lon told Tebba to slow Alpha's pace as they started moving again. The two companies had descended only another twenty yards before Tebba signaled that his men had found a concealed opening, and Lon halted both companies. They were still slightly above the forest canopy of the valley floor.

"We'll set up our line here," Lon told Tebba and Wilson Crampton. "Above that opening, and give it some room. Looks like we've got more soil to work with, so have the men dig in as well as they can."

"You want us to investigate that opening?" Tebba asked after switching channels to talk privately with Lon.

"We're not sending anyone inside," Lon said quickly. "Not while we've got the rest of this to worry about. Have your men hang a snoop into the entrance if they can do it without exposing themselves. And set up a couple of command-detonated mines in case we have to deal with a sortie from that opening."

"I'm going to move over to where they found the opening and have a look for myself," Tebba said. "And you don't have to tell me to be careful. I'm not going to stick anything out to get shot off."

"Yeah, well, I'll tell you anyway. Be careful. You do want to retire in one piece when the time comes." Inescapably, Lon toyed with the idea of going to have a look at the hole in the hill himself, but common sense held him where he was. That sort of operation was no longer his business. He had more than fourteen hundred men to worry about—his own battalion and Colonel Crampton's militiamen.

The sun was low enough in the west to shoot beams under the trees on the hillside. Bright sunlight and deepening shadows, extreme contrasts that taxed the ability of helmet optics to resolve satisfactorily. Lon found himself minimizing the polarity of his faceplate so that the shadows could hide nothing, then squinting against the sun.

Lon was still waiting for a report on the hole when Captain Roim called from *Long Snake:* "That unidentified ship has altered course again and it's accelerating—it looks like full out. It's either going to use Bancroft to slingshot it out of the system, or it's going in close to launch shuttles or fighters. If it holds course, it'll come within one hundred and fifty miles of the surface at its closest approach—four hundred miles southwest of your location—in a little more than three hours."

"Is either *Long Snake* or *Taranto* in position to intercept?" Lon asked.

"Beamers and missiles, at far more than optimal range. If that ship has a hardened skin, the way ours do, our weapons probably won't be enough to stop it. *Taranto* can't get Shrikes close enough to do the job either—not before that ship reaches the likely launch point, if that's what it intends."

"What about the Shrikes we've got down here? Can they get up to intercept?" Lon asked.

"Wrong munitions load," Roim said, so quickly that he had to have considered the possibility before. "The missiles they're carrying aren't designed for antiship use. They're carrying ground-support warheads."

"They could deal with shuttles, if that's what the ship

launches," Lon said. "Keep them from getting down here to cause us grief."

"*Taranto* is set to launch Shrikes to intercept anything that ship drops," Roim said. "If necessary, *Taranto* can put eight Shrikes out, though that might short you on cover later. It's your call, Colonel."

"I'm not going to overrule the experts, Captain," Lon said. "We'll do it the way you laid it out. Maybe you'll get lucky and cripple that ship."

"At least we should be able to keep it from crippling us, Colonel," Roim said. "She doesn't show any obvious armament, and if we're too far away to be certain of hurting her, there's even less chance for her to hurt us."

"We've got that hole ringed and ready to plug, Lon," Tebba reported several minutes later. "It does look like a cave. I inspected it through the snoop's optics and couldn't see how far it goes. The opening is large enough for two men to go through standing up. Then the hole slopes down and to the south."

"I don't want it plugged, except in an emergency, Tebba. Just as long as we can slam anyone trying to come out hard."

"We've got two mines in place, and several extras close enough to stop a second or third attempt."

"Good enough." Lon told Tebba about the extra ship coming toward them. "My guess is they're going to launch reinforcements—either troops or aerospace fighters."

"How large is that ship?" Tebba asked. "What's the most trouble they might be able to throw at us?"

"CIC says maybe four hundred men if they've got them packed in," Lon said. "That's just a guess, though. They still haven't matched it against any known types."

"They check that database you brought back from Earth?" Tebba asked.

"I'm sure they did. It's in the computer."

• • •

It was three hours past sunset before the ring was complete. There had been nothing more than scattered skirmishes during the movement of mercenaries and militiamen. They had not encountered any opposition larger than squad strength. Nor had anyone seen evidence that there might be several hundred of the enemy inside the extended perimeter.

"I know we have to check it out," Brock Carlin said during a conference that included the two colonels and all of the company commanders, "but the feeling I have is that we've got a lot of nothing. The raiders must have pulled out early."

"Don't let that feeling make you careless, Brock," Lon said. "We'll pull the perimeter in the way we planned, but move as if you knew there was a battalion of soldiers in there somewhere, with mines and booby traps every step of the way. We *know* these raiders have planted some of those.

"We leave half the men in position, watching in and out," Lon continued. "Move the rest in slowly, toward the ridge. I don't want anyone rushing this. We'll take all the time we need to do the job right. Mines, booby traps, snoops. There might even be snipers left, or cave entrances. Those don't have to be in the side of the hill. They could be anywhere, a small hole in the ground leading down to maybe an intricate system of caves. Check everything!"

"When do we start?" Colonel Crampton asked.

Lon hesitated. "Some of the men have been on the go for nearly twenty-four hours. Much as I want to get this operation finished, we've got to let everyone get some rest. We put the men on half-and-half watches, and bed down until dawn—unless the raiders decide not to let us take that much time."

Lon was surprised that the night *did* pass without major

incident. There were only a couple of shots fired by snipers well outside the perimeter. No one was hit. Most of the men managed to get at least some sleep during the night. Even Lon got a couple of hours.

24

Lon did not get nearly as much sleep as he had hoped. He had been wakened by news of the strange ship in the system. The plan to intercept it, or any shuttles or fighters it might launch, had failed. "I don't know whether that ship's captain is a genius or a suicidal fool," Captain Eldon Roim said when he gave Lon the news. "Maybe he's a little of each."

The ship had made several more course corrections, aiming closer to the edge of Bancroft's atmosphere, and had continued accelerating, long past the time when the computers in the Dirigenter ships said it would have to start braking or change course to avoid going too close to the planet—to avoid being burned up in the atmosphere like a meteorite. The ship had launched six of the small attack shuttles the Dirigenters had seen before forty minutes sooner than CIC expected, so the plan to intercept them became impossible. The ship itself—its skin glowing red from heat friction in the thin upper atmosphere—had come to within forty miles of Bancroft's surface, still accelerating, before its speed and course carried it out of range of the DMC ships and Shrikes.

"Our computers went haywire over the data," Roim said. "By every standard I know, that ship should have broken up or burned."

"Forty miles, that's still pretty high, isn't it?" Lon asked. "I mean, there's not a hell of a lot of air that far above the surface. Even twenty miles up you're basically talking a pretty damned good vacuum. There's certainly not enough air to breathe. Why not take a ship that close?"

"That ship was traveling forty thousand miles an hour when it got that low, sixty percent above escape velocity," Roim said, his voice rising in what sounded like complete indignation. "There are still enough molecules at forty miles to do major damage to an object that large moving that fast, more damage than I could expect a full salvo of every energy weapon aboard our three ships to do."

"So he did something we couldn't do . . . or wouldn't attempt," Lon said. "What's the ship doing right now?"

"It has stopped accelerating," Roim said after a slight pause. "It even appears to be decelerating slightly, now that it's safely out of our reach."

"What about the shuttles it launched? Were you able to track them to where they landed?"

Roim's hesitation was considerably longer this time. "We weren't able to track them all the way in," he admitted. "A combination of factors—the early launch point, the course the shuttles took, electronic countermeasures used by both ship and shuttles. Damn it, Colonel, we just weren't ready for what they did. That's the up and the down of it. They caught us with our pants down."

"It happens," Lon said. "We'll just have to deal with it."

"On the plus side, Colonel, we *are* making progress with our analysis of the raiders' stealth technology. The lab got its best clue from the captured helmets you sent up. They use white-noise generators to cancel out electronic emissions. The algorithm appears to be orders of magnitude better than what we can manage—and that's just from empirical testing. We haven't been able to crack the code yet and may never be able to. Assuming that the same basic technology is used in their shuttles, that minimal static we've been able to detect on some occasions is the extent of the lag between emissions and blanketing, or some slight imperfection in the implementation of the technology. With helmet electronics the lag is too small for us to find it at any distance. Your men have had to be, what, within fifty yards to catch any of it? Ten years ago we wouldn't have been able to detect as much as we can now. Ten years from now we might be able to do better. I don't suppose there's enough left of the two shuttles you destroyed to give us much help."

"Not much. After the explosions, both burned. We get a chance, we can have technicians look it over, but I wouldn't expect much."

"My tech officer would love to get his hands on an intact specimen, Colonel. He was salivating at the prospect."

Lon chuckled. "We'll try to accommodate him, Captain."

Another six armed shuttles on the surface—somewhere—in addition to however many more the raiders already had. Perhaps as many as 350 additional soldiers—also in addition to previous assets; the raider shuttles were smaller than those the DMC used. Munitions and supplies. Lon shook his head as he thought through the possibilities. *And no idea where the hell they might be.*

"Nothing we can do about it right now," Lon whispered to himself. "We've still got whatever forces the raiders have in this area to worry about." But he was unable to get back to sleep. He gave Colonel Crampton the tactical news, and mentioned it to Tebba Girana when he called Lon an hour before dawn.

"At least we know they've dropped those shuttles," Tebba said. "We can quit worrying what that ship might or might not do. Gives us an upper limit."

"For now. Nothing says that ship can't come back and drop more shuttles. Or do something bizarre."

"Lon, you can't worry about the movement of every

atom in the galaxy. That'll drive you crazy."

"I know, Tebba. It's just hard to know where to draw the line sometimes."

Draw the line. Lon fixated on that for several minutes after cutting the link to Girana. Lon's men and the militiamen with them had drawn one line, encompassing a large section of the valley and the western flank of the next line of hills. There were at least two hundred of the enemy somewhere in the vicinity, though Lon was no longer hopeful that those raiders might actually be inside the territory his men had staked out.

There must be a base under these hills, he told himself. *It's probably not the* only *raider base, and it might not even be the* main *base, but it* has *to be here. They had those shuttles parked in the valley, and they had at least a company of men to guard them.* No other explanation fit those circumstances. There had to be an underground enemy base close.

Forty-five minutes before local sunrise, Lon passed the word to wake the men and get them ready for the morning's search. He ate a meal pack and did what he could in the field to make himself presentable with a little water and a lot of scouring. He even shaved.

Morning's shadows were still long when Lon gave the order to start searching the area within the perimeter. It was a painstakingly slow process, requiring men to literally look at every square foot of ground in an area of a thousand acres. After two hours Lon *knew* there were no raiders on the ground—on the surface—within the perimeter. As the circle contracted, he started moving patrols outside the original perimeter, looking for traces of which way the raiders might have gone, other than underground.

Two patrols had contact with enemy patrols, or lone snipers. Those incidents were widely separated.

"What about that cave entrance your men found last

night?" Colonel Crampton asked. "When do we explore that?"

"Not yet," Lon said. "I've got a supply shuttle alerted to bring down our echo-ranging gear. We've got the clearing on this side secured now, out far enough to minimize the chance of a raider getting a lucky shot with a shoulder-launched missile. We can do some mapping from the air, close in, and use equipment on the ground to get a more accurate picture. We map any openings we find on this side of the ridge. As soon as it's feasible, we send men to start looking for openings on the other side, and set up a perimeter there. Then we map any caves in the entire zone."

"Like you did nine years ago?" Crampton asked.

"Similar. The principle is the same, but what we have now is somewhat more sophisticated. We stick probes in the ground around the entire area, then use one large shock and measure the results." Lon paused. "Instead of doing it dozens of times to map out one small section at a time."

"How soon do we get to this mapping?"

"Unless we run into trouble, we should be set by the middle of the afternoon."

"More waiting, doing damned little constructive?"

"It's *very* constructive, Colonel," Lon said, trying not to let Crampton's impatience annoy him. "We'll have a large cleared area inside our perimeter then, have any obvious cave entrances marked, and be ready to take action once we have a map of any extended underground system. If the raiders we encountered yesterday are above ground and within three miles of our perimeter, our patrols should have them located by then." He paused. "There have been no new reports of raids elsewhere, and Long Glen remains secure."

"The raiders were able to land reinforcements without challenge," Crampton said.

"Only because that ship's skipper took a desperate

chance," Lon said. "An *insane* chance, according to the skipper of *Long Snake*. The fact that he dared do what he did should be proof enough that we're making a difference. He risked a large transport ship and however many hundreds of people were aboard on a one-in-a-million maneuver. Actually, I find the fact that the enemy is that desperate pretty damned encouraging." *Now,* after the fact, after losing sleep over the possibilities.

"Maybe," Crampton conceded. "Oh, hell, I just hate sitting around like this, waiting for something to happen."

"I know what you mean, but we're going at this the best way we can, slow and methodical. In the long run, that'll get the job done and keep the casualties to a minimum."

Slowly. Methodically. Painstakingly. It was past noon when the supply shuttle landed. Lon had men stationed near the clearing and well out along the craft's approach to provide security. The shuttle landed and unloaded gear for the attempt to map any subterranean voids—and two technicians from *Long Snake*'s crew to operate the equipment and help interpret the results.

Alpha Company and the militia 2nd Company had started searching the eastern slope of the ridge. By 1300 hours, two more companies of militia had joined that effort. By that time, more than four hours had passed without any contact at all with the raiders—not a patrol or a sniper. The Dirigenter patrols ranging out from the perimeter in all directions had found nothing to indicate the passage of large numbers of the enemy.

"You think they must have gone into the caves, then?" Colonel Crampton asked Lon during a conference that included all of the company commanders.

"It's possible, but I wouldn't say it's certain," Lon replied. "It wouldn't be impossible for even two or three hundred men to get beyond the area we've patrolled without leaving clear sign. Or our patrols might simply have missed the track they followed. We have to assume that they could hit us without a hell of a lot of warning."

"If we find that there is an extensive cave system under this ridge, with maybe several hundred enemy inside, do we handle it the same as the last time you were here?" Crampton asked. "Block all the exits but one and wait for them to come out?"

Crampton could not see Lon's frown. "I don't think so, not right away. My idea is to block *all* of the exits at once, dump enough rock over the openings to make it impossible for anyone to get out without days of digging. Listen for the sounds of that kind of work. Leave just enough men on site to man the equipment and warn us if the raiders try to bring in more assets to dig out anyone trapped. We can come back later to uncork the caves—and see if there's anyone left alive in them."

"Bury them alive?"

"We lost too many men doing it the other way, Colonel," Lon said. "If there are going to be casualties, I'd prefer they were the enemy."

The naval petty officer who came to report to Lon had a disgusted look on his face.

"There may be a cave system like you're looking for somewhere along this line of hills, Colonel, but you're not sitting on it," the petty officer said. "We got good echoes over quite an area—call it two thousand yards along the ridge and twelve hundred yards wide, extending into the valleys on both sides. There are a lot of little holes, but not connected. The largest gap we found is behind that opening you marked yesterday, and the one chamber in there is only forty feet in diameter, and part of that seems to be under water. No way several hundred men could be using it as a base. And, yes, before you ask, I'm sure, one hundred percent positive. Sorry, Colonel, you just don't have the right spot."

Lon nodded. He *had* been about to ask, knowing the question would have been . . . foolish. "We'll get you back up to *Long Snake*," Lon said instead. "You and your assistant. Thanks for the help."

The petty officer laughed. "Anytime, Colonel. This little detour qualifies us for a day's hazardous-duty bonus."

"Now what?" Colonel Crampton asked after the technicians had started down the hill toward the shuttle that was waiting to take them back to their ship.

"I don't think we're that far off target," Lon said. "Assuming that the prisoners we questioned were using that clearing down there, they said they were in a cave about an hour's march from the LZ, and the caves were east of where they got on and off the shuttle."

"We're too close," Crampton said. "Men could hike from the bottom of the slope below us to that clearing in thirty minutes or so if they weren't worried about running into enemy soldiers or some kind of trap."

"More or less," Lon agreed.

"So, what?" Crampton asked. "We hike up and down this line of hills looking for them? Or do we start thinking this isn't the place those prisoners were talking about?"

"Even if it isn't the place they were talking about, we know the enemy had two shuttles based here, along with fuel, crews, and more than a company of men to guard them—more like two companies. Even if we might have missed where those men went yesterday, if they've been here for any length of time, going back and forth between that clearing and their camp—under the ground or above it—there has to be a trail we can find."

"You figure to keep fourteen hundred men here looking?"

"A little longer, at least," Lon said. "Maintain our lookouts and hope to give everyone a chance to get more sleep tonight. Resume the search in the morning. Leave a third of the combined force here to maintain this position, split the rest to search both north and south along the ridge and in the valley, most on this side, a few on the eastern side. Put some of my best trackers starting at the clearing, looking for the cave—or whatever—the raiders used for the men who stayed here to service and protect the shuttles. I think we've got a damned good chance of finding that site.

"What else would we do—go back to barracks and sit around until the raiders start hitting villages again?" Lon asked. "Unless we're needed somewhere else, I think this is the best place for us—at least through the next day or two. I'll have Shrikes and shuttles in the air looking for the men who got away from us yesterday as well. We don't want to forget about them."

"Between two and three hundred?" Crampton hesitated for a few seconds. "No, we don't want to forget about them, but they could be thirty or forty miles away by now—or anywhere on the continent if they got somewhere their shuttles could pick them up."

Lon shook his head vigorously. "Not this time, Colonel. We kept too close a watch on the few clearings large enough to let a shuttle land anywhere they could have reached on foot. We spot them, we go for them, try to force them to fight or surrender . . . and the raiders haven't shown any great tendencies to surrender."

"No, they haven't," Crampton agreed.

"When we do meet them, I want the best odds possible going for us. That makes for fewer casualties among our men."

Lon lowered the level of alert for his men for the night. There would be no long-range patrols. Electronic snoops had been planted roughly two hundred yards from the perimeter, with enough land mines to make infiltration dangerous for any enemy force. And, instead of keeping half the men on watch at a time, he cut it to one-third—two men out of each fire team, four men per squad. With nearly eleven hours between sunset and sunrise, that would give everyone a chance for something close to a full night's sleep . . . if there were no alarms.

Maybe I'll even manage to catch up a little on my sleep, Lon thought. He set no regular watches for himself. One of his company commanders would always be awake, "on duty" to respond instantly to anything, to handle any questions. Gunfire, any noise, would wake Lon. Even dreamed noises might do that.

One squad from Tebba's company had been designated to provide security for the battalion commander—Lon—a final line of defense. They were arranged around him near the crest of the ridge. The squad, with the help of Jeremy Howell, had already spent several hours "improving" the position, scraping out trenches, moving rocks to provide more cover, even felling trees to use their trunks and larger branches as part of the defensive shield. Although they were far from the outer perimeter of the combined force, that squad would maintain the same level of alert as the rest, four men on watch at all times.

Lon spent nearly a half hour conferring with Major Osterman in Lincoln, and with the captains of the three Dirigenter ships overhead. The fourth ship near Bancroft, proven hostile by its actions, had moved to a position far enough from the Dirigenter vessels to make interception impossible, and had decelerated, assuming a highly eccentric elliptical orbit of the world.

Just give us a quiet night, Lon thought as he arranged himself in his blanket to try to sleep. *A quiet night and a measure of success tomorrow.*

He was tired enough that he got to sleep almost immediately.

25

The dreams came. They did not wake Lon, but did trouble his sleep. His groans were too soft for even the sentries nearest him to hear. Lon had gone to sleep wearing his helmet, the faceplate closed. The nightmare was an impossible mixture of reality and fantasy, set against a backdrop that had never happened. He saw himself and Lon, Junior; Matt Orlis and his dead son; Wesley Crampton and his son Wilson. They were all together in one location—which had never happened, *could* never happen. The affair seemed to be a father-and-son picnic at some undefinable location. Lon, Junior, looked much as he had when Lon had last seen him. Matt's boy looked to be about the same age, as did Wilson Crampton. Lon had known the younger Orlis at that age but had obviously not known Wilson Crampton as a teenager. There were games and races—all very pleasant—until . . .

It started almost imperceptibly, discoloration of the faces, but only in small splotches that grew slowly. Then there were bloodstains, missing limbs, screams of terror. It struck all three boys: Orlis first, then Crampton, and finally—despite Lon's silent screaming denials—his own son. When he saw all three boys laid out in a row, mangled and bloody, Lon woke in a cold sweat, trembling violently, clenching his teeth against a final scream that fought to erupt from his throat. Lon clenched his teeth and held himself as rigidly still as he could until the tremors subsided.

He squeezed his eyes shut. His heart was beating wildly. His lungs fought for air. The throbbing in his head subsided, but all too slowly.

Five minutes passed before Lon felt able to relax his body and open his eyes. The pale glow of the timeline at the top of his head-up display read 0358.

More than seven hours of sleep, he thought. *I don't often get that much at home in my own bed.* He did not feel rested, though. His breathing was not back to normal yet, and neither was his heart rate. "Damn." He had not intended to speak the word, but it came out on its own, soft but with some force behind it. *This isn't the time to worry about what Junior will do in the future. I've got enough to worry about right here.*

It was 0411 when Lon got the call from *Long Snake.* "Colonel, we have a sighting of men moving toward your position, east of the ridgeline and approximately two point five miles south of your perimeter. At least a company in strength. One of the Shrikes spotted them crossing a bare patch of slope. The pilot wasn't certain how much of the van he might have missed, but he saw enough to say that there are least two hundred."

"Thanks, and thank the pilot for me," Lon said. He had sat up while he was listening to the call. "Have everyone keep a close watch for other movements."

"Of course, Colonel. The weather is liable to get rotten where you are in a couple of hours. We're tracking a major cold front, and there are heavy thunderstorms now about forty miles west of you, moving at about twenty miles per hour. The cloud cover extends west more than four hundred miles."

"Which means you wouldn't be able to detect enemy shuttles anywhere under the weather."

"Sorry, Colonel, but we haven't been able to refine our search enough for that."

"I know, and I know you'll do what you can. Thanks."

Lon called Colonel Crampton first with the news. Crampton was also awake, and said he had been up for more than two hours. "I'm not all that used to roughing it," Crampton admitted. "I tossed and turned all night."

"Let's get all the company commanders on the link," Lon said. "We know there's at least one company of raiders heading toward us, and my guess is that they've got more coming from somewhere. Maybe those shuttles that made it down last night. They could hit the ground close enough to let their troops hit us at the same time as this other batch."

"How do you propose to respond?" Crampton asked.

"Circle the force we've located so they can't run away, then pound the hell out of them from air and ground until they surrender or can't cause trouble," Lon said. "Keep enough men in our current perimeter to make certain we're ready for any surprises on this side of the ridge."

"How many men do we send? All we have is a minimum on the enemy force, not a maximum. You don't want to send too few to handle the situation."

"We don't have to outnumber them on the ground, Colonel. I'm going to have four Shrikes and three attack shuttles available to provide close-in cover and hit the raiders from the air. I figure we send two platoons of my men and one of your companies east, to get below the slope and the enemy force. Send the same numbers along the western slope, ready to bend around behind the enemy. Hold off until they get close enough for our perimeter to use men on it to complete the ring."

"Okay," Crampton said.

"Fifteen minutes give you enough time to get your companies alerted?" Lon asked.

"I'll make it enough."

Lon selected two platoons from Bravo and two platoons from Delta. Crampton sent his 2nd and 3rd Companies.

They rendezvoused and started moving twenty minutes after the conclusion of the short conference the colonels held with their company commanders.

Lon vetoed the idea of hitting the enemy force from the air prematurely. "I *want* them to keep coming," he had told the commanders during their conference. "We start hitting them now, they might disappear again, and I want to take care of that force for good, all at once, while we've got the chance, not just chase them off."

The enemy's line of march was observed as closely as possible from the air. Three pilots were already on the job, staying high enough to avoid becoming targets, low enough to catch an occasional glimpse of men moving north along the slope of the line of hills. The men on the ground appeared to be taking no special precautions to stay out of sight.

That brought a frown to Lon's face. "They've never been that careless before," he confided to Tebba Girana. "Even if they were confident of surprise, you'd think they'd take elementary precautions to avoid detection. It's as if they *want* to be found, want our attention focused on them."

"If they're only one part of a coordinated attack on us, they might want us to look just at them," Tebba said. "Maybe draw all our people out of defensive positions. Maybe they want to end this game as badly as we do."

"Makes you wonder, though, just how many more men they think they can concentrate against us," Lon said. "Six shuttles, maybe three hundred men, wouldn't be enough— even conceding that this force we're watching might have as many as six hundred in it."

"Maybe there *are* caves with more men in them, out past where we searched, but still close by," Tebba said.

"I haven't forgotten that," Lon said. "There could be cave entrances within eighty or a hundred yards of the perimeter."

"Or closer," Tebba said. "I remember how well hid that one you found last time was. You said you damn near missed it from ten feet away."

"That's why we took so much time making sure there weren't any holes inside our lines yesterday," Lon said. "And why I had snoops put out so close to the perimeter."

"How much time you figure we've got before they hit?"

"A couple of hours, at least," Lon said. "I don't think they'll be able to manage anything before sunrise. They can bring their shuttles as close as possible under cover of the storms, put the men on the ground within five or six miles if they can—two hours' march. Of course, those people might not hit the same time as the others. If there are men underground closer, we could get hit first by the ones we can see, then the troglodytes, and finally this supposed force coming in by shuttle."

"Troglo-what?" Tebba asked.

Lon laughed. "Troglodytes, cave dwellers."

"No words that big in the *DMC Manual*," Tebba said.

Men ate breakfast while they could, scooping food in as if the attack might come any second. Dawn—a gloomy lightening of the night. The approaching storms were close enough that flashes of lightning were visible over the peaks of the next line of hills to the west. Thunder rumbled across the valley. *Thunder or heavy artillery,* Lon thought, *they sound so much alike at a distance.* That brought a memory of Earth and his days at The Springs, the military academy of the North American Union. During the summer after his third year, Lon had spent six weeks at the army's primary artillery training facility in the South Plains District—in what had once been the state of Oklahoma. Lon and the two hundred other cadets had been exposed to every kind of artillery the NAU army possessed, all the way up to 255mm self-propelled howitzers and the various types of rocket artillery. The noise was the dominant memory, extreme even with high-tech ear protection.

The rain arrived, light, windblown squalls followed by the heavier, more persistent thunderstorms. Those seemed to come in waves, each more intense than its predecessor, with only brief easing of the rain and wind to mark the progression.

"The rain's liable to continue all day," Lon warned his company commanders. "Thunderstorms off and on. Maybe some hail now and then. And CIC says a couple of the storm cells are intense enough that there's a possibility of tornadoes."

"Tornadoes?" Captain Magnusson of Delta repeated. "You've got to be kidding."

"A possibility, Ron," Lon said. "Only a possibility."

"Yeah, but how do we deal with a tornado if one does hit?"

"Hunker down and ride it out," Lon said. "Pick up the pieces afterward. There's nothing we can do about the weather. It's not going to stop the raiders, and we can't let it stop us. Our Shrikes can operate in just about anything except a funnel cloud, and Shrikes have the speed and maneuverability to stay away from them without completely leaving the area. Don't get sidetracked by the chance, and don't spend your time staring at the sky looking for one. If a tornado does appear, we'll have a little warning. The greater danger is lightning. This isn't a training mission back on Dirigent, where we can cancel training to avoid an electrical storm."

"We proceed according to plan in spite of the weather?" Tebba Girana said.

"Yes," Lon confirmed. "The rain is going to be an inconvenience, but it hits the raiders the same as it hits us, and they might not be as well prepared as we are. Stay low, stay focused. Visibility is going to be minimal. We might have to go to our night-vision gear if it gets too bad."

The units that had to move were on the way. The men who were remaining in the perimeter had shifted to cover the gaps left by the mercenaries and militiamen who were on their way to intercept the raiders coming north along the eastern slope of the ridge. Lon expected the first contact to come within the next ten or fifteen minutes.

The rain. Dirigenter battledress uniforms were designed to shed water rather than absorb it, but the protection was not quite total over extended exposure. In time, the fabric would begin to absorb water rather than repel it. And despite the best care, there could be some infiltration of water at the neck and wrists. But it was better than nothing. Dirigenter battle helmets shed most of the water that hit them past the neck. Faceplates were treated to prevent water from beading on them. An occasional wipe kept visibility from becoming impossible.

Mud was a problem only in the valley and on the lowest stretch of the slope, but the ground became soft and mushy wherever the rocky spine of the ridge had gathered soil.

CIC radioed Lon that the enemy ship was moving again, coming in toward the planet on a course similar to the one it had followed to deploy the shuttles. "We don't anticipate them launching significant reinforcements," Captain Roim of *Long Snake* said. "They shouldn't have many more shuttles available, likely just enough for the crew."

"Then why come in again at all?" Lon asked.

"It's possible that they might try to launch missiles at you," Roim said, "but our best guess is that the ship is merely a decoy, trying to draw our attention away from the action at your location, maybe hoping to get us to divert Shrikes from close air support to chase the ship."

Lon hesitated. "It would be nice to zap that ship, Captain, for a number of reasons."

"I agree, but . . . it's iffy at best, Colonel. Even if we

pulled all our Shrikes and spread them to give us our best shot at intercepting, we couldn't be certain of destroying or disabling that ship, and we'd rob you of most of your air cover."

"We can't go that far, Captain. Too many men on the ground here, but if we could move *Taranto* a little closer to the course that ship is on, maybe deploy four or six Shrikes, we might get lucky."

"We'll do what we can."

Mercenaries and militiamen reached their positions around the raider force—which had slowed its advance. The ring around the enemy column was virtually complete. The best estimates from the officers on the scene was that the enemy force consisted of about three hundred men. Their point squad had stopped completely, and the rest of the column was adjusting its positions rather than continuing to march north along the slope. The point was still three hundred yards from the perimeter of the main DMC and BCM forces.

"I think they're waiting for something," Lieutenant Crampton reported, to both his father and Lon.

"Waiting for another group?" Colonel Crampton suggested. "Coordinating their attacks?"

"Could be," Lon said. "Let's spoil their timetable. Two minutes, Lieutenant. From now." Lon noted the exact time. "I'll notify the other commanders. I want everyone to hit them at once."

Gunfire and grenade explosions. The coordination was better than Lon had allowed himself to hope. The two militia companies came in perfectly timed with the mercenary platoons. The difference in altitude among the various components helped minimize the danger of friendly-fire casualties—always a concern with an enemy force completely surrounded.

For thirty seconds the battle seemed completely one-sided. Lon could not distinguish the heavier sound of raider rifles. The only gunfire came from the Dirigenters and the Bancroft militia. Then, just as the encircled raiders started to return fire, gunfire sounded west of that fight, on the western slope of the ridge, south of the perimeter.

"They've come out of the caves!" At first Lon did not recognize the voice as Ron Magnusson's. His company was the closest DMC unit. "At least two companies, Colonel, maybe a full battalion. Some are moving up the slope behind our people. The rest are coming straight at us."

Lon did not have a chance to reply immediately. That was when the enemy shuttles struck from the west.

26

The enemy shuttles came in low and relatively slowly. By the time Lon heard the report that the shuttles had dropped three hundred men on rocket packs half a mile west of the perimeter, the shuttles' multibarrel cannons were already firing, chewing paths through the forest and up the western slope of the ridge.

Two Shrikes had started strafing runs on the raiders on the eastern side of the ridgeline just before the enemy shuttles were spotted. The Shrikes were coming out of their shallow dives after hitting the raiders on the ground with cannon fire and rockets as the enemy shuttles approached the crest of the ridge, climbing and accelerating, directly toward the Shrikes.

In virtually any other circumstances, the boxy raider shuttles would have been no match for the Dirigenter fighters. Shrikes were faster, more maneuverable, and better protected. But chance more than design brought shuttles and Shrikes together when the DMC craft were most vulnerable.

All four raider shuttles launched missiles—two apiece—at the pair of Shrikes. There were too many missiles, too close, for the Shrikes to defeat them with electronic countermeasures or evasive maneuvers. Both were hit more than once and erupted in balls of fire. Neither pilot had a chance to eject.

The nearest Shrike exploded little more than three hundred yards from Lon's position, less than a thousand feet above the crest of the ridge. Debris, much of it burning, showered down on the slopes. Luckily, most of the wreckage came down well away from the manned positions. None of it hit the few dozen men who were near the center. And with all the rain, the fires quickly burned out.

Lon took only minimal notice. There was too much happening all at once. The Shrikes had exploded. Their pilots had not ejected. He radioed that news to CIC, then turned his attention to the more critical problems on the ground.

The men caught in the middle of the two raider forces, high on the western slope, already knew that they were in the middle. The commanders were responding as best they could. On the perimeter, Captain Magnusson was doing what little he could to ease the pressure on the exposed mercenaries and militia without moving his remaining two platoons out of the perimeter to advance on the enemy force on the slope in front of his positions—a force that was also advancing toward him.

"Tebba, move your company south," Lon said. The last wreckage from the Shrikes had scarcely hit the ground. "Push through behind our people on this side of the slope. Try not to lose contact with the perimeter, though. And remember, we're suddenly short on air cover." There were still two Shrikes supposedly on station, and the shuttles that Lon had put in the air, but the loss of two fighters was still of major significance . . . apart from the pilots killed.

Lon closed his eyes and took a deep breath. The last force—so far as he knew—of raiders on the ground would need at least another seven or eight minutes before they could get close enough to the western perimeter to cause trouble, and the units closest to them knew they were coming. But the fact that there *were* raiders on that side kept Lon from pulling soldiers from there to help with the enemy on the south.

Do I dare strip men from the northern arc of the line?

he wondered. North and northeast were the only sections of the perimeter not directly threatened by raider ground forces. After a few seconds, Lon decided not to attempt it. Yet. Not until the situation was a lot clearer . . . or more desperate.

Four raider shuttles came back for a second pass. This time the Dirigenter shuttles and Shrikes were ready. The final two Shrikes overhead came at the raider shuttles from ahead and above. The mercenaries' attack shuttles came at them from the north. This time the results were more satisfying. None of the Dirigenter craft were hit, and two of the raiders shuttles went down hard. The other two reversed course and headed west, into the heart of the storm, at full acceleration.

The Dirigenters did not pursue. Instead, they turned to help the forces on the ground. The Shrikes took the lead, since they would have a better chance to avoid surface-to-air missiles.

There were plenty of those after the raider shuttles had cleared the area. Lon noted three, and heard reports of others. In all, at least a dozen SAMs were fired by the raiders—without effect.

The initial ambush that Lon had engineered had turned into a confused melee. There were four groups of soldiers more or less parallel, alternating, which left one combined force of mercenaries and militia between two enemy forces, and one raider unit also sandwiched. On the eastern side of the hill, the two DMC platoons from Bravo Company and the militia 2nd Company commanded by Lieutenant Crampton were trying to fight their way upslope to close with the enemy. That first raider column had been hit the hardest. The younger Crampton reported that the raiders looked to have suffered nearly 50 percent casualties, with the rest in considerable disarray. "We have fixed bayonets and are moving in for the kill," the young commander said.

• • •

On the western side of the hill, Lon's Alpha Company was moving through the perimeter, thrusting a wedge out toward the area between the other half of the initial ambushing force and the raiders who had come up from the south—presumably out of caves—to support it. Tebba was coordinating with Delta's platoon leader and sergeants, and the two militia company commanders ahead of him, letting them concentrate on the first raider force while he moved in on their flank.

That was when the final raider force joined the battle, firing rifles and rocket-propelled grenades from the west. The final force that the defenders had been *aware* of.

A new source of incoming fire on the northern end of the perimeter came as a complete surprise to Lon. For a few seconds after Captain Carlin reported it, Lon was silent, startled. Then he found a possible explanation.

"That first batch, Brock, from the other day. They went north instead of south. They've been lying in wait out there, somewhere. That has to be it."

"Maybe, Colonel, but I think there are more guns out there than the couple of platoons that went off that way could account for. This sounds like a full company or more," Carlin replied. "Just how many raiders *are* there here? They must be hitting us with every man they've got."

"Then let's make sure we do the job we came here for," Lon said. "Hang on while I get Sefer and Colonel Crampton in on this." The pause was not long.

"We need to shrink our perimeter," Lon said. "Pull back toward the ridge on the west and pull south toward my position on the north before we get too extended to deal with all this crap."

"I've only got two of my platoons here, remember that," Carlin said. "The rest are over on the other side of the ridge."

"I remember," Lon said. "Two of your platoons and two of Magnusson's. As you move back, I want you to slide up higher on the slope. Sefer, your people will fill the gap as you get back toward the base of the hills. Can you get a platoon out without them being seen to give us a better idea how many men we've got coming in on the north?"

"We'll find a way," Captain Kai said.

"I have three more companies alerted to come in here," Colonel Crampton told Lon. "Three—that's all I can move at one time, unless you want to use some of your shuttles. And then I'd have to start stripping garrisons from the larger mining villages—or even the towns. I can't pull the company that's protecting Lincoln except as a last resort."

"We're certainly not down to last resorts yet," Lon said. The two commanders were together now, only a few feet apart, behind a low wall of rocks and logs. As a matter of sound discipline, they still communicated by radio, whispering in the insulated security of their helmets, while they watched the perimeter and listened to reports on the action from their subordinates. "I don't think it's time to bring in the three companies you have alerted. It's enough that you've got them ready to move if we *do* need them. Right now I want to make sure the raiders fully commit themselves to this fight. All the eggs in one basket, so to speak."

"They're not doing anything anywhere else. From the reports we have, they must have more than a thousand men here now. That sounds like they are fully committed, as close as they're ever likely to get," Crampton said.

"And fully engaged," Lon said. "Look, we've still got numerical superiority on the ground. And we have more airpower than they have, by a factor of at least three to one, and one Shrike is equal to several of those small shuttles the raiders have, even after what happened before. If we bring in another six hundred of your people, the raiders might disengage too soon, and I want to finish this here and now, if we can."

"We can bring the extra companies in behind them, make sure they've got no place to go."

"Covering all the possible routes out would spread your men too thin. The raiders could break through. No point in taking casualties when it won't do the job, Colonel. We need to let this develop a little longer."

The first raider force, the one that had been observed moving north along the eastern slope of the ridge, had taken the heaviest casualties during the early fighting, but the mercenaries and militiamen were unable to contain the remnants. They fought their way south and then over the ridge, linking with the second raider force, the one Lon assumed had come out of caves. The first force left behind more than two hundred dead and wounded.

"My guess is that about a hundred fifty made it across to join the others," Lieutenant Crampton reported to his father and Lon. "At least that many, possibly as many as two hundred."

"What about your casualties?" Colonel Crampton asked.

His son hesitated. "I've got at least twelve dead and thirty wounded. Some of the wounded probably won't live long enough to reach trauma tubes."

"There's not much we can do about that," Lon told Colonel Crampton over their private channel. "We've only got eight tubes available here, and we can't get shuttles in close enough to evacuate the wounded to Lincoln yet. The raiders are between us and the clearing on the west, and it would take several hours to carry men to that clearing to the east, where you and your people came in. We get the wounded back here as quickly as possible, and hope the medtechs can stabilize them enough to keep them going until tubes are available. In a pinch, they can rotate men in the tubes, put them in just long enough to start the healing process, then move them out to help others."

"Can we air-drop more tubes from shuttles?" Colonel Crampton asked. "Any chance at all?"

"Not much, I'm afraid. They're too fragile for any kind of rough landing, even hanging from a parachute. Between the rocks and trees, not to mention the storm, probably not one in five would be in working condition when we got to it."

Slowly, Lon was getting better estimates on the raiders' numbers. The last force, the one that had come in from the north unexpectedly, consisted of about 200 men, equivalent to a DMC company—and approximately 300 had dropped in by rocket pack west of the combined DMC and BCM force. Between 150 and 200 men remained from the first raider force. And somewhere between 400 and 600 men in the group that had come up from the south, west of the ridge.

Minus casualties. Raider casualties were harder to get good information on, except where bodies could be counted. Ninety minutes after the start of the battle, the best estimate Lon could make—based on information coming from his men and Colonel Crampton's militia—was that the raiders still had more than 1,000 effectives, men still able to fight. The raiders showed no inclination to surrender, individually or in groups. The only prisoners taken so far had been men wounded too badly to escape.

The Bancrofter militia had a total of 21 dead and 75 wounded for the day. Lon's battalion had lost only 5 dead and 30 wounded on the ground. Between the mercenaries and the militia, the combined force still had more than 1,250 men in place.

The numerical advantage was too small to let Lon feel complacent. *We're supposed to be doing the hunting here,* he thought, *but it's the raiders attacking and us sitting on this hill on the defensive. What other surprises do they have waiting to spring?*

He tried to piece together the possibilities. The most likely scenario he could imagine was that the raiders had still more men waiting to enter the fight, whenever they thought it would be most advantageous. The second was that they had more armed shuttles available than the four Lon knew about, aircraft that would not be detectable in the storm clouds until they started shooting.

What else? Lon shook his head. The raiders still had a ship in orbit, moving in, but Lon could not accept that it might contribute a lot. It wasn't large enough to carry many more troops or the shuttles to carry them in. It might be able to launch missiles, but the opposing forces were too close together for that to be a particularly intelligent move.

Lon spoke often with Vel Osterman and with CIC aboard *Long Snake*, separately and together.

"Maybe you're reaching too far for an explanation," Osterman said during one of their conferences. "We assume that they know what happened to the raiders here nine years ago, right?"

"No way to escape that assumption," Lon said.

"It seems fairly clear that this batch of raiders wants to avoid making the same mistake. They don't want to get trapped underground, where they can't put their numbers to good use. They don't want to get sealed off and . . . whatever. So they have to force the issue on the surface, before we can whittle their numbers down by attrition or pin them in their holes. They tried to continue raiding as normal after we got here. That didn't work, especially after we learned that they had inside help and took measures to plug that advantage. They tried meeting us in small-scale fights. That didn't do them much good either. So now they look for one grand battle to give them a chance. If they can beat us and thirty percent of the militia, that gives them free rein. For a time, at least."

"Possible," Lon conceded, "but we can't rely on that."

"Lon, I read your reports on your first trip to Bancroft long before we got this contract. The raiders you encountered then showed no military discipline, no sense of strategy or tactics when they were opposed by a professional military force. They were just thugs who had been gathered to raid and loot. Is that what we're facing now?"

"No, of course not. We're facing well-trained, highly disciplined soldiers with solid leadership. Professionals as good as the militia here, and very nearly up to our standards," Lon said. "That doesn't necessarily square with risking everything on one throw of the dice."

"It does if a good analysis of the situation says that's the only reasonable shot you have."

After six hours of almost constant rain, everything was soggy. Even Dirigenter battledress had lost some of its resistance to water. Where there was bare soil, it had turned to mud long before. Grassy areas were soggy, spongy underfoot. Everything on the slopes of the ridge was slippery. At the foot of the slope, conditions were worse because water had been running down the hills since the start of the rain.

Thunderstorms cycled through the area, no more than forty minutes apart, sometimes considerably closer together. As the day warmed up, the storms became more intense, more violent, more frequent. The wind gusted as high as sixty miles per hour occasionally, and the meteorologists aboard *Long Snake* continued to issue warnings that tornadoes were "highly possible." Three funnel clouds had been detected, but the closest had come no closer than thirty miles from the scene of the battle.

Lon had pulled the perimeter in as tightly as he dared on the north and west, reinforcing the crest and the southern half of the perimeter, where most of the fighting was concentrated. Sefer Kai had managed to get one platoon out to act as scouts. That platoon had broken into its constituent squads, even fire teams, to be able to cover more ground.

It was one of those squads that spotted a new column of raiders moving toward the fight.

"Another company," Lon told Colonel Crampton as soon as he had the report. "Coming from the south-southwest, about a mile out from the perimeter now."

"Time to bring in my extra companies?" Crampton asked.

"We still can't put them on the ground close enough to get into action soon enough to deal with these men, but"— Lon hesitated for several seconds—"I guess it is time to get them on the ground here. They'll have to come in at that clearing east of here. That means a three-hour march to reach us, longer to circle around on the south to get behind the raiders."

"I'll have them in the air in five minutes. I've got them bringing extra trauma tubes as well. Six portables and two fixed units. Can we start moving some of the seriously wounded toward that clearing?"

"I'll have the medtechs work on it. We'll have to send a strong escort with them."

"One platoon to carry wounded, another for escort?"

The Shrikes had been relieved by others. The two currently available did what they could to damage and delay the raiders Captain Kai's people had discovered. Cannon fire and rockets. The Shrikes came up from behind, guided by the mercenaries on the ground. Behind them, two attack shuttles came in to add their measure to the attack.

It stopped the raider column for several minutes. Then three fire teams from Charlie Company started to harass the raiders from the flanks in a series of hit-and-run attacks.

Two raider shuttles returned to the attack on the ridge, but arrived too late to have a chance to go after the Dirigenter shuttles, and the raider craft were met by Shrikes. One raider shuttle went down in flames, almost hitting the column of raiders on the ground. The other shuttle turned and ran west again. This time the Shrikes stayed with it, close enough to keep it in sight, and it, too, eventually was brought down . . . after leading the Shrikes sixty miles from the main battle.

"Time to start trying to envelop the raiders on the south, Colonel," Lon told Crampton a few minutes later. "We've concentrated forces on that end. We can put nearly two full companies of my men and one of your companies into pushing down the slope into the enemy's main force. The rest of us will start moving down and into them from this end, leave just enough troops in the line to keep the enemy forces on the west and north from overrunning us from behind."

"My son's got 2nd Company in position," Colonel Crampton said.

"I'll have Captain Girana in tactical control," Lon replied. "He's in position, too, and he has two platoons from my Bravo Company as well." Delta's two detached platoons had moved back into the line with the rest of the company.

"How soon do we move?"

"We'll wait until we can make a couple more passes from the air," Lon said. "Two additional Shrikes are on their way down to relieve the ones here. Before those two go back up to *Taranto* to rearm, we'll use them in the softening up as well, along with the shuttles I've still got here. Five minutes until the air attack. As soon as the Shrikes and shuttles pull away, we go."

• • •

It did not go exactly as planned. As the aircraft came in for their runs at the main force of raiders, the enemy was starting a move of its own, pushing diagonally uphill toward the north, into the defense perimeter below the bulge that had been formed earlier. At the same time, the enemy forces that had been positioned to the west and north started advancing, moving in closer, using fire-and-maneuver tactics. And the final enemy column, its numbers reduced by a third after the air and ground attacks on it, was within minutes of being close enough to contribute to the main battle.

The security detachment around the two colonels was fully involved in the fighting now, when they could spot targets—difficult at extreme range in the rain. Lon was firing as well, except when he was too busy on the radio. He went through one magazine for his rifle and loaded another. Five feet from Lon, Jeremy Howell was operating a grenade launcher—and Lon had no idea where the corporal had come up with that. Jeremy had not been rated as a grenadier even before he had become part of Lon's headquarters detachment, but he was operating carefully, taking time to aim and loosing grenades one at a time, not emptying a five-grenade clip as quickly as he could pull the trigger.

Lon just happened to be looking toward Jeremy when the corporal jerked back and to the side, a bullet through his left shoulder, blood quickly blossoming out over the fabric of his battledress tunic. Lon quickly crawled over to Jeremy, forgetting everything else in his hurry to assist the young corporal. He ripped the younger man's tunic more, to let him see the wounds—entry and exit—better, and pulled pressure dressings from the first-aid pouch on his belt. He had just finished applying the bandages when he heard a high-pitched scream, so piercing that it was painful, over his radio.

"What was that?" Lon asked, switching to a channel that would connect him to all his officers and noncoms. "Who screamed?" There was no answer. Lon clicked a control to bring up a communications log on his head-up display, to determine what channel the scream had come over. Colonel Crampton and the company commanders from both Lon's battalion and the militia force were the only people with regular access to that channel.

Lon needed only a few seconds to cycle through the vital signs of his captains, to make sure that they were all still alive and healthy. Then he switched radio channels to talk to Colonel Crampton.

"That scream must have come from one of your company commanders," Lon said.

"My son doesn't answer," Crampton replied. "I can't get his lead sergeant either."

That conversation was cut short by the explosion of several grenades on the hillside, thirty yards below the two colonels, close enough to send shrapnel past them with enough speed to be lethal if it hit anyone in a vital area. Those blasts were followed by an intensification of the rifle fire directed at the defenders high on the slope. The raiders below were mounting their most determined assault yet on the shrunken perimeter of the mercenaries and militiamen.

Lon leaned close to Jeremy Howell for just a few seconds. "The wound is clean, in and out, Jerry. You'll be okay." Howell nodded, and Lon picked up his rifle again and got into a firing position over the low barricade in front of him.

For several minutes Lon had no time to worry about the scream, his wounded aide, or the progress of the battle around the rest of the perimeter. He answered radio calls with no more than a terse acknowledgment—luckily, none required more. The raiders had pushed up to the base of the slope, within thirty yards of the perimeter, and seemed determined to break through no matter the casualties they took in the process.

Two enemy shuttles appeared, firing cannons and rockets into the defensive perimeter. Lon's men were ready. Three missiles were launched at the shuttles. One exploded as it made a hard turn to the north, trying to escape. The flaming wreckage fell close, forcing defenders and attackers alike to duck away from the debris. The second was hit, but not decisively. It trailed smoke as it tried to escape west again, losing altitude rapidly. Lon did not see it finally come down. He used the momentary letup in the raiders' attack to pull the perimeter in more at the center, bringing his men and the company of militia that was closest up to the line he was on.

When the raiders started advancing up the slope, they came under heavy fire from three sides. The attack faltered, then came to a complete stop less than fifty yards from Lon's position. The surviving raiders took cover using the low ramparts the defenders had abandoned in their initial perimeter, but taking fire from above, those did not offer much protection. After several minutes the surviving raiders started attempting to withdraw—and took more casualties as they did. Of the three hundred or more who had launched the advance, fewer than a third made it out of the final crossfire.

Lon slung his rifle and went back to Jeremy. "Come on, kid, let's get you to the medtechs," Lon said. Howell was still conscious, but when he attempted to get to his feet, he got dizzy and almost fell. Lon supported him and moved him toward the crest of the ridge. The medical station had been set up on the eastern slope.

The medical station was overflowing with wounded—many clearly in worse condition than Jeremy Howell. A medtech took a quick look at Howell's wounds, said, "You're doing okay. We'll get to you when we can," and helped Lon set him against a rock, out of the way.

As Lon was turning to head back to his command post, he saw two men carrying a makeshift stretcher in from the south, with a familiar face walking next to it. Wil Nace, Alpha Company's new lead sergeant, was covered in blood—the sleeves and front of his battledress tunic were completely red. There were smears of blood on his helmet and on his face under the turned-up faceplate. Lon went toward Nace and the stretcher.

"What happened to you?" Lon asked, raising the face-plate of his own helmet.

"I'm okay, Colonel," Nace said. He gestured at the stretcher next to him. "Colonel Crampton's son. He's in bad shape." The stretcher-bearers kept going, hurrying toward the medtechs and the collection of portable trauma tubes. "I'm not sure if he'll make it." Nace shook his head. "Close as I can make out, two RPGs exploded pretty much at the same time within a couple of feet of him. Maybe three. Killed a half dozen men around him, including his lead sergeant. Blew off both the lieutenant's legs. Hell, half his left hip is gone."

"How'd you get all the blood on you?" Lon asked.

"His blood. I was about the closest man not wounded or shocked senseless by the explosions. I got to him and did what I could to stop the bleeding." Nace squeezed his eyes shut. "God, I didn't know I was capable of what I did. I had to reach inside the chopped meat those grenades left to tie off the arteries in his left leg—hip. That was the only way I could keep him from bleeding to death right there, and I still don't know if it was enough. There was nothing left to put a tourniquet on. The right stump at least had enough left for that."

Wil Nace turned to the side, away from Lon, and started puking, retching so violently that he had to drop to his knees to keep from falling.

• • •

Lon gave Colonel Crampton the news about his son while he was on the way back to his command post. "He's alive but in very bad shape," Lon told him. "He may have lost too much blood before they got him to the trauma tubes."

There was a long pause before Colonel Crampton said, "Thanks for telling me. I'll get over there as soon as I can. I can't let go right now."

"You'd better go now," Lon advised. "I'll keep you posted on anything going on you need to know about."

There were reports from company commanders. The raiders were moving uphill again on the southwestern front, where they had the bulk of their troops. Some of the fighting was already hand-to-hand.

"We'll leave one company of militia and two platoons of our people to guard the medical station," Lon said. "I want everyone else pushing toward the main enemy force. Let's finish the job here and now. If anyone hasn't done it yet, fix bayonets."

Lon attached his bayonet to his rifle as he spoke. When he got to the squads that had moved back toward his command post, it was only long enough to collect those men and start them moving south, along the side of the hill.

Toward the enemy.

The raiders were concentrated in a wedge, 300 yards long, 150 yards wide at the base. The apex had reached and penetrated the defensive line through the middle of one of the militia companies but had bogged down there, unable to turn to roll up the line on either side of the break-through. While Lon was concentrating his forces, the raiders were attempting to broaden their attack, widening the wedge. The last members of the other raider forces were converging with the main body. *All their eggs in one basket, just the way we wanted it,* Lon thought.

At the sides of the raider wedge, mercenaries and militiamen worked to turn the corners back, fighting to compress and contain the enemy. Lon led the men he had gathered near his command post—a mixed force of Dirigenters and Bancrofters—toward the center of the firefight, the point where the raiders had broken the defensive line. There were already six platoons—two mercenary and four militia—trying to push the raiders back out of the gap. Captain Magnusson had taken command of the joint effort, bringing two platoons in to plug the original penetration and then gathering the nearest militia platoons to try to repel the enemy. Lon added the men who had come with him.

The raiders resisted with as much determination as any soldiers Lon had ever encountered, as if they knew they had nowhere to go, no escape. Even when some of the enemy ran out of ammunition, they continued fighting, moving closer to use bayonets or belt knives.

Slowly the raiders were forced back toward the south and down the slope, fighting every step of the way, taking and giving heavy losses. Only after more than an hour of this deadly close-in fighting did some of the raiders—individuals, then small groups—start throwing down their weapons and surrendering. They were stripped of helmets and any remaining gear and moved away from the fighting. Those raiders who were too badly wounded to move on their own were left where they lay, with the dead.

The fighting ended suddenly, after nearly ninety minutes of hand-to-hand combat. Two piercing blasts on a whistle were followed by a loudspeaker announcement from within the concentration of raiders—an order from the ranking officer for his men to lay down their weapons and surrender unconditionally.

27

It was nearly sunset before the rain finally stopped, leaving water dripping from trees and running down the slopes of the line of hills for hours afterward. Water was slow to seep into the saturated ground. There had been none of the magical cleansing of a poet's springtime rain. This left only mud and dirty puddles, many of them tainted by blood.

The fighting was over, but not the work. Shuttles had been operating in relays carrying the wounded back to Lincoln and Bancroft's other towns—anyplace with medical facilities. Dirigenters and Bancrofters were given priority. Wounded prisoners went afterward, to be treated when possible. The location of the main raider base, two miles south of the area Lon's people had searched, was discovered easily. Several wounded raiders were anxious to tell where it was after being reminded that they couldn't be treated without the antidote to the nanotech self-destruct mechanisms they had been infected with. Several portable trauma tubes were found in the caves, as well as tons of metal and minerals plundered from Bancroft's mining facilities.

Manning reports were compiled for mercenaries and militiamen. Lon grimaced at each detailing of the dead and wounded from his battalion, though the numbers were not as high as he had feared they would be. Thirty-seven Dirigenters had been killed in the day's fighting, 140 wounded or otherwise injured. The three companies of militia had suffered slightly more casualties, both dead and wounded. Lieutenant Wilson Crampton had survived, though Lon's senior medtech said it was the most extraordinary survival he had ever seen. "It's a bloody miracle he made it," Sergeant Carvel told Lon. Colonel Wilson Crampton echoed that sentiment.

"The miracle was one of your sergeants," Colonel Crampton said when he and Lon met to go over the reports they had been receiving. "One of my son's men said he saw one of your sergeants go to Wilson and stop the bleeding—said if he'd been five seconds slower he wouldn't have made it."

"Company Lead Sergeant Wil Nace," Lon said. "I saw them when they got to the medtechs."

"I want to thank him personally," Colonel Crampton said. "I owe him more than I can ever repay."

"I'll arrange it," Lon said, looking away for an instant, remembering that it might be *his* son in similar circumstances . . . in not too many years.

Raider casualties took longer to enumerate. Dead, wounded, captured. The raider force had suffered more than 50 percent casualties—dead or wounded—in the fight. Some of the wounded might have been saved had it not been for the toxins their leaders had infected them with to keep them from talking. Many of those who had been seriously wounded died before the antidote could be located and brought to the medical stations to allow treatment of the prisoners.

The prisoners were kept together and guarded through the night. Stripped of their helmets, weapons, and most of their other gear, they posed little threat. By morning, many of them were willing to talk. The other raider bases, the locations of the remaining shuttles, even schedules for transport ships were learned in the first few hours of questioning.

"There are a few officers among the prisoners," Colonel Crampton told Lon after they had all returned to Lincoln. "It looks as if we'll even get the names of most of the agents the Colonial Mining Cartel managed to plant here." Colonel Crampton had been spending most of his time with his son. Wilson would need two months or more of trauma tube treatment to fully regenerate his legs.

"That's good. We won't have any trouble clearing the rest up either," Lon said.

"What about that raider ship?" Colonel Crampton asked.

"Shrikes from *Taranto* managed to disable that yesterday," Lon said. That news had come as something of a surprise to him after the battle. Somehow he had completely missed the reports on that ship from Captain Roim of *Long Snake*. The Shrikes that had been assigned to intercept the raider ship had not been able to destroy it, but they had crippled its propulsion system. It was locked into a very eccentric orbit around Bancroft. "We haven't received a surrender from them yet, but we will. Either that or we'll finish the job."

"I hope you can get them to surrender," Colonel Crampton said. "We can use that ship, once it's repaired. Get men trained to crew it. That ship could give us the protection we need out in space . . . some of it, anyway. We'll be ready when the next raider transport comes to make a pickup, and we'll make it harder for those bastards from Earth to try something like this again."

Lon smiled. "We'll see what we can do for you, Colonel."

Phip Steesen was not so easy to appease. "You kept me out of the big fight on purpose," he charged, the first time he managed to be alone with Lon after everyone had returned to Lincoln. "You stranded me back here so I wouldn't end up like Dean."

"I didn't know this was going to turn out to be the big fight when we left here, Phip," Lon explained. "And no, I wasn't trying to keep you out of anything."

"Like hell you weren't."

"It didn't even *occur* to me."

Still, for the next three days Phip spoke to Lon only when duty demanded it.

Cleaning out the remnants of the raider force, recovering material they had looted and the munitions and supplies cached in their various strongholds, and taking the two remaining attack shuttles left to them took nearly two weeks. The crew of the ship needed twelve days to decide to surrender. The ship had been boarded and the crew taken off. Engineers from *Taranto* and *Long Snake* had already started repairing the ship's propulsion system. Bancroft had contracted for an engineer and two officers from *Taranto*'s flight crew to stay over for six months to train Bancrofters to operate the ship. Those Dirigenters would return home when a supply ship came to bring new weapons and four Shrikes. Eight Bancrofters would be going to Dirigent for flight training. A dozen others would go for more extensive training in ship operations.

"A most profitable addendum to a successful contract," Lon noted in the last report he dispatched to Dirigent via message rocket. "It seems unlikely that Earth's Colonial Mining Cartel will attempt to attack Bancroft again, but if they do, Bancroft will be better able to defend itself."

The prisoners, nearly seven hundred altogether, including twelve families of recent settlers identified as agents working for CMC, would be routed back to Earth—as transport became available—except for several dozen men who asked to be allowed to stay and settle on Bancroft. The government of Bancroft also began distributing detailed reports of the activities of the Colonial Mining Cartel to other worlds, and it sent an official diplomatic protest to Earth . . . for what little good *that* might do.

There was a formal ceremony at Government House to mark the successful completion of the contract. Governor Sosa announced a large completion bonus for the men of 2nd Battalion, 7th Regiment, and one further honor. Lead Sergeant Wil Nace was awarded the Medal of Valor of the Bancroft Constabulary Militia.

It was sixteen days after the climactic battle that an MR arrived from Dirigent, carrying—in addition to official mail—personal mail for the men of 2nd Battalion. There were two message chips for Lon among the personal mail, one from his wife and children, the other from his parents. In a rare gesture of self-indulgence, Lon postponed reading his official mail and turned to the family letters first. Lon was used to the segmented nature of the letter from his family. Sara had recorded a number of sections in private. Lon, Junior, and Angie had also recorded private messages. In addition, there were joint sessions, with all three sitting around talking more or less at once. They talked about the details of daily life, and about the things they had been doing with the elder Nolans. All in all, that letter ran for nearly an hour. Lon was tempted to replay the entire thing immediately, but took the chip from his complink and inserted the chip from his parents.

"God, it's good to have them on Dirigent," Lon whispered while the second letter was playing. He hardly noticed the tear at the corner of his left eye, wiping it away absently.

His parents were full of cheery news, their discoveries, their "exploration" of their new homeworld. Several times Lon found himself chuckling over their exuberance. But one passage—his father speaking without his mother present—almost brought Lon to tears.

"I've spent quite a lot of time chatting with Junior. He's been full of enthusiasm for your outfit and swearing that he's going to enlist the day he's old enough. I know how much that troubles you, but I think that maybe there's hope he'll change his mind. Junior has talked a lot, but he has also done a lot of listening—not your strongest suit when you were his age, if you remember. I've talked about my teaching, and about the options he has here. Given him a different perspective on a few things, I think. Maybe it sounds different coming from an old geezer like me rather than a certified hero-soldier. There's no guarantee here, son, but the last few days Junior hasn't been quite so absolutely adamant about becoming a soldier."

"I hope you're right, Dad," Lon whispered to the complink screen. "I *pray* you're right."

The Dirigenter ships started for home three weeks before the end of the originally contracted three months, their job finished. Lon paid his first visit to the section of *Long Snake* where the Dirigenter dead were being stored for the trip home. There were too many dead—one was too many—but he consoled himself with the knowledge that it could have been much worse.

He sat alone in the antechamber for more than an hour, staring at the hatch that led to the bodies. *How many fathers and mothers have to mourn?* he wondered.

Maybe, subconsciously, I was *trying to keep Phip away from the fighting,* Lon thought—honest in proximity to the dead. *Colonel Crampton nearly lost his son. Jerry was wounded.* Lon shook his head. There was one problem he still had no answer for. "How can I convince Junior there are other things to do than be a soldier like his father?" Just the hope that maybe *his* father would make the difference.